D0556321

Fictional Film Club

Copyright © Mark Savage, 2019

All rights reserved.

ISBN 978-1-949127-06-5

Second edition

Edited by Ariel Kusby, Bobby Eversmann, & Mickey Collins

Book design by Mickey Collins

Cover image: *Paramount Theater 3 Albilene, Texas* by Nicolas Henderson (flickr.com/photos/texasbackroads/14657358754/). Used under Creative Commons 2.0 (creativecommons.org/licenses/by/2.0/legalcode). Image was brightened.

Published by Deep Overstock, Portland, OR.

deepoverstock.com

Fictional Film Club

a novel

Mark Savage

7:18 XxxXX

FICTIONAL FILM CLUB

Contents

INTRODUCTION

Or

THE CHOCOLATE CASSETTE

In my dream last night there was a film being shot near some train tracks, on location somewhere in Eastern Europe. The director, a serious grey-haired man in a black turtleneck, sat on a high chair watching with trusting urgency as the crew prepared the next shot.[1] They moved lights, arranged trees, paced out measurements and taped down cables. Alongside the train track a makeshift second track was being built for the camera to run along on a small cart, to give a fluid movement to the shot. A train pulled in, slowly. It scraped and squeaked as it moved. It was a series of boxcar carriages with large side doors, yellow but rusting to brown in spots. It wasn't period perfect: the scene was supposed to show prisoners arriving at a concentration camp, and this train was at least thirty years too new. But the director nodded. This train conveyed something of the necessary industrial horror. The lumbering anachronism would add weight.

There was a flash-forward: to a school, after some apocalyptic event. Dozens of families were living there. They had adjusted to the new world, and there was a feeling of tentative détente, a wary peace. The school had a farm with a few animals. Crops grew. Sunlight came in the tall windows on a winter morning, warming the hallways. A second flash-forward showed, very briefly, a man sitting on a sofa. His

[1] *director.* Picture Ingmar Bergman if you like. He is the perfect shorthand for *the director*: the high, smart, forehead, the quick eye, thinking, listening, enjoying the process because it is what matters in art and in life. The more I try to remember the director's actual face, the more it is obscured. I see the puffy jackets of the people on set. The overcast sky, perfect for shooting. But the director hides in plain sight, featureless and serious.

wrists were bleeding. A third cut showed two men. They were on a balcony of a hotel room, several flights up. Police were moving into the lobby below. The men jumped for a neighbouring building and missed, falling to the street. The authorities moved in to arrest the injured men, and take away their briefcase.

The man on the sofa, I somehow knew, with that dreamy certainty, was the director's son, in the future. It became evident that the director, troubled by this vision of his boy trying to commit suicide, was making a film about the end of the world. As if his invented holocaust might have such miserable power that it would shock this tomorrow from his mind. Prevent it, even. I saw a second image of the son on the sofa. He was stirring, and medics were tending to his wounds. Now I was beginning to wake up, and was aware, however abstractly, that I was dreaming, and so maybe this reassuring image, the son surviving, was my invention, my own director's cut, a happy ending to appease my inner test audience.[2] I hoped that the two men who jumped were

[2] *inner test audience:* I realised at this point that I'd been pushing the narrative in a dozen tiny ways throughout my dream. When I became concerned that a real train might come along the tracks and smash the production to smithereens I noticed, away to my left, a junction from which a further set of tracks branched out from the main one. These tracks looped through the trees beyond the set, before rejoining the original line at a safe distance, several hundred yards away to the right. A real train could avoid us, I was now assured. This extra track appeared as if in answer to an unasked question, as if it was invented by myself to reassure myself. Another person dreaming the same dream wouldn't have needed it, perhaps, but might have imagined fireproof clothing, or a catering company, or a very comfortable and unoccupied bathroom, depending on their particular worry fetish.

villains whose evil plans had been prevented. But I suspected that they were heroes of a failed resistance attempting to prevent a global catastrophe. Because without this apocalypse, the optimistic sequences in the school did not make sense. They could not happen.

***

Describing a dream (aside from being self-indulgent and generally tedious) is like describing a film in which you recognise the actors' faces from other films but cannot name them. WG Sebald said that *dreams are the one place where we might be viewer, lead actor, writer and director, all at once.* Brazilian poet Machado de Assis, a man whose writing frequently broke the fourth wall and addressed the reader directly (not unlike a dream in which I can both be watching a scene and in it), said that *dreams disdain fine lines and finishing touches on landscapes – they content themselves with thick but representative brush-strokes.* In Clark Campbell's *O Alienista!* (1975), Ossie Davis, playing de Assis, says *dreams do not allow for detail in our backgrounds; stare too closely, and one can see the thick paint of the mind crudely creating the trees and streets of our youth.*

Carl Jung had a feeling during childhood that he was two people: Number One was a fine upstanding Swiss citizen, and Number Two was a dignified figure from the eighteenth century, with a natural authority.[3] The return to waking from dreaming, he suggested, felt like

---

[3] *with natural authority: Memories, Dreams, Reflections,* Pantheon Books, 1963.

switching from one to the other, although as a grown man his ideas about these two selves were more complicated. Important in the act of waking was what he termed *Schlussszene*, loosely translated as *final scene*, by which he meant imagining a satisfactory ending to an unfinished dream.[4] This was necessary, the young Jung thought, to keep his personalities intact and effective. Marcel Proust: *I often wake up with a feeling that the dreams I can just about grasp as I emerge from them are slipping away, and as I remember them, clarify them, write them down even, they are preserved, but in a state which undermines their original nonsensical perfection.*[5] Like a film in post-production, where hot pos-

---

[4] *Schlussszene: Memories, Dreams, Reflections.* I often woke up from a nightmare (sometimes having wet the bed) after my parents' divorce. (I'm not sure the divorce *caused* this; in fact, linking the two feels a little too narratively convenient, like the flashback montage that all too neatly explains how the murderer ended up like this in *Wrong 'Un II* (Les Clay, 1993).) Although she'd never have got it from Jung, Mum told me about this technique of writing a happy ending to my dream. *Imagine that the bullies with knives were really...rabbits with carrots, or teddy bears with chocolates.* After one dream in which I flailed in the shallow end of a pool, I laid in my damp bed until I'd written a sequel in which I swam so fast I took off out of the water. My impotent gun would be loaded with bullets, second time around. A monster would be unmasked; it would really be Dad, playing around, surprising me even though he wasn't supposed to visit until next weekend. That said, my saddest dream experiences were, as now, the happy ones that are interrupted by waking, just like Tinto (Alex Spec) in *Elfelejtett Dolgokat (Forgotten Things,* Rudi, 1967): *I'm at a party with an old school friend, or a dead relative. I become aware that the scene cannot be happening, and that twenty years have passed since I saw them last. I focus on the walls, the clothes, and the conversation. I do this to fix these details, to make them true, but the more I focus the more the space flickers and threatens to vanish.*

[5] *nonsensical perfection: Swann's Way* (Grasset, 1913), translated by C.K.Scott Moncrieff, 1922. In 1981 Terence Kilmartin revised Moncrieff's translation. He replaced the phrase *non-*

sibilities are lost in pursuit of something concrete.[6] Kathy Acker: *Maps are dreams: both describe desire, where you want to go, but never the reality of the destination.*[7]

***

Like my dreams, I don't always remember if I saw a film in black and white or colour. Or where, and with whom. On a big screen, a TV, a laptop. I'll often forget that a film might have been compromised in some way the first time I saw it, like the films that were recorded on video, and had their ends chopped off, or the scratched DVDs that skipped an entire scene, the follow-ups to jokes that I didn't hear because I was laughing aloud, alone, or the many, many lines of dialogue I missed because of a fidgeting popcorn eater in the dark, or a giggling couple, or a ringing phone.[8] I find it easier to recall the locations

---

sensical perfection with *weird exactitude. Nonsensical Perfection* (1999) and *Weird Exactitude* (2003) were later albums by producer and rapper Lucky Richard, consisting of covers and interpretations of French songs translated into English.

[6] *concrete:* Sometimes I wake up with a phrase in my head that I know is the key to unlocking a whole narrative, and repeat it to myself over and over. I come up with an abbreviated set of code words to help me recall the phrase, and an acronym of those words, sometimes. But it all slides away, like the tide, leaving something on the beach of morning, something interesting, debris, messages in bottles.

[7] *reality of the destination: A Map of My Dreams* (Poetry Mailing List, 1977), p.49.

[8] *or a ringing phone:* I inherited a black and white television set around my ninth birthday. It was the one that my Mum had taken to the petrol station where she worked to watch the wedding of Prince Andrew and Sarah Ferguson in 1986. Any Royal Wedding, perhaps because I've never sat through one since, is tied in my mind with a picture of Mum at her desk adding up numbers

within the film. These are what fill my dreams. My reactions to films such as Andrei Tarkovsky's *Stalker* (1979), Andrzej Zulawski's *Possession* (1981) and Hans Wilmots' *Die Stadt, La Ville, The City* (1985) were, initially at least, based on their *spaces*. All, in different ways, show

---

on a calculator with dizzying speed, *taptaptaptaptap*. My sister and I spent a lot of time after school or during holidays at Mum's various workplaces. I'd draw pictures. Robots. Cars. War scenes. One day I realised I was making decisions, choosing when to start a drawing, and when to stop. Like any truth it was obvious and entirely unoriginal, but it felt like I'd come up with it completely by myself.

A few years later that TV ended up in my room. Often I'd fall asleep inches from the screen, and wake up a little later to find a film had begun. The sound levels of a film are lower than other television shows, and much lower than adverts, and sometimes the drop in volume would wake me up. If I'd missed the beginning of a film I might not know what it was called. If the newspaper was still around I might be able to find out. Someone at school might have seen it. But often I saw films and didn't find out what they were called. Or if I did, it was years later. There's the one where the kids break into what turns out to be a horror house, with the emaciated kid living in the walls (*The People Under The Stairs*, Wes Craven, 1992). The one with the man with nine lives performing dangerous jury duties in mob-ridden Chicago (*Disclaimer*, Tommy James, 1954). Or further examples, untagged: the one with Jeff Goldblum in the desert, young John Brix as a scientist, an older Sophia Loren in prison. Mae West in a cowboy hat, Chris Fast in a Dodge, Elliot Gould as himself. A character actor I recognised from a kid's film where he was Santa, now playing a gangster. Some are still lost, just vague structures of image and movement, evoking that line about memory being what is left when something happens and doesn't completely unhappen. I forget who said it. Hybrid scenes, overlapping plots, snatches of story. I started keeping track of films I had seen, films I wanted to see, and films I wanted to make in a notebook. I wrote in it every day until I filled it, when I transferred everything to a ring binder, so I could add pages whenever I liked. If I could inexpensively make this book look like that one, I would. I consider it to be the true original unexpurgated *Fictional Film Club* and mourn its loss (in a train carriage between Canterbury and London Bridge, January 2000) more than many deaths.

a crumbling post-industrial Europe. *Stalker*'s post-nuclear lost space. *Possession*'s dead-ends, where the Berlin Wall has truncated city streets and tracks, creating a dead zone. *Die Stadt*'s layered city levels that go on and on, like Borges' library of Babel, with balconies you could fall from and continue falling forever. These are all ambivalent areas: not simply barren, or violent, or impossible. All seem familiar somehow, as if a wrong turn in any city could lead you right into them. They are quietly uncanny, not specifically Gothic or distant. They are worlds that contain possibility, that do not seem hemmed in; they exist beyond the frame, and before and after the time-frame of the film. These *zones*, to borrow *Stalker*'s terminology, are so affecting, I think, because, like Walter Barch's eerily calm civil war canvasses, or the deceptively benign blue planet in Joel Scott's *New Hebredaeia* film cycle, they appear so *ordinary*. They are seen in grey daylight. Their otherness is established without the fantastical tropes we recognise from other films. They are like a part of the world where two edges meet, and the volume drops, and nobody quite notices.[9]

---

[9] *where two edges meet:* These films remind me of the walk home from school that I would make when I was fourteen and living in Nuneaton, Warwickshire. Instead of a more direct route, I'd walk they way my friends did, towards town. Into town, often, which was way out of my way. We'd loiter on a corner, by the graveyard, or in the subway under the train tracks. What were we waiting for? Only what all fourteen-year-olds are waiting for. Drama, comedy, sexual excitement. Anything. We'd sniff out the merest suggestion, and that was usually all it was. Eventually we'd head off in different directions to our homes.

I would then make a long solo journey back out of town, itself far longer than a direct path from school to home would have been, starting across the large empty car park, past a garage that was usually closed, down a side road next to L's house, then down the slope past the overgrown brambles and high fences with barbed wire by the railway. Then I would pass through the long narrow subway tunnel under the tracks (and this part feels especially like *Stalker*, the trickling water dripping past the yellow lights in the otherwise dark tunnel, the graffiti so thick it was illegible, just messages on top of each other, bands, football teams, loves, hates, spite, now all a Jackson Pollock tangle) before coming up another angled ramp into a new street which started as a dead end (and now we're in *Possession* territory, roads just coming to a stop in the middle of town, commercial buildings of some kind, apparently abandoned, the feeling that it isn't just the time of day that makes it quiet, but the era and the epoch) and would end as a dead end too, once it went past Jo's house and the cemetery, which was not remotely spooky, but modern, polite, and dull (evoking *Die Stadt*'s banal municipal tidiness). The road, the one with two dead ends, would give way to a gravel path, which then turned into a muddy track through grass, then past some trees and over a second railway track which was not in use, and down towards a small brook. A small wooden footbridge crossed here (your booming footsteps echoing like the room with fake reverb in *Die Stadt*), and on the other side was the new housing estate, built in the 1980s, Horeston Grange. The estate was named, like so many conquering developments, after what it replaced, the manor house and its land. This small wooden bridge then, was a boundary (not guarded, like the no-man's land of *Possession*, but there nonetheless). Standing on the bridge and looking north, you could watch the small brook as it trickled under Hinckley Road, by the roundabout where it meets Higham Lane. The water trickled through a concrete cylinder (*Stalker* again).

Horeston Grange had two main roads that made two horseshoes through the red-brick houses, but never met. Each one had many *culs-de-sac* budding from it. I'd cut through the pedestrian walkways, until I got to the allotments at the other end, cross them, and climb over my back fence. (In Agata Pyzik's *Poor But Sexy: Culture Clashes in Europe East and West*, she talks about both *Possession* and *Stalker* in the context of, among other things, a fetishism regarding the Soviet years by both the East and West. Am I guilty, accidentally or otherwise, of conflating my memories of a small town in England with an exotic [to me] series of elsewheres? If so, my confusion was aided and abetted by the planners of the estate themselves, who decided to name the roads of Horeston Grange after towns in Devon and Cornwall, 180 miles away, and with no obvious link.) I'd get home nearly three hours after school had ended. When Mum asked me what I'd been up to I would answer, truthfully (and just like the boy in *Teenager* [Soriano Rocha,

✳✳✳

When the spaces in novels deceive me, it feels like a failure of my imagination. Every time I tried to picture the house while reading Gabriel García Márquez's *One Hundred Years of Solitude* I could only see my Nan's old house in Portchester, England. It couldn't be more different from a wooden structure in the rainforest. Similarly, the Stamper residence in *Sometimes A Great Notion* shares a layout, to my mind, with the first house I lived in, despite the former being a lopsided wooden building in the Oregon woods and the latter a semi-detached brick house in suburban England. I haven't seen the film version of that book, but I did picture Paul Newman as Hank as I was reading, because I knew he was in the film. An actor can be resolute and clear in your mind, even when you haven't seen all their films, or cannot tell their films apart.

✳✳✳

A recent dream brought to mind a drunken brawl from a black and white film. At first I thought it was from *Top Banana Got Shot* (Ken Wall, 1952), but there is no fight scene in that film. It isn't *Johnny Guitar* (Nicholas Ray, 1954) either, for while the architecture of the setting is similar, with a structure built right up against a rock for protection, that film is in livid Technicolor. It is easy to search the internet for *best westerns* or *the films of Nicholas Ray* but at this point in our history,

---

1962]), *nothing much.*

searching for video of a bar fight that matches your memory using only keywords is difficult. Eventually, when thinking about something else, I remembered. It is Billy Wilder's *Temperance* (1949). Two characters duke it out in a pioneer wilderness. Horses reel wildly at gunshots. The wrestling men finally fall through the doors of a minimal hut-cum-bar, in a frantic embrace. In this new environment, their behaviour suddenly seems absurd to them. They stop, sit at the bar, ask for the bottle, and share a drink. It is as if they've landed in a different scene in a different film, and when my memory places them in *Johnny Guitar* or *Top Banana,* then in a way, they have.

***

What are our favourite films? Are they the ones we watch the most, or the ones we think about the most even though we've seen them only once? Are they the ones we buy on cassette, and then again on DVD, special editions, Blu-ray, and save to the cloud? Are they the ones we keep close at hand, on display, next to the television? Next to my Mum's TV there are various musicals, family comedies, her wedding tape. Mum and my stepdad got married when I was eleven. A camcorder was operated by several people throughout the day. The camera work includes many amateur flourishes, now quite dated: long, slow pans from one side of the room to the other, and back again, endlessly. Extreme zooms wobble into the faces of talking guests at a distant table (followed by the cameraman laughing gently to himself, or offering a commentary on the action, until the subjects notice they are being filmed, and then mug for the camera, or feigning annoyance, pretend to hide their faces) The original video was damaged some years ago. The soundtrack is still clear, but the picture is hidden by rolling bars of colour. Now, you can hear my narration, squeakily pre-pubescent, as I intrude on my sister getting changed into her evening dress, and you can hear her screams, as well as the laughing screams of my cousins, but you cannot see my sister jumping to hide behind her bed. The video was converted to DVD a decade ago, but the transfer did not fix the tracking problem. As a visual document it is useless. But now we can watch the DVD reproduction of broken video textures on a large new TV with a stereo sound-system. We have done this as a family more than once.

A moment that ages the tape specifically: Grandad's mobile phone rings during the ceremony. Everyone laughs. He is the only person there with a device like this, and the shock is obvious. A ringing phone at a contemporary wedding would barely be noticed, with the owner of the phone generally excusing themselves or fumbling in quiet embarrassment until the noise is killed. But amongst the ensuing good-natured derision on the video are at least two voices who suggest that my Grandad has phoned himself, just to be seen to be important enough to have a mobile phone, and to be called on it. The glee, the excitement, the wonder of this novel technology, is evident. Today, no-one would behave in this way.

***

Artist Hans Tefl collects homemade videos like this. Weddings, school plays, holidays. With footage of Disneyland trips sent to him by hundreds of families, he made a thirty-hour piece called *The Kids at Space Mountain* (2005). Child after child passes by us, excited to be in the Magic Kingdom, smiling at their parents who hold camcorders or phones. *Watching it is like a dream of a perfect childhood moment, forever*, Tefl says.[10]

***

In Tefl's uncharacteristically breezy history of man and technology, *Selfie*, he lays out his fascination with on-camera behaviour by those unaccustomed to it. The book, as well as including photo essays about Tefl's own Stuttgart apartment, sets itself up as a kind of study of the *presented* self. *Look at the Victorians stiffly posed for group photographs, or paddling children on whirring Super 8 home movie reels (that default setting for* nostalgia *in Hollywood films, irrespective of era). Then there is the news footage of those men and women in line to buy copies of Lady Chatterley's Lover in 1964, after a judge said it could be legally sold again. Then contestants on reality television. Then self-taken images of one's new haircut taken in a restaurant bathroom in the 21st Century. This progression shows us a degradation of the relationship between technology and humanity. As technology improves, our reverence for it grows, and*

---

[10] *Tefl says:* Interview at filmfanblog.com, April 2008 (www.filmfanblog.com/interviews/2008/4/tefl2)

our suspicion of it lessens. It is easy to identify the era when a recording was made, even if we cannot see the image. Just hearing the comfort of the talkers, the formality of their speech, clues us in completely.[11] This is not just true of the average person, Tefl says, but performers too, those whose possession of their own image one might expect to be stronger. *Compare the almost lazy, comparatively unaffected (incompetent even) miming of The Rolling Stones or the Kinks on television in 1965 with any music video made in 2015. Any individual who has grown up in the era of the music video knows instinctively the postures required to portray anything. Even confusion and reluctance have codified gestures that have developed with each technology.* In the 21st century, we are not surprised by cameras at events. Our reaction is likely to be to pull out our own and record too. A wedding in 2015 will produce thousands of photos and footage from any number of sources, the guests, and will rarely all be pulled together into a complete project. *Perhaps social media will help us collaborate on the biggest film of all time. Perhaps we are already doing this, but are too close to the screen to see the image,* Tefl says.

***

Are these the films of the future? Incomplete collage recordings created in a nebulous cloud by a team of amateurs? Would this be so far away from the work of Alex Aliyeva (page 53) or Tom Grimini?[12] In *VHS*

---

[11] *clues us in completely: Selfie* (Paragon Books, 2011).

[12] *Grimini:* I do not refer to the early acclaimed Glasgow-set punk films like *Play The Roy Race Card* (1978) and *Chechen Burr* (1980) for which Grimini is best known. Those leave me

Minutes (1985) Grimini visits his family and with a series of cameras, recording devices, and notebooks attempts to record every aspect of their behaviour over a weekend. He fails, of course. As did scientist, actor and philanthropist Edward Titchell, who experimented with gramophone recordings in the first decades of the 20th century.[13] Marcel Proust dedicated his time to compiling his memories, and felt a failure. Proust fan and filmmaker Barry Bishopsfield has dedicated most of his creative life to amending and correcting one piece of work. His *Tom*

somewhat cold, being perfectly arthouse in every way, perfectly imperfect, and thus somehow hermetic. His later works, specifically *VHS Minutes* and *Bundle* (both 1985) are less sure of themselves, and much more interesting.

[13] *Titchell:* In his *Collected Diaries* (Vintage Books, 1949) Titchell says *at Christmas 1914, war had broken out, and my extended family was to be holidaying en masse at my uncle's estate in Gloucestershire. I knew I would never see all of these people together again in one place. Some were soon to be doing their bit overseas, some on the verge of moving away to Canada and Australia. My uncle himself was elderly and ill. The gaudy dinner table repartee I grew up around would be lost. I took along on the journey from London as much of my recording equipment that I and my men could fit into a third-class compartment, and set it up around the house; in the dining room, the study, the kitchen. I wanted to capture as much of their conversation, their off-colour remarks, their wonderful jokes, for myself. But during that holiday, even with all of us there, it was too late. Father, a fine storyteller, did not have the patience to socialize anymore, and Mother hadn't the energy to cajole him. But still I looked at them, and the others, and tried to remember every detail. I managed, at great expense, to capture hours and hours of their voices, but still found it missed so much. I was initially disappointed. The wit contained within is a pale shadow of that which I knew and heard for many summers. But I would also put forth that those recordings contain far more life, humour and telling revelations about the human condition that any London show I have seen to date. And I would wager that my family is not uniquely brilliant; that in all families, everyone is a clown and a storyteller. Everyone knows the script, and can recite any part. All families have perfect timing, especially when they talk over each other.*

Keeps Score (page 215) has been endlessly remade, re-edited, perfected, and re-perfected, ever unfinished. Bishopsfield says *so many of the artists that intrigue me, real or imagined, are obsessed with memory.*[14] *Fictional Film Club*, despite its speculative nature, is actually an act of memory.

***

I had a premonition when I was ten. I was riding my bike to the shops. I knew, suddenly, as I rounded the long curve past the roundabout by the Harvester (where the Long Shoot meets Hinckley Road and Eastboro Way) that I would grow up to make a film called *Chocolate Cassette*. I didn't know where the words came from, or what they meant, but by the time I had gone inside and bought a loaf of bread for Mum and two Biscuit Boosts for myself, I had seen in my mind's eye, over and over again, a cassette, made entirely of milk chocolate, being placed into a Walkman, which was made of the regular combination of plastic and metal. It would fit perfectly, spin, and slowly melt. *Chocolate Cassette.* The image stuck with me. The words had power.[15] I would imagine the chocolate cassette inside the pocket of a sweating spy walking through

---

[14] *obsessed with memory:* Taken from Bishopsfield's blog entry dated May 2001. (www.barrybishpsfield.com/blog/5-15)

[15] *words had power:* In the 1998 film *Lipstick Fibrosis*, Jayney, guitarist in the titular band, says: *This is how bands should be formed. Name first. Someone, in a state of enlightened stupor, puts together two words, perhaps three. They are so beautiful and threatening that they hang in the air like a dare, at least until the band is formed, and friendships and livers are ruined forever. For a higher purpose.*

Berlin Tegel airport. Or locked in a temperature-controlled vault behind a large canvas in a billionaire's study. Or being discovered in a quarry by a gang of tearaways. In all cases, it contained a recording that could only be played once. A song, a code, a secret, which is heard, then eaten. Melodies built around lost chords, or numbers that describe the edge of the universe, ingested and gone. The eternal McGuffin. These scenes stretched in my head and became wider narratives. Films with sequels that always involved tense face-offs between smoking men. *The Search For The Chocolate Cassette. Return Of The Chocolate Cassette. Chocolate Cassette At The Beach.* The delicacy of the delicacy was never forgotten. But what would it sound like? I was never sure. All along, I wondered if I hadn't seen the title *Chocolate Cassette* on a video box, or on a book cover. I remember, as a test, asking David H, a local pop culture authority, if he had heard of *Chocolate Cassette.* He said *yeah, sure, why not?* Characteristically perhaps, I didn't see this as an exposure of David H, but as a confirmation of the power of imagination.

Years later on my first trip to New York I was on a subway train. Lights and colour flashed by as we passed through a station. A film poster flew by. There was a blonde head. Some words. *Chocolate Cassette*, they seemed to say. It's easy to see, now, with the internet, that it doesn't exist. But it does exist too, because I thought of it.

So *Chocolate Cassette* is my favourite film, at least until I see it. I've thought of it as a cool title, a terrible one, a clever one, too clever, dumb. It doesn't matter. *Chocolate Cassette* is a mantra, a promise. *No matter how bad things are, don't worry. One day you will make* Chocolate Cassette. The few friends I've told about it ask what it is about, or ask if I've got any film equipment, or money for the production. This misses the point. *Chocolate Cassette* exists. If it was made it might not. It is the eleventh film in the top ten, the empty place at the table for the guest who doesn't show up, the prayer you don't say aloud. It is my all-time favourite film that does not exist, and the best tribute to it is to leave it out of this book.

***

Picking a favourite film from a selection of films that were never made is tough.[16] What do you leave out? There's so much. I have decided, in

[16] *tough:* I could explain my process. I made a document called CONTENTS with a long list from which I would make the final selections. They were ordered chronologically. (By the year of their fictional release, not the order in which I wrote them.) Some of them were just a name with no film attached. I liked looking at the names in different fonts of varying authority. I liked the page that said CONTENTS so much that I added to the document some of my writing about the films I had selected. I put them in the correct order, with suitable fonts. I printed it out. I did no further work that day. The printing felt like enough. I had achieved something. I had, on paper, the bulk of my manuscript. Now theoretically I could carry it with me, look at it on the bus, maybe edit it with a red pen in the staff room at work; inspired, I might take bathroom breaks and pull a folded page out of the inside of my shirt and add some notes. I could take it anywhere now, rather than wait until I got home to my computer to work.

But once I'd printed it out, I couldn't imagine leaving the house without it, and didn't for weeks, during which I did no work on the pages. None. And also, because I'd printed the document, I couldn't work on it on the computer, because then the printout would be wasted, and I'd be carrying an expired version, useless. I had to be carrying the latest version, and I was, as long as I didn't change it. So while having the manuscript in my bag meant that I could edit it on

this book, to only include films up until 1970, with later films presented in further volumes at some point. My only real disclaimer is that if any of these films are actually real ones, I apologise. I have no way of knowing. I am reminded of the time that I first moved, in a childhood filled with moves, from one school to another, miles away. I walked in on the first morning to see my new head teacher who had actually been my old head teacher at my old school, but she had left the previous summer, apparently to work here. *We can help each other find our way around,* she said. I was six. It made it clear to me that people didn't just disappear when they left my life. The world exists beyond my classroom, beyond my school, beyond my house. But there are only so many people and places. More than you'll ever see, but still. Every list has an ending. This is both terrifying and reassuring.

---

my journey to work, it also meant that I would not. If it is in my bag it is safe, as long as I don't take it out and attempt to improve or finish it. After a while I tried carrying my laptop around with me, so that I could work anywhere. The laptop fit in my bag, but nothing else would. I couldn't take lunch or another book or a notebook with me. The weight of the unfinished book was literal and metaphorical. I pictured the horror and relief of manuscripts lost in two films: at sea in *The Second Draft* (John Loose, 1999) and floating in the breeze in a parking lot in *Wonder Boys* (Curtis Hanson, 2000). I imagined my laptop dropping off the top level of a multi-storey car park and smashing into pieces with some satisfaction.

THE MESMER

Louis Grenier, 1894

I always knew I could make something of myself, even if it was something false.

Louis Grenier

When people first hear about Louis Grenier, they tend to be taken by the peculiars of his case (the disappearance-slash-death of Grenier and his wife Annabelle Newton), and I was no different. It was years before I found myself finally able, or willing, to locate him in a wider context.

1894 was before the Lumière Brothers and Thomas Edison set the 20th Century in motion. The future was still to be invented.[17] Most people hadn't seen a projected image on a large screen. Louis Grenier, an amateur magician from Paris, had, and saw great possibilities for its use in his stage act. He arrived in New York that New Year with pages

---

[17] *20th century:* If we accept that *recorded* time is a human creation, then it is clear that the invention of cinema was what started the 20th century. In the same way, the 1950s did not begin until Elvis Presley appeared on the Ed Sullivan Show in 1956. the 1960s did not begin until The Beatles charmed America in the JFK vacuum of early 1964; the 1970s didn't begin until Watergate; the 1980s until MTV first broadcast in 1981; the 1990s until Bill Clinton's election, or the début of *Friends*, or until I moved from Nuneaton in Warwickshire to Worthing in West Sussex. The rather arbitrary way we divide the decades is both convenient and false. The 20th century, as refracted through her pop, jazz, television, and cinema, is resolutely *about* time. It is also about *recording*. Sinatra on wax. TV footage of the moon landing and the Berlin Wall falling. These are all *records*. The first rock'n'roll single was *Rock Around The Clock* and it was about movement, about energy, about two minutes long. About time.

of designs for a piece of machinery that would augment his act. His Octoscope II used a flip-card technique to turn the stills, which were projected onto a screen using a series of mirrors. It was limited, but Grenier knew that if used carefully, successful illusions could be created that would help launch a career in magic, like his hero Jean Eugène Robert-Houdin.

From a modern perspective, it might seem that Grenier lacked the vision to see what projected pictures could and would be; that his ideas steered him towards the cul-de-sac of novelty, rather than moving him forward into the widescreen dreams of the future.[18] After all, there is nothing more Victorian than a stage magician. But this seems a cruel reading. Grenier's biggest misstep might be that he did not let his audiences draw breath. The invention of cinema was so large that people had to understand it, let it sink in, before being asked to move forward. And in 1894, they didn't—couldn't—yet. The following year in Paris, the Lumière Brothers' film of a train arriving at a station would cause people to flee their seats in fear of the train hitting them. Audiences had yet to learn to *watch*.[19]

---

[18] *future:* The Lumière Brothers themselves said *the cinema is an invention without a future.* Edison, the better businessman, saw otherwise.

[19] *to watch:* The Lumière Brothers first showed a program of films in 1895 that included *La Sortie de l'Usine Lumière à Lyon* (Workers Leaving the Lumière Factory). They brought their show to New York in 1896, two years after Grenier's disappearance. It is striking that the first film showed people leaving work. The implication (if we were to search for one) might be that technology would free us from the factory; the reality might be that it helps us (with smart phones

Novelty must be allowed to percolate. Grenier was arguably not behind the curve, but too far ahead. Most celebrated pioneers are rarely the first in their field. They are usually in the peloton, catching up with the breakaway riders. They move the gestalt to reveal the path, shift the gaze to show a trail that somebody had already taken, but unseen.[20]

***

The written word, as Victorian thinker, novelist, and activist Elizabeth Bart said, *is a rigidly linear form: left to write, left to right.* The sequence of letters tells us a story, in order. The novel took us away from the village, away from society, into ourselves. The novel, when it works (which is not necessarily the same as saying when it is good, or when it is done

and iPods) tolerate the commute.

[20] *shift the gaze:* Take The Beatles. Their global sphere of influence is so large that an American president's performance is now more likely to be informed by the words and style of John Lennon than Theodore Roosevelt. What blend of elements made The Beatles so popular? We could argue all day. But at their core, there are enough distinctly recognizable parts: the Chuck Berry riffs. The Everly Brothers' harmonies. Music hall. Spike Milligan. An easy handsome charm. (Add in, I suppose, a kind of gang quality, the necessary role for every member, and the suggestion, to paraphrase Ian Svenonius, that the group as an *idea* is more powerful than any member – one can imagine John, Paul, George, or Ringo sitting on the toilet, but it is impossible to imagine *The Beatles* doing so.) They wove in newer ideas and technologies throughout the sixties with a playful confidence that never alienated, unlike the work of, say, Yoko Ono (the pariah in their story for three crimes: being Japanese, being a woman, and being interested in the avant-garde). Because they were trusted, by the mid-sixties The Beatles could lead us into more outré territories. But no matter how expansive and experimental they were, they always existed in a recognizable pop idiom, albeit one they were rapidly helping to reshape. Deliberately or otherwise, they followed Harry Houdini's showbiz maxim that you *have to let the audience see that the rabbit has disappeared before you make him reappear.* Grenier did not.

well), performs a mind-meld on the solo reader, in secret. It might do it a million times over, to a million different readers, but the process is fundamentally one that exacts itself in solitude.

Marshall McLuhan, who borrowed some of his best riffs from Bart, said *technology brings us together, but in an illusory way.*[21] Which is more dangerous than not at all. The new is as satisfying as it is distressing. Henry Ford: *If I had asked people what they wanted, they would have said faster horses.* Or better novels. More ambitious painters. But they got those too, and one could argue, *because* of the technology. George Bernard Shaw said that *art has many blind midwives pulling it from the neoplasm of vague channels into a clear bright world.* The step into the cinema era can scarcely be imagined to have been imagined completely, even by the protagonists.[22]

---

[21] *The Medium Is The Message* (Penguin Books, 1967) p.67. McLuhan's *The Medium Is The Message* seems very of its time now, but in many ways it is essentially Bart's *A Victorian Audit* (self-published, 1884) redux, with added puns. Both were fearful of the impact of technology on our lives. Bart's primary concern was the seismic transition from painting to photography. McLuhan gets credit for coining the term *Global Village,* and for predicting the internet (and its effects) in the middle of the twentieth century. But here is Bart, more than eighty years earlier: *Now one can foresee another way in which we might be complicit in our own downfall, not from war, but from leisure. Not from guns but from distracting entertainments. Comforting, delightful, distracting entertainments.* (*A Victorian Audit*, p.456.)

[22] *scarcely be imagined:* In his 2012 book *Likes* (Random House), Anton Burbank suggests that inventors seldom understand their creations: *Pictures of cats, romances with old school friends; the Amazon monolith; old TV clips on YouTube; being at the beck and call of a boss outside the office as well as at work; this is where the Internet is. The liberation we hoped for is buried in a snowstorm of 'likes'. The word 'like' has, like, become, like, punctuation in both spoken, and,*

***

Louis The Magic was the name of Grenier's first show using the Octoscope II, and it appears to have been a simple spirit illusion using a projection of a dancing girl. The Octoscope II was cumbersome, noisy, and incredibly hot, and drew attention to itself wherever it was placed in the theatre. In other shows that year Grenier employed similar effects and had similar problems: *The New York Buzzard* described *The Queen of Sheba* as a *disappointing fizz of non-technologies* while *The Manhattan Fidget* called *Resurrection* a *blasphemous cuss at the black art of entertainment.*[23]

The Mesmer was a huge step forward. It was a show that acknowledged Grenier's failures as both a magician and a scientist. Alongside Grenier was stage star Annabelle Newton, quite the coup

---

like, written language. It is therefore completely appropriate that Facebook users are allowed to 'like' a comment, or a band, or a post. Because this action does not mean a firm commitment; it is peripheral, milquetoast, and essentially, a brief comma in the structure of one's life. In this way, a strong political statement, a work of art, or a complaint about the weather are all reduced to the same level. (Likes p.56)

[23] *newspapers:* The number of newspapers that sprang up in New York in the last two decades of the 19th century is worth commenting on here. Many of them, printed several times a day, were owned by successful businessmen such as William Randolph Hearst, who saw an opportunity to have a direct mouthpiece to the ears of the people. These newspapers' blend of optimism and scorn is familiar to tabloid readers of the later 20th century. As well as those mentioned above, the list of newspapers that reported on Louis Grenier include *The Downtown Fibber, Sullied Victoriana, American Tat, The Brooklyn Brag, The Gotham Bugle, The Big Apple Vigilant,* and *The Williamsburg Soothsayer.*

as her New York fame drew crowds.[24] Grenier performed a series of illusions that initially seemed familiar, with Newton disappearing and reappearing in different areas of the theatre. But then, after entering a large wardrobe, she could be seen on a screen above the stage. In pre-recorded reels, she danced to the music of the orchestra in the theatre. The musicians themselves timed silences to coincide with parts of the film when Newton appeared to be frozen, and sped up to a frantic pace during a sequence when the illusionist himself appeared on screen and repeated, at exaggerated speed, the illusion performed just five minutes earlier in the theatre, only in reverse. At this point, both Grenier and Newton, according to a breathless report in the *Queens Inquisitor, reapparated there upon the brocaded balconies of the real world Palace Theater, in fully three dimensions, plausible and verified by those sound gentlemen in proximity.*

The trick was repeated, but with masterful variations—at one point, looking confused, Grenier left the stage and approached the Octoscope II. The house lights came up. He apologized to the crowd, turned the machine off, and appeared to puzzle over its non-functioning innards, with loose reels and cogs falling everywhere. As people began to boo and leave, an image of Grenier appeared on the screen,

---

[24] *Annabelle Newton:* Annabelle Newton had a familiarity for me that I placed only recently. She had the same peachy cheekbones and small eyes set wide apart as a girl I went to school with, L. But only in *this* film. An internet search yields a range of Newton images that look nothing like the memory I have of L. It is as if, in some way, she plays L in this film. The bobbing hair just below the chin. The slow blink. The blush.

shouting instructions to himself below in the theatre about how to fix the machine.[25]

The Mesmer was a great success, and Grenier and Newton toured the country with it, marrying on the road in October 1894. The Grenier-Newtons were cover stars of magazines, and a recording of a performance of *The Mesmer* was made using Edison's Kinetoscope, which itself played up and down the East Coast.[26] This version of *The Mesmer*, a recording shorn of the live action element, was among a rotating set of films played on Edison's increasingly more robust machines. Next to such plain, single-shot action reels as *The Duel* and *A Family Walking*, it must have appeared vague and unclear, like a kind of stage set without actors. Here, *The Mesmer* sequences lacked context

---

[25] *fix the machine:* Judging by some reports, the crowd did not understand the technology enough to fully appreciate the mastery of Grenier's illusion. If one does not understand how the Octoscope II works, even superficially, could one be impressed by it apparently working even though it was broken? As Houdini said, *the crowd member must at least feel like he is able to guess as to the machinations of the trick; if one makes the Sun disappear, staggeringly impressive as it may be, the crowd might feel short-changed, as they cannot even begin to understand how it might be done.*

[26] *the East Coast:* This recording, which lasts for seventeen minutes, huge for the time, is what contemporary reviewers refer to when discussing the film *The Mesmer*. It is of course, a film of a show involving film, and as such is an early example of *Filmism*, the movement championed by the Spanish New Wave in the early fifties: Filmism was a post-modern attempt to examine the art of cinema by filming screenings of films. A split in 1960 between *Real-Filmists* (those who shot the theatre, the audience, and surroundings, as well as the feature) and *True-Filmists* (those who only permitted the feature itself on-screen) caused ripples throughout intellectual Spain. Both parties remained fans of *The Mesmer*, however.

and content, like a record sleeve without the record.

The Mesmer show was successful but expensive, and the Grenier-Newtons' debts grew. In 1896 Annabelle took up an offer of a contract to appear in some of Edison's Biograph movies and Grenier announced one final farewell performance of *The Mesmer* at Brooklyn Hall on October 26, 1896 that would *bury the ghost of magic.*[27] Highly publicized, the show sold out; but despite hundreds of witnesses, there is much conjecture over what actually happened that night.

Most agree that Grenier and Newton performed better than ever, and despite the rumoured strain on their relationship, the horse-play and chemistry between husband and wife was unnaturally natural. The trouble appeared to flare in the third act, at the part when Grenier came into the audience to fix the broken Octoscope II. As usual, the images on the screen somehow continued even after Grenier turned the machine off to examine it, and as ever, he argued with the image of himself on-screen. But then something different happened. Newton appeared on-screen too, and to much laughter, argued with both of her husbands about the best way to fix the problem; the joke, of course, being that there was no problem if they were both on the screen. Then the fake problem appeared to become a real one. Or did it? Did the device

---

[27] *bury the ghost of magic:* Grenier used this term ironically, as Edison had supposedly described stage magicians like Grenier as *ghosts* that his inventions *would bury.* Grenier disliked Edison and must have been troubled that the Grenier-Newtons' finances were so dependent on Annabelle's acting gigs in Edison productions.

spin into life, knocking out noise and heat, causing the projected pair to double, triple, quadruple, and play at super speed, dancing and dancing, faster yet, causing the applause to grow to crescendos? Or is this myth-making, caused by confused or melodramatic witnesses?[28]

Firemen came to confront the blaze, and while no audience members were hurt, the Grenier-Newtons were never seen again. Nor were their bodies found. Eyewitnesses report seeing Grenier dissolve into the wall, fly through the air, or erupt in a cloud of smoke as his likeness burned on screen. Or they say he was carried out in an ambulance, he was mingling outside with his wife after the show, or he made a hasty exit through a backstage door. They can't all be true, and might all be wrong. A cab driver who claimed to have driven the pair to Grand Central station later that night was proved to be a drunk. Did Grenier fake their deaths to escape debts? Or kill his wife and himself in an elaborate double bluff? Periodically, internet sleuths will report uncanny likenesses of the pair in the background of a film from the early decades of the 20th Century; he as an unnamed bar patron or cowboy, she as a Ziegfeld Folly girl or a masked beauty in a harem. Some of these claims are compelling, but no sighting has been verified.

The Big Town Sober Judge offered a sentimental reflection sev-

---

[28] *melodramatic witnesses:* One said: *Before we knew it, the cursed contraption was a heap of hot yellow. This caused the images on the screen to melt and distort, spinning the dancing images into new confounding shapeless peoples, before exploding into snapping stars. The smell of burning filled the lungs of the patrons, and the slides burned, burned, burned* (*"Death Blaze Envelops Magician, Wife" American Tat*, October 27th, 1896).

eral weeks later:

> *It is as if, undone by the real world, failing at life,*
>
> *Grenier conjured a feat beyond any: He man-*
>
> *aged to vault himself and his wife into a deathless*
>
> *afterlife, a constant invisibility; and in this burning*
>
> *heaven of celluloid and wood, where she dances*
>
> *and he draws rabbits from hats, the words Louis*
>
> *the Magic and legend are never separated.*[29]

***

The feeling persists that Louis Grenier doesn't fit into cinema history. That he's not allowed to count. He isn't *cinema*. But in a time when film and the edge of its territories are vaguer than ever, maybe the difference between experimental oddball and visionary future geographer should not be drawn so starkly.

The Mesmer

Directed by Louis Grenier. Produced by Louis Grenier, Thomas Atherton.
Written by Louis Grenier. Starring: Louis Grenier, Annabelle Newton-
Grenier. Biograph/ Black Maria Studio. Release Date: 1894 (US). 20 mins.
Tagline: Come And See The Greatest Conjurer in New York. . . Bury The
Ghost of Magic!

---

[29] *"Editorial Opinion" Big Town Sober Judge*, November 12th, 1896

ARIPILE INVIZIBILE ALE COLIBRI

(THE INVISIBLE WINGS OF THE HUMMINGBIRD)

Dmitri Loao, 1913

Nothing whets the intelligence more than a passionate suspicion.

Stefan Zweig

When Vincenzo Loao fell from his horse and subsequently died near Bucharest in 1913, the story made the front page of most of the newspapers in Romania. Loao was a baron of some wealth, and a cousin of Prime Minister Ion I.C. Bratianu. If he was known outside his home country it was because he was a prominent practitioner of *Tigan Tau* (loosely translated as *gypsy Tao),* a fad in parts of Eastern Europe during the early decades of the 20th century. But his place in film history might have been forgotten were it not for the detective work of self-described *shamanistic historian* Nicolae Nicolescu half a century later.

Nicolescu pursued an obsessive interest in the Loao case for many years, seeking to understand the baron's cryptic dying wishes. Suffering from the head wound that would kill him several days after his fall, Loao wrote out the message he wanted for his headstone, in weak cobwebby crayon. It was a mixture of Romanian, Portuguese (the language of his grandfather) and several indecipherable words. Sweating and feverish, he insisted that everything be reproduced exactly as he had drawn it. His younger brother Dmitri dutifully saw that a stonemason reproduce the message exactly, despite not understanding it all himself. Fragments could be made to make sense; one line seemed to say *the hummingbird cannot be seen to move* although some argued that it was more like *the hummingbird moves so quickly that no one can see* – a subtle difference, but a difference all the same.

Nicolescu thought that Tigan Tau would be the key to translating the message, but the religion confounded him. *It is a derivation of Eastern transcendentalism fed through a Dead Sea gauze and winged with Romany blood rituals and flower-theory. As far as I can tell,* he wrote. *I may be wrong.* He was about to conclude his research when, he claimed, news came that changed his book. In March of 1966, a publican in Bucharest found two reels of film in his basement that he was not able to identify. Rather than handing them to the authorities, he was persuaded by a customer to let them be taken to the University of Bucharest, where they ended up on the desk of a scholar referred to by Nicolescu as *Mr Gheorghe,* but who we might reasonably assume is actually Nicolescu himself.[30]

Gheorghe identified the main actor appearing in both films as Vincenzo Loao, the exotic part-foreigner who died fifty years earlier. His striking black features and his long frame (Loao being, by various accounts, anywhere between six and seven feet tall) were verified by many in Loao's hometown, just twenty miles from the capital. Gheorghe

[30] *is actually Nicolescu:* Film scholar Teuton L. Bosch (who presented *Aripile Invizibile Ale Colibri at* MOMA in 1999) feels strongly that Gheorghe is Nicolescu. In 1990 Nicolescu had revealed, after all, that he often used pseudonyms during his research, because of his concern about the Communist regime's interest in his activities. His other names included Roberto, Mr Put-Put, Gris, and Gheorghe Lupescu.

noticed that some locals superstitiously refused to look at the films, despite the fact that each of them was only seven minutes in length, and contained apparently innocuous footage of Loao walking, dancing and performing a quiet array of poses for the camera.

Frustrated by the reluctance of the locals, Gheorghe was about to leave town when, according to his account, a mute and nearly blind man beckoned him into the woods. He led Gheorghe through the trees in near dark until they came to an abandoned barn. He gestured for Gheorghe to go inside, where there was nothing except a pile of wood in the centre of the building, prepared as if for a fire. The old man walked to the pile, lifted the wood and pulled out a can of film. On it was drawn a small white symbol. He pointed to this carefully, and then placed the film in Gheorghe's hands, gesturing for him to leave quickly.[31]

---

[31] *to leave quickly:* Bosch didn't necessarily believe this particular part of the story. He wrote in his labyrinthine history of film *VIZ-A-VIZUAL* (Intelligentsia, 1994) that Nicolescu had a flair for the dramatic too. Bosch and Nicolescu arranged to meet in West Berlin in 1982 to talk about the *Aripile Invizibile Ale Colibei* reels and several other films that Nicolescu was keen to keep out of the hands of the Ceausescu regime. Bosch was left waiting in his hotel for several days by notes left at the front desk postponing their meeting. On the last morning Nicolescu appeared at Bosch's breakfast table wearing a cape and carrying a long staff. As Bosch spoke German, English and French, and Nicolescu spoke Romanian, Albanian, and a little Yiddish, they struggled to communicate, and commandeered a Turkish waiter, who had some Albanian and German, to help. *Nicolescu took pains to always tell me that he was working on behalf of Mr Gheorghe,* Bosch wrote, *although he could have been talking about the weather too at times, and I wouldn't have known* (*VIZ-A-VIZUAL*, p.745). Bosch safely transported the films, and the two stayed in contact, with Bosch receiving postcards signed *Mr Gheorghe* and postcards signed *Nico* for several years.

It was another film of Loao. Also exactly seven minutes in length. Although the film was slightly deteriorated, the long dark gentleman could be seen throughout, performing several deliberate poses like a slow-motion martial art. It still made little sense.

But then in 1967, Gheorghe received an anonymous package. It was another film, much like the previous ones. Another arrived a month later. Weeks after that he received a tip-off of a Loao film turning up in Sarajevo, and retrieved it by train. Another was sent to him by an acquaintance in East Germany, who had no knowledge of his search. Later that year, when Gheorghe was interviewed over the phone by Greek periodical *Filmdat*, he drew attention to the films, and received an influx of new material. A stockbroker in London sent him a piece from his collection, which showed Loao on a horse approaching a castle; a projectionist at a picture house in Queens, New York, sent a film to Gheorghe that had been found amid reels of fading previews and crumbling B-movies.

In all, there were twenty pieces of film of Loao. Gheorghe put them together as best he could, but could make no sense of them.[32] He

---

When Nicolescu died in 2002, the correspondence from both stopped.

[32] *could make no sense:* According to Nicolescu, Gheorghe had worked in military intelligence for the Romanian government during the Second World War. He made these claims for himself too, saying he had solved the German *Reservehandverfahren* (a scrambled word code system used when no Enigma machine was available) before the British. Bosch quotes Nicolescu: *Deciphering codes has been my life, for better or worse (VIZ-A-VIZUAL, p.751).*

Mine too. My first Valentine was written in code. I received it when I was fourteen.

was convinced of a narrative, but could not recreate it. Nicolescu writes:

Gheorghe tried it all; tried playing them in every possible

order. Still, they only glowed with suggestion. But then,

something strange happened. When Gheorghe was trying

to change from one reel to another, his projector chewed

A little context: my attendance at school had always been patchy, but never more so than that previous year, since I'd perfected Mum's signature and written a series of notes excusing myself. As I had a history of minor and less-minor sicknesses, my teachers accepted these letters without question. But on that particular day I was there, and waiting in my seat before Geography. As the other kids came into the classroom, and began getting their books out of their bags, my friend Jo walked in with a large envelope and threw it on my desk. *It's not from me,* she said to the room, stepping back in order to be clear. *I'm just the messenger.* I thought of the naïve boy who plays the titular role in *The Go-Between* (Joseph Losey, 1971), and how he has no idea about the torrid love affair for which he is an unwitting conduit. I wanted to hide the card and study it privately at my leisure. At the bottom of the field maybe, or in the trees near the river. I would open it slowly, sniff the dried saliva holding down the envelope, stroke the handwriting inside like Siri Hansen in in Claus Johnsson's *Widow One* (1967) when she receives what she knows is her husband's suicide note. But my classmates crowded round, and quickly the card was being pawed at and wrestled over by many hands. It almost got ripped in a tug-of-war. Then Mr Davison came into the room, and they all scrambled back to their seats. *What's all the fuss about,* he asked. *Mark got a Valentine, sir,* they said, singing it like it was the funniest joke in the world. *Did Mark deign to bless us with his presence, today,* he said, *looking straight at me. Nice to see you for a change.* Mr Davison told everyone to sit down, and then picked up the card. *Should we read it and see who it is from,* he said. Everyone said yes except Jo and me. *Sorry Mark,* Mr Davison said, and winked, as if I was in on the humiliation, and not the focus of it. He put on his glasses slowly, and with a theatrical flick of the wrist, pulled the card from the envelope. He squinted. Everyone sat in anticipation for what he was going to say, like the guests at an award ceremony. *Who is it from, sir,* someone shouted. Mr Davison closed the card and put it on my desk. He took his glasses off. *It's written in some kind of code,* he said. *I suppose it's a message just for Mark then. Okay everyone, the fun is over! Open your textbooks to page 15, we've got a lot to cover today.*

the two reels and threw them onto the screen simultane-
ously; the two images (one of Loao performing an odd
karate; one of Loao miming fishing) were combined,
and created an entirely new shape: and behold! when
Loao moved into a lotus position, and this was now
juxtaposed with him riding a horse near a castle, one
could see something forming: new shapes, appearing like
hieroglyphics, his body shapes forming letters, sentences:
there is an A, hard and angular, there is a C, soft but
clear. And then Gheorghe remembered Loao's epitaph,
regarding the hummingbird, and pondered that the film
stock may be wings, which, when beaten together at fero-
cious pace would cause order to come... and after many
weeks of re-watching and watching, viewing the films in
different orders, laying them over each other on-screen
with two projectors, Gheorghe discovered the statement
that he believed that Loao had left and hidden. The sped-
up images of contorted body parts combined to spell out
the following:

I have nothing to say... There is no more... my body is
dead... I cannot believe in a world that exists without
me... therefore I must be alive... forever more.

Aripile Invizibile Ale Colibri

Directed, produced, written by, starring: Vincenzo Loao. ACE Films.

Release Date: 2002 (US) (the layered Gheorghe cut is credited Vincenzo Loao/Mr Gheorghe and is the only version to be commercially released, being shown at MOMA in 2002). 43 mins. Tagline: none

ваш фильм (YOURFILM)

Alex Aliyeva, 1922(?)

Bearing witness to the travelogues of others is one thing,

but when one can self-document a unique passage in

light and colour, does one not hum contentedly?

Gilles Deleuze

A ll audiences are frustrated by their inability to act, said famed acting teacher Brixford Hander. *They want to be involved more than they can be.*[33] But is this always true? Are video games so popular because we have a thirst for media we can interact with, manipulate, and control? Even at this point in the 21st century, when we can engage with quite sophisticated interfaces, more passive forms like cinema and television (and sometimes even novels and plays) sustain an interest. Perhaps Hander is wrong. But perhaps he is right, and part of the appeal of placing ourselves at the mercy of an artist or group of artists is the feeling of our hands being bound, our eyes being held open, to be made to sit and bear witness.

It is easy to think of cinema as a heritage art form threatened by more recent phenomena such as video games (just as theatre was threatened by film, and painting by photography and live music by recorded music and vinyl by cassette and cassette by compact disc and compact disc by downloads and streaming), but notions of interactive

---

[33] *Hander's Stagecraft* (1952, Penguin Books).

cinema are as nearly as old as cinema itself. Aleksandra 'Alex' Aliyeva was a Ukrainian who invented the YOURFILM technology in 1922. Utilizing brain pads that were attached to the heads of the viewers, YOURFILM technology changed the action according to the emotional reactions of the audience. What happened on screen, after the initial default image of two lovers on a battlefield (*Love and War are the beginning for all stories*, according to Aliyeva), depended entirely on how the assembled reacted.

Years after the technology had been destroyed, Aliyeva, an exile in France, gave an interview with *Cahiers du Cinéma* in which she described YOURFILM:[34]

[34] Andre Bazin: *"Big Ideas: Interview with Alex Aliyeva" Cahiers Du Cinéma*, December 1960. The library in Nuneaton was at the bottom of the high street, close to a roundabout on the ring road. (This might not seem immediately relevant. But as the hero [Gordon Jackson] says before his final speech about his childhood in *Dove Stiamo Andiamo* [*Where Are We Going*, Lucio Fulci, 1975] during which he reveals that he is actually the killer: *a tangent, perhaps, but indulge me, please.*) The roundabout had a stone monument that said *Welcome to the Geographic Centre of England, Please Drive Carefully*. When I didn't go to school I'd tend to go to places I wouldn't be seen, across the farmland north of school towards Higham-on-the-Hill, or along the brook in Weddington where I'd eat my sandwiches in the concrete drainage tunnel that ran under Hinckley Road if it was raining. Sometimes I'd be bolder and walk into town, where I'd usually end up at the library, as it was free and dry. I'd read biographies, history, short novels, the newspapers that we didn't get at home, the weekly comics, the monthly magazines that I'd never seen anywhere else: *Pop Situation, Sight & Sound*, and the compendiums of *Cahiers Du Cinéma*. I'd write lists of films I wanted to see in my notebook, and write reviews of them once I'd seen them (using a complicated scoring system that I won't elaborate on at this point).

Once when I was touring my usual spots of the library to find a particular volume of *Cahiers Du Cinéma* that I'd been reading the previous day, I saw David H sitting at one of the tiny tables on the rainbow carpet. His knees jutted high above the round table and he sat engrossed in a large picture book. I recognised it as one I'd enjoyed as a young reader: a bear decides to learn how to bake cakes but no animal will teach him as they are scared of him. It ended, I remember, in a strangely unresolved fashion, with the bear stowing away on a boat to head, he hopes, to the city. The last image made the sunset in the distance seem anything but welcoming, much like the last shot of the boy following the bus in *Forza Lagos* (Azu Uche, 1987). David H looked up from his book, saw me, unfolded himself from his chair and walked over. He grinned. *Good place to hide, eh? They never look for skivers in here do they?* I didn't tell him that I came here on Saturdays too. Most of the people that David H hung around with wouldn't talk to someone like me, but my parents knew his and had made us play together when we were small, and as David H had no anxiety about his place in the social food chain, he'd say hello. He got expelled for sniffing glue in the caretaker's office when we were twelve, but he would still show up at our gates after school with pornographic magazines from his lending library which he said was as tall as his bedroom cupboard. He had videos you could borrow for fifty pence, including the complete list of the video nasties banned by the Thatcher government. Whereas music cassettes were easily copied and consumed—a quick overnight double made on high-speed dubbing, renegade sounds hidden with headphones—films were problematic. Getting unfettered access to the family video player was tricky. But David H would offer thorough accounts of a film's plot, dialogue, décor, acting choices, and grand themes as he sat on the railings outside school. He'd string us along sometimes, turning a simplistic plot into a nuanced serial of ten-minute episodes each afternoon. *We see you more now than we ever did when you went to this school,* Mr Davison would say every time he saw David H (a line I'm convinced was a reference to the brutal deputy headmaster in *It's Doin' Me 'Ead In* [Tim Bosworth, 1974], perhaps Mr D's subtle way of saying that he was being indulgent with David H, but I never asked). Certain films David H described scene-by-scene I've since seen, and they were just like he said. *A Clockwork Orange, Risky Conquistador,* and *A.C.R.O.N.Y.M.* are all films I in turn described to other kids at length before I ever saw them, and my descriptions, written out carefully and put in my binder, were David H's.

David H leaned on a bookshelf and looked at me. *The girls at Etone are way fitter than at Higham Lane,* he said. *Best move I ever made.* I nodded. *Got any action yet,* he said. He rubbed his jaw in anticipation. But I had no news on that front. As I started to talk about the rogue *Cahiers du Cinéma* that I really had to find, the seedy glimmer in his eyes started to fade.

concept but more like Monet in its colouring and blurring of fantasies. Like melting clouds... one minute our heroine was running through a field, before the swaying wheat became a sea. The amazing thing was that the screen appeared different to each viewer at the same showing: what you saw

---

Wait. There is something, I said. I didn't want to lose his attention.

Ushering him over to a quiet aisle, I pulled out the Valentine. He took it like it was an important document, and held it delicately. He lowered gently to the floor and placed it on the carpet. We knelt over it. He smoothed out the creases that had been caused by the melee and gently fingered a small rip. *What have we here then,* he said, and we both sat over the card like any number of treasure map scenes from any number of films. *I can't understand it,* I said, when he opened it to read it. He stroked his face as he looked at the jumbled text. He stared at the page for a few seconds, then looked at me. *Twenty pence,* he said, and held out his hand. I paused, and he wiggled his fingers. I felt around in my pocket for some coins.

Dear Mark...roses are red, violets are violet, I'll be the plane if you'll be the pilot. I want to kiss you every day love L--- xxx. David H threw his head back and laughed.

It doesn't say that, I said.

It does too, he said. *I swear. It's written in Iggedy. Some of the girls used to write me messages in class with it when I was still at school. Your school, I mean.* He laughed again. *God, L--- really fancies you.*

L---?

Yeah. Dark Hair. To the chin. You do know her, right?

I paused, trying to appear cool with the whole subject. *I think so,* I said. *Do you think... it's really from her?*

Clear as day, he said. *I didn't think her taste would be so... sophisticated.* I thought he was teasing me. As a gesture of integrity he told me to keep my money, that this translation was free.

Just make sure you let L do everything she wants to you, he said. *She's a goer.*

and what your neighbour saw was different. You

agreed on the principles...or did you? One time a

group of drunken sailors turned the story into a

tawdry strip show through their bustling brainwav-

es (this happened quite a lot actually), but another

time, the same story reached a fetid nirvana of

absurdities with a crowd of minor geniuses. I wish

I could see that version again and again. But it is

gone.

A keen student of the work of Sigmund Freud, Aliyeva saw YOURFILM technology as an experimental art form that could expand humanity's horizons. But while Aliyeva was interested in the psychedelic uniqueness of each experience, and its meaning, the Soviets saw other possibilities, including the subliminal spread of propaganda. A few years later, Eisenstein's *Potemkin* and *October* would offer heroic socialist images, but in 1922, the Soviets felt that Hollywood studios were way ahead in the skillful way they hid covert political messages inside glamorous and humorous star vehicles. Perhaps YOURFILM could render such passive cinema old-fashioned, and put the Soviets at the forefront of the entertainment field. It was also potentially the symbolic embodiment of the socialist ideal: art with a collective author. By the people, and for them too.

But fate turned against YOURFILM. When Maxim Gorky

returned from Italy to the USSR in the early 1930s, his rejection of fascism and (re-)embrace of communism was such a propaganda boon that the writer was given the Order of Lenin. When Gorky compared YOURFILM to the *distracting trinkets of Coney Island* and called it *another time destroyer, a waste*, YOURFILM's days were numbered.[35] It was an indulgence, with one prominent critic too many.

The appetite for YOURFILM seemed to fade away. Funding was ended, Aliyeva moved to a new department, and the YOURFILM technology was put into storage. Officially, at least. But Aliyeva believes that the authorities were actually very excited by her work, and took the machine away from her in order to develop it into something she would not: a weapon. She asserts that huge, disorienting YOURFILM projections were thrown across the sky above the Germans in Stalingrad to confuse and scare them, the doctored technology working with and multiplying the fears of the invading troops.

She suspects that after 1945 it was co-opted by American agents, and that more-developed versions were used in Korea, Saigon, Nicaragua, and Iraq. She also claims to have spoken to North Vietnamese soldiers who have suggested that their enemies were somehow tooled with Soviet brain-pads in order to convince them that they were seeing huge ten-headed Communist hydras or futuristic tanks against them. *An ideal as a hologram,* she says.

---

[35] Maxim Gorky, *Notes on Exile,* Gosizdat S.P., 1935.

Aliyeva fled the USSR in 1955: *I was escaping from a regime that only had nefarious uses for my talents. That of course, may well be true everywhere,* she said. An interview in the UK in 1962 is worth quoting at length:[36]

> *Where did your studies into the YOURFILM technology begin?*
>
> I was a chemistry student and a fan of cinema. I had a friend in my class that I would go to the movies with. We were watching a film with Buster Keaton and Fatty Arbuckle. The one in the hotel...
>
> *The Bellboy?*
>
> Yes, yes. *Third rate services at First Class prices.* Ha. I'll never forget the moment when the horse-drawn elevator breaks and falls, causing the plank to throw the girl up in the air, and onto the elk's head on the wall. At that point, my classmate gripped the arms of the seat and convulsed in what seemed like laughter, but was a seizure. Later, after she recovered, she couldn't remember the film very well, and described sequences that weren't there. I was curious. Her medication subsumed her brain activity to prevent an attack. Not that we understood epilepsy then. We don't now, really. What I

---

[36] Tom Strand, *"From Behind The Curtain: Alex Speaks," Sight & Sound The Film Quarterly,* Winter 1962-1963.

started to do was to make a series of experiments that were really a search for a reverse medication. I attempted to create beautiful seizures in myself.

What do you mean by seizure?

A fit. A grand mal. But what happened wasn't, I thought, as strong. It was more like a drunken dream. And it wasn't for long. But then after, I was left with a curious sensation... that I've never felt again, but... it made me push on.

So how long did this experience last?

About eight minutes in total. In further experiments I made it longer. Then I made the real discoveries with pH balances and how they controlled the *texture* of the experience. But it was never quite as simple or precise as plotting certain narratives, as some people think. It was more of... a feeling.

So a pleasant narrative as an alkaline, say, and a negative one as acid?

Well that's the thing. Plotting an audience's emotional response to a film isn't simple. We recorded their behaviours, made readings. Temperatures, synapse readouts, finger pulses, interviews. Any discharge, really, was not only noted but sampled.

When did the authorities begin to take notice of your activities?

Well, in a sense, they always had. The university was government-funded. But one must remember that the Bolsheviks, in common with almost any government in the world, especially one that seizes power, are less interested in intellectual activity than one might suppose. And so being a scientist or a poet at a university is one of the more free places, because no-one in power is really looking much.

Which is why students lead so many protests around the world?

But any protesting group is always labelled *students* by authorities. The authorities know that to many people, the word *student* means lazy, inept, unrealistic, and naive. Amateur, and most of all *jobless*. If you're learning, you're not an expert.. And as we can see from talk shows, the *expert* has become a most privileged position. An expert can tell us that smoking kills. It takes another expert to tell us it does not.

Did the Soviets steer your research? Or try and stop it?

At first they made some good points. For example, that being scared in a horror film is not the same as fear of losing a job and not being able to feed a family. It is more like enjoyment. The man from the government who spoke to me, he was a small man in round glasses, and he was not a scholar, but he was smart. And he said to me: *smile, cry, laugh, punch the air; they all bought a ticket at the same price, did they not?* The problem for me was where they went with that.

Where was that?

I was interested in how different groups affected the film together, but the Soviets, ultimately, were interested in how a film might be used to affect a group of people. This is far less interesting, intellectually. But they were never intellectuals. They realized that what matters more than the reaction a program causes its audience is the fact that they are watching. Similarly, a regime can do whatever it wants to its citizens, as long as they are in power.

So the Soviet regime, you are saying, is an extension of this?

And beyond. Television is where we end up. A passive medium that cannot be affected. Unless we turn it off. And we don't.

Do you still hold out hope for technology such as

YOURFILM?

Even if—and I do not make the supposition lightly—
even if a group of people could find a way to harness
it—and I think we were very close—I'm far less optimistic about its application now. Our capacity for
wonder with regards to technology has diminished, for
a start.

***

Subsequent audience interfaces in cinemas have met with limited success. Generally they have been on-rails narratives that bear little relation to YOURFILM's free-wheeling possibilities.[37] Gimmicks like 3-D
glasses, scratch-and-sniff cards, and multi-screen projections are all
variations on a theme. They all say, in their way, that the film itself is not
enough. YOURFILM seemed to say that the film could be everything.

Aleksandra Aliyeva died in Paris in 1985. Up until her death,

---

[37] *possibilities:* The on-running *Choose Your Own...* series (in which each film stops at various
points for the audience to vote for whichever pre-recorded scenario they desire) has been resur-
rected many times since its 1954 début. For decades it was a forgotten gimmick but briefly came
back into fashion following its use by Robert Rodriguez in the retro *Naked Naked Sex* (2004) and
Six-Gun Pizza (2005). These experiments had fun with how hilariously outdated the mode is, but
also served to highlight how far ahead of her time Aliyeva was. Similar to the *Choose Your Own...*
films, the adults-only *Top Or Bottom?* spin-offs in the seventies quickly lost their novelty, with
audiences frequently taking the most savagely deviant option at every opportunity, causing the
films to be little more than the same sequence of melodramatic, sexual, and violent events each
time, just like any conventional B-movie, but with a dozen intervals during which only the click-
ing of keypads can be heard.

she was trying to resurrect interest in her old technology. She made a couple of regular narrative films to generate attention, but they flopped. Her paranoia about the negative uses of her work might be a touch hysterical. But maybe not. What may be true is that YOURFILM's audience-curated spaces have been with us all along, in ways that we can't even imagine. Or *are* imagining, and don't realize it.[38]

---

[38] *imagining:* Phillip Brent: *When I first mentioned the* Plot Program *in the late nineties, studios denied its use. Now, its use is wide and not even controversial* (*"The Way Of The World," Sight & Sound,* June 2017). The *Plot Program* is software that generates films by culling and collating ideas from previously successful scripts, removing ambiguities, and offering improvements by comparing the structure of the new film with thousands of others, all ranked by their box office success. This results in jokes, one-liners, and action sequences being used again with few changes. In some cases, even the same footage is used. Brent: *Beyond the obvious questions of artistic value, this technology raises other concerns. Green-screen and CGI can already convince an audience of almost anything: that an actor is in space, or on a dragon, or twenty years younger. A star that dies can have several films released in his wake* as *his wake, each tagged and marketed as his last performance.* But what if, say, a bankable star can no longer perform to the standard required? Could computer work convince an audience that Robert de Niro in his seventies has the same commitment and intensity that he had in his thirties? Could a variation of YOURFILM technology pick up on the audience's huge desire for him to be as good, and provide an assisted performance, so that the De Niro in front of us is merged somehow with his younger self, harmonising like an empathetic auto-tune? (The leeway given to those who once did wonderful things suggests that *this does* happen, technology or not. We might only be interested in Paul McCartney talking about his new record because he made *Revolver*, and we might only interested a little bit, and be keen to hear him talk about *Revolver*, but we'll listen all the same. Because Paul McCartney made *Revolver*.) Taking the thought further, is it possible that some stars may not be real? Might they be made out of our idea of what a *star* looks like? Of press releases, vitamin B jabs, and glue? Hazy dreams of Hollywood suicides, blurred headshots, and B-roll?

ваш фильм YOURFILM

Directed/Produced by Alex Aliyeva. Written by Alex Aliyeva / The Audience. Starring: Konstantin Eggert, Olga Tatiana. Mosfilm. Release date: 1922(?). 23-44 mins (short version) or 61-75 mins (deep version). Tagline: Your Dream. Your Idea. YOURFILM.

MENSCH VERSUS MITTWOCH

(MAN AGAINST WEDNESDAY)

F.G. Hoch, 1930

Abraham Lincoln sagte: "Du kannsyt der Verantwortung von heute nicht entkommen, indem du es morgen meidest"

(Abraham Lincoln said: "You cannot escape the responsibility of today by avoiding tomorrow")[39]

The Landlady, *Mensch Versus Mittwoch*

There is a sequence in F.G. Hoch's *Mensch Versus Mittwoch* in which Eli, played with brilliant care by Emil Jannings, leaves a bar and walks drunkenly down a Berlin alleyway. He is set upon by an unseen assailant, who beats him to a bloody mess. The attack is shown reflected in the eye of a cat, who watches the action before turning away to toy with a dying mouse. It is such an extravagant piece of camerawork, stepping way beyond the usual stark theatricals of the Weimar Expressionists towards something quite new, that it threatens to rip the film almost completely away from its own narrative.[40] This stylistic

---

[39] *by avoiding tomorrow...* The landlady has, of course, got the quote wrong. When her tenant Eli points this out to her, she says: *You're still in bed at noon and I'm the one who is back-to-front?*

[40] *from its own narrative:* The only other contemporary example of something similarly striking might be *Alice dans le Pays des Merveilles* (Man Ray, 1929). My English teacher Mrs White had the poster of *Alice...* in her classroom. The image, with a Mad Hatter that looked more like the vampire in *Nosferatu* (F.W.Murnau, 1922), was pinned to the wall behind my chair. Once, during a group discussion about war poetry, I raised my hand to volunteer an opinion on the imagery used by Siegfried Sassoon. I was interrupted by laughter from Mrs White.

I'm sorry, Mark, but the way you're sitting, it looks like you're part of the poster and

exuberance has its critics. Tony Deflower described the sequence as *an ostentatiously decorated Christmas Tree in August: beautiful, distracting, and completely out of place.*[41]

Several meanings can be inferred though, surely: by obscuring the brutality of the beating, director Hoch might be suggesting that the violence is too much for us; or, with the cat's disinterested stare, that the violence is banal; or that the viewer is complicit, because we *want* to see Eli beaten because we go to the cinema to see *action*; or all of the above. Hoch invites this kind of examination in the very next scene, too. A bloodied Eli limps into his room, and falls down on his bed. He reaches for a blanket to cover himself, but drops it. There is a knock at his door. It is his concerned landlady. She asks if he is ok. *Yes, of course,* he says. Fade to black. This scene takes two minutes. It is then shown again, in its entirety: Eli limps in, falls down on his bed. Drops the blanket. A knock at his door. It is his landlady. *Bist du ok? Ja, naturlich.* Fade to black. Many first-time viewers claim to miss this repetition, this record-skipping break of the verisimilitude. It is as if the brain corrects itself to believe that the scene only played once, similar to how it combines the information from two eyes into one picture.[42]

---

wearing a top hat. You look uncharacteristically sinister.

    I didn't raise my hand in lessons after that.

[41] *out of place:* Tony Deflower, *"Hoch Deflowered," Film Styles* Vol 3 Issue 4, Summer 1975.

[42] *fade to black:* Psychologist Berndt Schwartzer, in a 1962 study, claimed that, *when shown the same film twice consecutively, subjects are likely to argue that they were different.* They also

To Tony Deflower, this repetition was even more egregious than the beating scene. He called it a *pointless trick*. But isn't it an imagi-

---

frequently feel that the second film was shorter. Schwartzer called this the *Wayback Feeling*, because a journey on a previously unfamiliar road seems to take less time on the return trip, due to the surroundings having already been seen and catalogued in the brain. I watched *Mensch...* twice. The first was at my Nan's on TV one Sunday afternoon. At the time I was drawing a picture of a soldier being shot (in careful detail), so I mostly only heard it. The second time was with broken headphones in the dark boxy TV room at the library. I was watching a German film in lieu of going to my German lesson. I felt that this excused me somehow. I came out of the library into the rain, fingering my left ear which had been bothered throughout my viewing by a low buzzing noise. I walked down the ramp to the underpass, and saw a bunch of kids from our school, their red shirts showing under their coats. I was surprised to see them, as I thought that the film would finish long before school was finished. I thought that they were bunking too, but the clock face above the town hall said it was nearly four-thirty. Later than I thought. I was on my own time. *Wayback Feeling.*

The group came closer, and I stood tall and sucked in my tummy. They were from the year above. Vicki was with them. She was L's best friend. She was considered more pretty than L, in the cannibalistic (and widely understood, despite never being explained) playground ranking system. But she had a blankness to her. She never smiled with her eyes. She whispered with the group, and then waved me over. She'd never acknowledged me before. *Didn't see you in German today*, she said.

No, I said.

Going to the arcade later, she said.

Maybe, I said.

We might sneak into the George after, she said.

Cool, I said. The older kids laughed.

Have you ever been in the George, one of them said.

Not for a while, I said. But I didn't even know where it was. They laughed. But they seemed to buy my story, and I walked on. I felt like the kid in *Hhhh* (Sara Gillespie, 1991) who convinces a peer that he can tell the time by the sun to the exact minute, all the while sneaking glances at his digital watch.

native evocation of Eli's concussed confusion? This is a film that is very much a meditation on the inevitability of the calendar. In this context, the repetition seems considered and absolutely relevant. Deflower's dismissal seems hasty. And when you consider the use of such stylistic devices as flashbacks and dream sequences (which are widely understood by viewers despite their inherent *falseness*), it is surprising that this kind of nuanced duplication hasn't been explored more often since.[43]

Hoch was rarely so bold again. As film scholar Joseph Pranden said when reviewing the downward spiral of the filmmaker's career, *the early prognosis of 'terminal genius' was premature, and with time the outlook receded to become something less spectacular.*[44] Those extreme spells of inspired sickness included *Gestalt Honey* (1932) and *Zwölf Jünger* (*Twelve Disciples,* 1935), but by the time of *Kiss Killer* in 1950, Hoch was in pot-boiler territory, and would never leave.

Hoch's departure to a new beginning in America in 1937 was

---

[43] *surprising:* Or is it? Maybe it is limited for storytelling purposes. Maybe we need new information each time. In Bergman's *Persona* (1966) an eight-minute scene is repeated, but this is so we can see the faces of both Liv Ullmann and Bibi Andersson in turn. There are any number of films containing *Rashomon*-style retellings of the same situation from different points of view. But the only example of the same scene repeated twice in *exactly* the same way like *Mensch...* that I can think of is in *Rappaport* (1982), when Alun Armstrong's depressed detective suffers a series of Deja-vu moments. They are Deja-vus for the viewer at least, as the character doesn't seem to ever notice.

[44] *Film As A Popular Art Form*, 1971, Scholar Books. I read this book at the library when I was once again bunking off school. Inside was a message. *Spoken to her yet? Y [ ] N[ ] Kissed her? Y [ ] N[ ] Tongues? Y [ ] N[ ] DH.*

actually an ending. Far from flourishing in Hollywood like his friend Fritz Lang, he struggled. But *Mensch...* is Hoch at the summit of his powers. His confident direction is fully backed by Weimar studio Ufa, and *Mensch...* was one of their last great pictures before the subsequent suppression of the Nazis.

In the film, Eli experiences the week as seven individuals, each with a distinct personality and agenda. These seven people visit him in the same sequence, over and over. At the beginning of the film, the meetings appear to be random and accidental: Tuesday runs into him in the marketplace, Wednesday in the café, Thursday at the entrance to his building. Each seems polite, at first. They all wear their own colours, but it seems as if Eli is the only one to see this. (When sitting at a table in a restaurant with his acquaintance Strom, Eli sees Tuesday and points him out. *See that man with the yellow flower on his lapel? No? Over there. The band on his hat matches it.* Strom says, *Him? It looks brown to me. Green even.*)[45]

---

[45] *it looks brown to me:* Hoch, like Gyorgy Ligeti, Franz Liszt, and Eddie Van Halen, experienced visual synaesthesia. *This scene is a recreation,* Hoch said, *of discussions with Fritz Lang about the colours of weekdays. Fritz insisted that Thursday was duck-egg blue. A scandalous lie* (*My Life In Cinema,* Hippo Books, 1963).

We learned about synaesthesia in science late that February. Encouraged, I'd started going to school more since the valentine landed on my desk. L was in my science lesson, and I now sat in a seat vacated by a kid with a long-term sickness (Rich with glandular fever? Tom with shin-splints? Rob with measles?) that offered a better view of her. Mr Harris tried to get a class discussion going, with his usual agitated energy: *Do any of you have any colour feelings like this? Anyone? Come on, people!* (clap) *What colour is happiness?* (clap) *death?* (clap) *Monday?*

Each of the seven visitors has their own personality. Monday carries a red pen and a ledger. A name tag says *Gedanken Editor* (Thought Editor). He wears thick spectacles. He tells Eli that his shortsightedness is good for his job, because he only needs to look at his page, up close: *I need only see in two dimensions; across the ledger, and down the page to the bottom line.* Tuesday, more reticent, is always a few steps behind. Wednesday and Thursday often get themselves confused, but crucially never arrive in the wrong order. Friday is a boisterous drunk, Saturday too. Sunday, the only female, offers a haven for Eli.[46]

He picked on L. She blushed. She was usually quiet in class. But after some prompting she went on to talk more than I'd ever heard her talk before. Her voice was scratchy and thin, and her sentences would periodically drift into uncertain noises, rather than come to a deliberate end. But her ideas were quite original, and I could have listened to her for much longer. To her, Monday was dark blue, Tuesday was yellow, Wednesday orange, Thursday brown, Friday green, Saturday black, and Sunday white. An animated discussion ensued, as members of the class volunteered their own thoughts. One kid disagreed completely with L's version. I put my hand up to say that I agreed with L that Tuesdays were yellow. (While I remember her spectrum well, I don't remember the rest of mine, perhaps because I wasn't as taken with the premise as she; perhaps because I was more taken with her than the premise. I do remember that none of my days were black or white, and that Saturday was, and remains, Ferrari red.) I glanced over. L wasn't looking, but Vicki was grinning at me. *We agree on Tuesday,* I thought. After that, I examined our behaviour more closely than usual on Tuesdays, looking for examples of extra rapport. One Tuesday in early March, L swung her bag onto her shoulder and it lightly hit my arm. *Sorry,* she said, and looked at me very briefly. *My fault,* I said. I began to imagine that our first kiss would be on a Tuesday, but then I realised that any focus on this idea removed six days from the calendar of potential.

[46] *a haven for Eli:* In *Anthologie de l'Humour Bleu,* (1942, Roman Books) Andre Breton said that Hoch and writer Lisbeth Heinz's characterisation of Sunday as female was indicative of a *petit bourgeois conservatism. One of the premises on which the Surrealist Manifesto was built*

She is calm and apologetic, and meets Eli in parks and cafés, trying to explain that the increasingly frightening mixture of petty punctuality, brawn, and casual indifference that the others display isn't their fault. *They just do what they do, Eli. You have to understand. It isn't personal.* Eli tries to persuade Sunday to visit more frequently, maybe twice a week. But she runs away, telling him that he knows when he'll see her next. *This is how it must be, Eli.*[47]

Eli wants to run away with Sunday. He makes a plan. He figures that Wednesday is the most timid of the rest of the days. If he can avoid Wednesday he might disrupt the chain, and escape the clutches of routine. The spell broken, perhaps he'll then be able to spend weeks on end with Sunday with no threat of Monday arriving. But where can he go where Wednesday cannot find him? Week after week goes by, and there is Wednesday, following Tuesday, followed by Thursday, in the gardens, in the streets, in the woods. No refuge can be found. Eli changes his regular paths. He throws everything out of sync to surprise even himself. He loses his job and friends. *Is it a girl, Eli?* his boss says, after reluctantly firing him. *It's always a girl. No,* Eli says. *I just need more time.* But still, the days always catch up with him, and their aggression

---

postulated that the days of the week are all women (p.78). It is hard to argue with such absurd defiance.

[47] *this is how it must be, Eli:* It is possible to read this exchange as a warning of the organized violence of the Nazis that was on the horizon, and the part the German people would play in letting atrocities play out. Hoch denies this: *Critics give me too much credit. I wasn't smart enough to see them coming.*

grows. Eli drinks and tries to sleep through an entire twenty-four hours, but wakes to find that one of his assailants has visited, destroying his room. *What day is it*, he asks the landlady when he gets up. She shakes her head at him. *Shouldn't you be at work?*

He resorts to a final plan. He barricades his room. He locks the door, shutters the windows, and waits. If Wednesday can't find him, Eli wins. He sits and reads. Noises occasionally distract him from his book (itself a distraction from the situation). He inspects the kitchen, the bathroom, the bedroom, then returns to sit. Repeat. Sickeningly slowly, Hoch allows us to begin to realise what Eli will, a beat or two behind us: someone else is there in his small apartment. It takes an age, but when Eli finally turns his back on the dark bedroom, Tuesday steps out from behind the long curtains. Tuesday quickly and quietly unlocks the apartment door for his eternal successor.[48] They nod familiarly, their

---

[48] *eternal successor:* This moment, in which Eli almost finds Tuesday, but turns away, has divided critics. James Anchon, writing in the *New York Times* after the film's screening at the Vision Festival in New York in 1968, complained (in the manner of many viewers of horror films ever since), that *for a man so careful to suddenly be so careless destroys the tension of the film completely and utterly.* He talks about Eli, but could mean Hoch too. Victor Perkins however, in his masterly *Film As Film* (Da Capo Press, 1972), countered that rather than being a poorly made sequence, it might represent a considered choice. Perkins suggests that Eli's oddly mannered turn away from the curtain, the one that prevents him from seeing the interloper, actually reflects a change of heart. As if Eli knows Tuesday is there, and cannot look for fear of confirming his suspicion; that he saw what he didn't appear to see: *Indicated to us by a lingering look at the floor, it is as if Eli has arrived at the conclusion that he cannot reject the sequence of events that is happening, and will continue to happen. Rather than asking why Hoch allows Eli to appear so careless when he almost trips over Tuesday's shoes but does not find him, we should ask why Eli*

celestial relay handover as smooth as ever. And Wednesday enters, knife drawn.

Mensch Versus Mittwoch

*Directed by F.G.Hoch. **Produced by Franz Lammer**. Written by Lisbeth Heinz, F.G.Hoch. Starring Eli Jannings, Maly Delschaft, Max Hiller, Werner Krauss. UFA/ Goldwyn Distributing Company.Release Date: November 1930 (Ger). 87 mins. Tagline: Tomorrow Won't Wait.*

---

would be so blind at such a moment. For surely it is easier to believe that Hoch the film-maker is making a deliberate decision here, that late in the day, Eli knows that Wednesday must come in. Is already here. Was always here (p.234). Like a Greek Hero, Eli's fate was cast the moment he tried to fight. He is a man who sees things others cannot, and cannot see the one thing the others can: that one day will follow another, until it does not.

DIJONNAISE

Walter Friend, 1933

I once knew a girl who needed constant praise

And fillings in her sandwich, mustard, mayonnaise

Her bread it always landed butter side up

There ever was a suitor with a complimentary cup

Of ketchup

Noel Coward, *Condiment Cathy*[49]

Underground legend Walter Friend's interest in the minutiae of existence was first displayed in this experimental short, shot in an afternoon in 1933. *Dijonnaise* is twenty-four minutes long, and shows an unnamed man eating a meal, in the grainiest black, white, and grey. It is a completely and absolutely quiet film that hits curious spots of tension because of what is left out. Which is *everything else*. The danger of offering so little is that an audience will sink away, indifferent or bored; but *Dijonnaise* sustains interest, and has even acted as a provocation to discourse and conflict.[50]

---

[49] *Condiment Cathy:* Coward's satirical swipe at certain high-society individuals who attempted to hide some of their rather more lowbrow tastes was, according to Walter Friend, playing on a gramophone at the party during which he came up with the title for *Dijonnaise*. One of our dinner ladies used to reference the song (which none of us kids knew) if any of us took more than one sachet of ketchup in the canteen: *Want a burger with that sauce, Condiment Cathy?* L, I noted from my seat near the door (the one with the best view) took mayonnaise and black pepper for her chips, and ate them with a knife and fork.

[50] *discourse and conflict:* There was a scuffle at the first showing of the film at Harvard University in 1935. This may have been a prank instigated by friends of Friend, but disorder and petty vandalism also occurred when the film was shown in New York and Philadelphia that same year.

Friend was a student of the *Diktat School*, a group of expat Americans in Paris between the wars who idolized both Renoirs, Robert Bresson, and Henri Cartier-Bresson, and saw through them a way

People see things in it, Friend said when asked about the trouble. I first saw *Dijonnaise* in Mr Price's art lesson. At the beginning of Spring term the school juggled our days and I ended up in this Friday afternoon class. I was delighted, as L was in it too. When I first walked in I felt L look up. I praised myself for refraining from returning a glance. Mr Price liked to drag in the television set for this last lesson of the week, draw the curtains, and show us a film of significant value. *Here is another film of significant value,* he'd say. During *Dijonnaise,* one kid wanted to know what the man was eating, and so walked right up to the screen and stood on his tiptoes, his shirt hanging out behind him like a flat tail, to try and spy into the bowl. *Aha! What does Joel's action remind you of, class? Anyone? We watched it last term! Doesn't he look like the little boy in Don Carpone's* Le Donne Della Mia Vita (1964) *trying to look up the actresses' skirts on the cinema screen! Ha!* Vicki, sitting next to L, said something. Mr Price, who rarely lost his temper, shouted. *Get out of my classroom, you vile child.* Vicki spent the rest of the screening in the corridor making cross-eyed faces at L through the window.

At a screening of Friend shorts at the Curzon in Soho in the late nineties, a couple behind me sustained a whispered argument that covered everything from who the man on the screen might be, to the nature of the male member of the couple's feelings for a mutual friend, to *everything else* (their walking pace down the street, her choice of shoes, his need for a haircut, which of them was speaking the loudest and annoying the rest of the audience, *his* constant talking about nothing, *her* constant talking about everything but nothing). Maybe Friend's films demand that we try and fill the silences. Friend made a film called *Blank Canvas* in 1943. This involved a painter pacing back and forth in front of a blank canvas for twenty minutes, occasionally putting paint on his brush, and lining up his first stroke, but then pulling away, never actually applying the first touch. This deliberate series of actions and inactions made me think of Mr Price in class, trying to show us an educational video but struggling to get the machine to work; he would point the remote at the video player, move, and then do it again, only squeezing the button harder. The similarity was only fleeting, but the fact that Mr Price had been the one to introduce the films of Friend to me in an art lesson certainly underscored the link. I can't see *Blank Canvas* without imagining an off-screen schoolgirl making fun of the artist.

to breathe humanity into American cinema. The *Diktat* members were privileged sons of wealthy Americans, with all the cocksure playfulness that that can bring. *We thought we could do anything,* is one of their abiding slogans. They returned to LA where they set about making short films with borrowed equipment from the large studios, equipment that they gathered with charm, ingenuity, and trespass. *We saw ourselves as dark horses stalking Hollywood,* Friend said. In *Dijonnaise,* the protagonist wears the same coat that Humphrey Bogart wore in *The Maltese Falcon,* a deliberate confession, Friend said, of the fact that he had borrowed so much Warner Brothers' gear.[51] Fellow *Diktat* filmmakers John Vigour and Herb Silence shot their shorts *Arrows* (about lost Native Americans) and *Sebastien* (about the legendary drag cabaret star) in the same week as *Dijonnaise,* and with the same equipment. The filmmakers quickly got a reputation far bigger than the small audiences

---

[51] *borrowed so much Warner Brothers gear: Playboy* interview, March 1969. During one Mr Price lesson I saw L accidentally knock a pen off her desk and not notice. At the end of class I waited until everyone had left and picked it up. It was a good pen, a green rollerball that moved very smoothly across the page. That night I wrote with it in my journal, feeling L residue flow from the ball point to my page. I closed my eyes as I wrote, like the hack in *Ghostwritten* (R. Simac, 1987) who can conjure up dead geniuses to help him write his successful novels, at least until he moves house and the spirits don't follow. I wrote quickly and then examined the work, scanning it for traces of L. I slept with the pen under my pillow, curious as to whether the proximity of the object that had had such proximity to her might infect my dreams.

The next day I was using it in class when Vicki came over and pulled it from my hand. *That's my pen,* she said. *I know 'cos I stole it from my brother. Thanks for keeping it safe for me.*

for their films would suggest. This caused celebrated film historian Dizzy Bordell to call that manic period of filming as *the shots heard around the world, but never seen.*[52]

Dijonnaise's title has no obvious connection to the subject matter, unless we see it as a clue to what is in the man's bowl.[53] The cut-and-shut combination of the words *Dijon* mustard and *mayonnaise* was actually a Friend invention, and he sold the name to Heinz in 1951 for an amount far greater than anything he received for his film. He

---

[52] *At Them There Movies: The Collected Dizzy*, Roger House Publishing, 1966. Dizzy Bordell here argues at great length for an alternative version of history—one in which his favourite things are recognised as the most important.

[53] *no obvious connection:* This kind of titular misdirection can be appealing. Terry Gilliam's *Brazil* (1985) is not about the country. Oscar Vengkat's *Norma Jean Baker* (1962) has no obvious connection to Marilyn Monroe. Renata Adler's 1976 novel *Speedboat* has only fleeting paragraphs set on a boat. These titles feel borrowed. They are careful deceptions, the right labels placed on the wrong parts of the map. A step even further is wholesale appropriation: Bob Jones' *Beatles For Sale*, The Replacements' *Let It Be*, and Lipstick Fibrosis' *Led Zeppelin IV* are all records that steal titles from more popular works. When I moved and started at school in Nuneaton, I replaced a kid called Sam who had moved away. His Dad had got a job down south. Because I sat in Sam's seat in Mr Price's art lesson, and because Mr Price was bad with names, he called me Sam Two. It was a joke with staying power, as kids delighted in calling me Sam so much that even teachers in other classes picked up on it. One not-so-bright kid was amazed at the coincidence that the previous boy and I had the same name. Some remarked on my physical likeness to him. This went on for years. Occasionally, someone would talk about an event that happened at school before I was there as if I should remember it. *Come on Sam, you were there. You threw the first rock!* I learned about Sam through the kids' expectations of me. He was a loveable idiot who enjoyed breaking things. I was quiet. I didn't stand a chance.

And the first time L said my name, it wasn't my name:

Move, Sam. Other people need to use this corridor too.

repeated this trick of collapsing words together to invent a new one in order to title his next film, *Brunch* (1941), in which we see a woman eating a meal that is neither breakfast nor dinner, but somewhere in between, and with *Ham-Fisted* (1943), in which we see a man with a ham for a paw attempt, clumsily, to eat himself. The films were screened in basements and bars, or they would be sneaked into studio screening rooms late at night, an audience assembled by word of mouth, the titles being whispered like new words in the language for the first time, because that's what they were.

Even Friend's lesser works contributed to the lexicon. *Brynner* (1944) was not a word that passed into common parlance (there was already a word for the meal between breakfast and dinner—it was known, to 1940s Americans at least, as *lunch*). But it did become the in-joke stage name of upcoming young actor Yul Jones, a friend of Friend, who later starred in *The King And I* (1956), *The Magnificent Seven* (1960) and *Stone-Cold Leprosy Soundworld* (1971).[54]

---

[54] *Yul Brynner:* Brynner died on October 10th 1985. Orson Welles, his co-star in *The Battle of Neretva* (Peter Branch, 1969), died on the same day. Brynner appeared in the Welles-directed *Perseid* (1967), which was part of a sequence of interlocking narratives called *NOTES*. The series contains six finished movies, an unfinished seventh, a stage-play, and a cryptic novel. There is a link back to Walter Friend here: he was approached by Welles to assist with the cinematography of several of the movies, but Friend resisted. *I took my Mount Olympian bulk to the Zeus of underground cinema; but Zeus was hiding in the sewers,* Welles said about Friend's rejection (*LA Times* interview, *"I used to have friends in this town"* Sam Goldman, July 12th 1973). His quasi-memoir *Well, Well, Welles: Reasons to Disbelieve Or: A Life Against Hollywood* (Penguin Books, 1977) is full of *F for Fake*-style sleights of hand, arrogance disguised as self-mockery and vice-versa: *I see*

Friend went on to make the lyrical *Intern-net* (1957) and *Motorhead* (1959), speculative fictions about trainee psychic fishermen and electric skull replacement surgery respectively. Perhaps Friend's most lastingly memorable piece was *At The Drive-In* (1959), a documentary recording of a screening of *Rebel Without A Cause* at a drive-in theatre in California. After some shots of cars arriving and young couples buying popcorn, the camera finds a spot and doesn't move. Unlike much of the distracted audience, it simply watches the screen for the duration of the film. The Technicolor melodrama of *Rebel* seems so distractingly different when seen in greys, and Friend's

---

my younger self, and I see a boy wanting to turn everything full cycle. Wanting to explode cinema to such an extent that future generations would believe the medium to be a myth; Billy Wilder would seem like Bigfoot, and the Gish sisters a pair of gorgeous Loch Ness monsters, imagined only (p.302). In so many ways, the existence of Welles himself seems dubious; he is The Great Orsini, the man whose personality and presence almost rubs itself out. Can anyone see *Citizen Kane* without knowing that is supposedly the greatest film of all time? Does that matter? Welles' subsequent work, and everyone else's, lives in its shadow.

Is there a footnote big enough for Welles? Big enough to include his desolate *Non Quixote* (1947), or his barmy *Remain Cordial To The Stick Incest* (1962) which was savaged by the LA Times, who headlined their review *Welles Has Run Dry*. Notable too is *Bellerophon* (1944): Pearl Stringer, later a star of stage and screen, appeared in it as Bellerophon's unlover Anteia, but no-one noticed her at the time. It was only later, after her Broadway albums and Oscar nomination for her role in Vincente Minelli's *At Hard Park* (1965) that her appearance in *Bellerophon* began to appear on her resume. Welles' take in his book is priceless: *The studios and the press were so determined not to give me any praise at that time that they seemed readier to suggest that there was a time-travel conspiracy involving me going back twenty years and casting Pearl Stringer after she was famous, than to give me credit for discovering her. (Well, Well, Welles*, p.491)

detached presentation of the excitable youths on camera (and on the screen on camera) articulates the confusion of the generation gap almost as well as Nicholas Ray's masterpiece itself, but from the other side: by this point Friend was well into his fifties.

He stopped making films shortly afterwards, and wrote a memoir about alternative American Cinema called *A Bit Of The Other*, in which he expressed regret that, as he saw it, he had never topped his first film. *It was never bettered. I have played with the ingredients, jumbled my technique, started the whole thing from scratch, not measured anything at all, measured everything; but nothing in my career is as sweet as that simple, wonderful,* Dijonnaise.

Dijonnaise
Directed by Walter Friend. Produced by Walter Friend, Herb Silence. Starring Samuel Hartley. Diktat Pictures. Release Date: Winter 1933 (US). 24 mins. Tagline: None.

OPULENCE

Josef von Sternberg, 1937

I can see heaven as no man has ever seen... I have

burned in the sun's outer rings... charred my wings on

re-entry, fallen to Earth with a crash... but I can see

heaven...

Queen Adeline, *Opulence*

Josef von Sternberg's final creation around Marlene Dietrich's hollow stare was his most decadent and ambitious production, if we take those words to mean, in the context of a Hollywood film, both large and expensive. But as much as the film itself seems to demand it, it is hard to dismiss *Opulence* as a mere extravagance. It offers passionate commentary on unrequited love, the loneliness of the adored, and the dissatisfaction of comfortable living. That these subjects were unfashionable then and still are now should not distract from its achievements. Dietrich is Queen Adeline, a ruler in a mythical kingdom.[55] The people

[55] *mythical kingdom:* The kingdom is a brilliantly hodgepodge mixture of hokey exoticas. This infidelity upset some contemporary critics, who could not place the city in the real world, and some modern ones, who do not know on behalf of which people(s) they should be offended. But its patchwork Greek/Roman/Egyptian/Chinese/Intergalactic mythos never allows the viewer to settle and understand the world, and by so doing, does something larger: it lets the impossible drift into view.

The House of Laser at the top end of town also had quite the collage feel inside. The entranceway and long wide staircase was part of the original ballroom structure, but there were clues everywhere to its other uses over the years: unplugged neon signs, walls that hadn't been painted over, walls that had been revealed, notices in the bathrooms for ancient events, and various fixtures that suggested disco, bingo, and more. Big Gavin said his Dad used to go to see wrestling there in the seventies, and that he was there the night a train derailed over by the Leicester Road Bridge. The wrestlers went to help pull survivors out of the wreckage while still wearing their leotards. (This is very similar to a scene in *Wrestling Is Real* (Bob Hurt, 1986), and it seems possible that Big Gavin, or his Dad, had been confused.) Little Gavin said his parents got married in the main hall back in the sixties. It was possible to feel, as each iteration of the building was replaced by another, that a particular community's ghosts were locked in, mourning the loss of their version of the building. The ballroom dancers, oldest of all, seeing us kids with our pretend guns as just the latest in a series of indignities. The House of Laser never felt permanent, it never felt finished, and much as we loved it, we knew somehow that it couldn't last. The large main hall was painted completely black, with occasional daubs of neon paint on the corners of the wooden maze to help navigation. You'd clip on your plastic chest piece and gun, both of which had flashing lights to give away your position, and run around, trying to zap each other. I'd tend towards a careful approach, finding a safe corner position from which to pick off kids running past. Sometimes, when it was quiet for thirty seconds or so, the illusion of the place took over, and as I hid in the dark it was possible to feel like I was embedded in the computer like Jeff Bridges in *Tron* (Steven Lisberger, 1982). Once I sat there for so long that a creeping sense that everyone was gone rose up my back and became undeniable. I stared up at the ceiling, listening out for sounds of shuffling feet or screaming laughter. I noticed for the first time a large rectangle shape across the back wall, like a screen. Had this been a cinema too? The area was painted the same black as the rest of the walls, but seemed to glow, like a TV screen that has just been switched off. Each game lasted thirty minutes, but it was so hard to tell time in the chaotic dark that it always felt like the siren announcing the end could come at any time. But just then, in my silent nook, it seemed possible that at any moment one of the building's ghosts, say a ballroom dancer, or a disco dancer, or a wrestler, or a bingo player might come around the corner, or even someone from a future version of the building, as if it hosted both past and yet-to-come memories in some way, like the room that records trauma in *The Stone Tape* (Nigel Kneale, 1971), or the time-travel gate in the warehouse in *We Contain Multitudes* (Val Stech, 1962). Suddenly I wasn't in the House of Laser anymore, but a large retail space, filled with aisles and aisles of miscellaneous fickle objects. I closed my eyes to hold the illusion and investigate it further.

Buzz-buzz.

systems, and ended poverty. Opposition forces have melted away. Her approval ratings are nearly one hundred percent. But she is bothered by the lack of perfection in these numbers. *Why don't they all love me,* she says. *They do, they do,* her aides insist, and they are almost correct. Almost. She orders the building of ever-grander arenas and forums, bestows on the citizenry a multitude of gifts and throws them lavish balls. And the people have never been so happy. *But are they the happiest people ever,* she asks her mirror. *How can we know?*

When a plague arrives, thought to be a distinct impossibility with the extensive hygiene reforms implemented by the queen, a minority of the people threaten revolt. She tries to placate them. *Should I give them all diamonds? Should I pave the streets with gold? Should each citizen get a night with the queen?* Her beloved adviser and town planner Abraham (Lionel Atwill) says that whatever she does, *like children, they will resent you for the one thing you cannot do... guarantee them against*

My chest-piece shook. I had been shot. I spun around, and saw a laughing figure disappear behind a wall. I turned to pursue but tripped and dropped my gun. I fell to the floor, and my chest piece vibrated again. *Buzz-buzz.* And again. *Buzz-buzz.* When I looked up, several people were now standing over me, taking turns to shoot me and earn cheap unsportsmanlike points. *Buzz-buzz. Buzz-buzz. Buzz-buzz.* In the dark they were just flashing red and blue lights and grotesque green smiles. I tried to roll over to get up but I slipped again. Someone laughed. Someone else said *I think we got him enough. Leave him, V.* I got to my knees and looked up. The figures had scattered except one: it was L. She had her weapon pointed at me, and held out my gun to me with the other hand. *Truce,* she said.

They're going to turn this place into a supermarket one day, I said, reaching for my gun. She withdrew it at the last minute, shot me again, *buzz-buzz,* and turned and ran.

death.

True or not, Abraham's words stay with Adeline. After throwing her biggest feast yet, a sixty-day orgy of food and love, Adeline is distracted by the one member of the hundreds who doesn't appear to be having fun. When she disguises herself and approaches this woman, she hears that *the Queen has brought this on us: this plague can only settle in well-fed bodies.*[56] Discouraged, the queen closes the doors of the palace and becomes a recluse. Her plans don't stop, although now they are only for herself: inside the palace she builds a holiday planet of gargantuan excess. Over the ensuing thirty years, shown to us in a dizzy fifteen-minute montage, her army of designers, artists, and labourers construct one thousand floors of golden heaven. One of the delights of Sternberg's direction here is that he sympathises so much with the queen.

---

[56] *this plague can only settle in well-fed bodies:* In his book *Making Meaning* (Harvard University Press, 1989), critic David Bordwell dismissed *Opulence* as being *window dressing built around this simplistic moral: that wealth is a sickness. Making Meaning* was essentially a criticism of many contemporary film theorists who, in Bordwell's opinion, spent a lot of time constructing meaning to shoehorn into elaborate readings of movies. While there was, and is, undoubtedly something to what Bordwell said, his examples were not necessarily well chosen. Scholar V.F. Perkins replied to Bordwell in his seminal essay *Must We Say What They Mean?* (*Movie Magazine* Vol 34-35, 1990), suggesting that *Opulence* contains a complexity of ideas and that *to suggest that this one sentence is the film's key is to assert a meaning in exactly the manner that Bordwell takes issue with.* In the same essay Perkins also famously argued with Bordwell's assertion that the *meaning* of *The Wizard of Oz* lay in Dorothy's words *there's no place like home.* Perkins suggests that Dorothy's preference for Oz might be seen to be *substantially qualified by the film's other data* such as Judy Garland's acting, the soundtrack, and the use of colour during her time there.

Her vanity is not portrayed as a simple flaw, but as something more complex and human. More than ever, Dietrich seems to be playing the director himself. By the mid-thirties, Sternberg's delirious, grandstanding vision was increasingly unfashionable next to the snappy comedies and austere *noirs* of the day. His films are if anything even less credible now, so much so that it is unfathomable that any Post-war director in Hollywood could recreate *Opulence*'s damaged innocence without turning it into a tediously judgemental morality play about wealth. Dietrich herself describes *Opulence* as her favourite film, and suggested in 1984 that:

> *Modern Hollywood talks socialism; no big movie can*
> *be made that doesn't root for the little guy, and bash*
> *the powerful. And yet they are funded by the biggest*
> *and richest. Hollywood is a rich man dressed as a poor*
> *man, and Josef was a poor man dressed as a rich man.*
> *They hated this... and they hate it even more now. Josef*
> *is seen as morally conservative because he wanted to*
> *make grand pictures. But he was a rebel, a dreamer, and*
> *always foreign.*[57]

---

[57] *New Yorker* interview, April 15, 1984. This was shortly after Dietrich had surgery for bladder cancer. It was later revealed that she had been very close to death, but in this interview, she brushed off the rumours of her ill health. The nearest she came to addressing her mortality was in a television interview with Johnny Carson in November 1984, when she said that *sometimes people must remember that we are all human. And that if Dietrich can die, so can I.* Abe Fuller, entrepreneur, claims to have sold 500,000 t-shirts bearing the iconic *If Dietrich Can Die So Can I*

For me, a strength of *Opulence* is also a point for which it
received criticism: there is no explanation of *where* the money comes
from, of how the country gets its riches. The *film noirs* were about the
bad things that people would do for cash, but *Opulence* imagines a
world where there is endless money. Desperate everyday calculations
about work and finances are removed, and citizens have more time for
pleasure and contemplation. This allows us, and them, to focus on the
real question: if we have everything we want, what comes next? Isn't
that an important idea in itself? But as audiences we've been trained to
view wealthy characters with suspicion.

The film also evades easy feminist readings—for although
the queen is powerful, she is also beautiful, and loves her people; she
leads without sentimentality, but cares, even though the act to which
she is driven might be reckless folly. In a great crescendo inspired by a
dream the queen has (inspired in turn by a dream Sternberg had), she
draws plans for an entire planet that can motor through the heavens
under its own influence. But when Abraham jumps to his death from
the tallest tower of the palace in horror at the never-ending vastness of
these ideas, she is distraught: her ambition cannot be sated, she cannot have victory over herself, and she can only lose. The final sequence
of the film follows Dietrich from her forty-poster, forty-meter bed,
up a spiralling staircase moulded entirely from diamonds that cut her

---

slogan since 1985.

feet, through a cavernous parlour the size of The Vatican, into a great hall the size of Switzerland filled with an army of one million blonde children, through a hundred-acre interior orchard filled with hand carved wooden trees, golden apples and felt grass (which she points out to a guard and says *have you touched my grass. It simply must be felt,* and laughs sadly when he does not), along a pathway studded with sequins, through a flea zoo, an elephant zoo, a Victorian toy room, a midget funfair, a hall of mirrors, entire floors filled with water, or food, or bean bags, or nudists, up through levels of complete darkness (for quiet contemplation) and levels of brilliant, shadowless light (for honest self-evaluation), up a slide that inverts gravity, through ever grander and more plush dining rooms and lounges, bedrooms, and halls, until finally coming to a silk-lined elevator large enough for a single occupant that goes to floor 99999. When she gets out, it is onto a scaffold structure. She looks up; and we can see how close the construction is to the moon itself, which hovers mere feet above, like a slice of George Melies' *Voyage dans la Lune.* Dietrich climbs up onto a wooden platform, reaches out above her head, and lays her hand on the surface. She sighs when she touches it; and then, after a pause, pulls off a handful of dusty cheddar, and greedily gobbles it. With tears in her eyes, she chews on her handful of mooncake, and utters the final, famously stuttered, words:

It. Needs. Salt. The Moon. Needs. Salt.

Opulence

Directed/Produced by Josef von Sternberg. Written by Josef Louys. Starring Marlene Dietrich Lionel Atwill. Paramount Pictures. Release Date: March 1937 (US). 97 mins. Tagline: I Can See Heaven.

BEHOLD THE AWESOME

MOUNTAIN

Dexter Himmler, 1938

Inadvertent magic is, we think, the best kind: the hazy
coincidence, the series of signs not quite decoded. It can
be the first recording of a song, before the words have
clicked into place, when the flawed syntax catches the
edge of a chord, and the hum of a misplaced microphone
spills into the mix. But there comes a point, and this can
be dangerous, when the artist can fall prey to a confi-
dence borne of this early fizzing success: she wants to
harness the power without understanding it, and seeks a
do-over, never understanding that the misplaced passes
and fudged lines of the imperfect first incantation were
vital to its construct.

Greil Marcus, *Lost Locales*

Dexter Himmler's *Behold The Awesome Mountain* is about the reconstruction of a scene. It is an attempt at discovery through rediscovery, and vice versa. Insight through repetition.[58] It revels in

---

[58] *repetition:* Andre Bazin said that *Cinema begins with repetition;* that the image on the screen is not Humphrey Bogart and Lauren Bacall, say, but is their double. If the magic of theatre lies in watching an actor transform in person, then film, by removing that presence, must give us something else. Not a replay of a performance, but a piece of false life all of itself. On the screen, we do not watch an actor *pretend;* we watch a star *be.* This does not require an audience. We can imagine endless reflections of Bogart and Bacall playing out in bright 2-D without imagining anyone watching. These repetitions and doubles are not unique to cinema of course (see Shake-

classically cinematic themes of doubles and exotic locations, but also erasure and regret.

An expedition led by Jan (Lukas Bronowsky) goes missing in the Himalayas after an avalanche. The only sign of their party is a mule that walks down the mountain carrying packs that include several unexposed rolls of film, apparently taken by the group's photographer Nicolas (Pieter Wiki). Jan's sister Olga (Anna Buchwald) and Nicolas' brother Otto (also played by Pieter Wiki) arrive from Europe and develop and examine the photographs for clues that might help them mount a search party. But guides with local knowledge say that the places photographed by Nicolas suggest that the party were travelling into uncharted territories, and that following them would be suicide.

Follow them they do, of course, tracing their siblings' course as suggested by the photographs. There are many pompously heroic pictures of Jan standing tall against striking views, which confuses Olga as she says her brother was always humble and hated having his photograph made. The pair also begin to realise that the shots taken by Nicolas are astounding. Not only did he follow the expedition up a

---

speare, or Bacon, or Tryst) but the medium is prone. Brian De Palma's best films are the ones that not only confess their inspirations, but display their entrails brazenly, like a killer who wants to be caught. But they are crimes of passion. *Cut-Up* (1988) took De Palma's Hitchcock obsession, seen earlier in the giddy *Suspicious Windows* (1977), *Dressed To Kill* (1980), and *Body Double* (1984) to its natural end, by remaking *The Birds* and then ripping it apart and reassembling it. *Blow Out* (1982) is De Palma's cover of *Blow Up*, which itself contains knowing nods to *Behold The Awesome Mountain*.

mountain, but at points he leads, dragging his tripod and camera over ledges first to look back down and record the arrival of the party on a previously untouched spot, led by a proud Jan. *He must have smoothed over his footprints with snow in order to make this shot look perfect,* Olga says at one point, referring to a composition called *The Arrival.* As the search goes on, they discover that some of the shots defy physics, particularly an image of Jan and the party on top of a peak looking up to the camera high above them, an effect that might be achieved with a modern helicopter shot.

Otto, fascinated by his brother's work, is determined to press on. His likeness to his brother, who appears only occasionally in the photographs, begins to unnerve Olga. She becomes convinced that the search party is heading for the same fate as the expedition. *It would have a certain symmetry,* says Otto.

The local guides are convinced that their trek has become pointless and suggest turning back when a storm approaches. Olga agrees, but Otto continues with one Sherpa, beguiled by his brother's images.[59] He is particularly taken by a self-portrait that was double-

---

[59] *beguiled by his brother's images:* Jean-Luc Godard said that this is the moment when the film becomes truly diverting: *the movement from a search-and-rescue narrative to a more nebulous metaphysical one, from the objective of the brother to the object of the photo, is when the film steps beyond the theatre and becomes an idea* (*"Dexter Himmler: Appraisal" Cahiers du Cinéma,* January 1954). One day at the library I took my notebook out of my bag and a photo fell out. It was of L. She was wearing a bikini top that revealed the curved scoop of red on her chest where she'd worn a swimsuit and got burned the day before. I looked around to see who was looking.

exposed, leaving two Nicolases blowing heat into their gloves on a trail. As Otto arrives at the locations in the pictures he recreates the poses as best as he can. He takes ever more care with this ritual. *I need to see what the expedition could see when the camera was seeing them,* he says. *The storm is coming,* the Sherpa says, over and over.

Otto sends his guide back and climbs on alone. *He was always half in love with the potential for his own destruction* he says about Nicolas, while holding up a picture of his brother. *Do you, dear diary, resent that you have to carry all that photographic equipment,* he says directly into the camera. As the weather gets heavier and the going slower, Otto becomes convinced that he is too late. But not because his brother is dead. He is convinced that Nicolas and his team have had great success and found some snow-capped Eldorado. He wishes he had been with them. He mourns the victory he feels his brother had without him. But he also regrets missing the lesser details: the consultations with Nicolas over maps, the passing of brandy, the games of ping-pong and shuffleboard at base camp that never happened. He imagines his brother's responses at every step, and acts them out, making memories that didn't ever happen, pulling fraudulent texts from his boots and fake stories from the snow. He curses his own mistakes. As the storm gets

No one was. I tilted the photo trying to see more of her chest, just like that boy in *Le Donne Della Mia Vita.* I knew it was from L's trip to Minorca with her cousins the previous summer. I'd overheard her say that it had been her first time abroad, except for Scotland. I slipped the photo inside my *Halliwell's Film & Video Guide* that I always had in my bag. Was it a signal from L? Who else would put it there?

worse, it gets harder to recreate the poses of the previous expedition. He takes the wrong route, his compass spins, his angles are skew-whiff. He stumbles into a small cave that bears a likeness to the location of Nicolas' penultimate shot. With conditions worsening and supplies dwindling, he looks into the camera for the last time:

> *I just know that there is a warm safe place here where*
>
> *nobody but me can find him, napping and content... and*
>
> *I also know that I may never find it...*

Otto walks out into the white.

Back at base camp, Olga and the search party return. When she reports that Otto refused to stop searching for his brother, she is told that records that have arrived from Europe say that Otto Nicolas Baumann, sometimes known as Nicolas Otto Baumann, had no siblings.[60] Olga cries in confusion. The film ends with a shot of the double exposure photograph.

Himmler shot the film in English, despite a German cast, contrived a fictional crew member that he claimed was lost on location to drum up publicity (even occasionally claiming this person was his twin brother), and never made another film. He attempted to remake *Behold The Awesome Mountain* in America in the early seventies, but failed to find the funding; this time, his previous tracks really were covered over,

---

[60] *had no* siblings: This ending has its critics. Blogger X.Friedrichstrasse argues that it *turns an intriguing and wonderfully ambiguous story of devotion into a two-bit campfire ghost story* (www. friedrichsays.com/reviews/5/02/behold).

never to be followed.

Behold The Awesome Mountain

Directed by Dexter Himmler. Produced by Fritz Loger, Dexter Himmler.

Starring Anna Buchwald, Pieter Wiki, Lukas Bronowsky, Fabrice Democ-

coli. FDF Pictures. Release Date: Feb 1938 (Ger). 83 mins.

Tagline: So white. So empty.

M. JAINET'S ETERNAL ZIGZAG

François Lepin Eziot and

Françoise Lepin Eziot, 1941

...an hour later they of course loop back and, finding the intersection they made earlier, exclaim 'More tracks!... A second car joined the first one.' As the hours go by they rejoin their own tracks again and again, believing each time that the highway they are following has grown busier and busier. This brilliantly allegorical scene is endlessly regressive: what Thompson and Thomson are doing is failing to recognize that they are not only reading their own mark but also reading their own reading of their mark, their interpretation of their own interpretation. Tintin, crouching over the tracks, realises what is going on but has no means of communicating. Then the Khamsin whips itself into action: a ferocious sandstorm that soon wipes all tracks away. An orgy of marking, reading and misreading, followed by total erasure, total inscrutability. As Tintin huddles, despondent, endless grains of sand hit his eyes and mouth, like so many illegible tracts.

Tom McCarthy, *Tintin and the Secret of Literature*

P lot-wise, this is as simple as those early cinematic experiments called *Tennis Match* or *The Motorcar Departs*: one man pursues another, endlessly. No context is offered. Our sympathies are pricked by the details: the clothing that suggests that the chased man might be a member of the resistance. Might the chaser be a Nazi spy-hunter? Or a hunter of Nazi spies? The runner is called M. Jainet, and he will run and run and run. The pursuer has no name. A caption at the beginning tells us that *The war is over, but M. Jainet continues to flee.* Why? We never know.

The Eziots take this simple stylistic concept and hold it for 85 minutes, like captains clinging to the mast through a storm. Each scene takes place in a different location, and is made up of a single shot, usually with an unmoving camera. Sometimes, a scene can sit empty for minutes: an abandoned market at night, a doorway outside a glowing bar, a tow-path along a canal at dusk. But almost always, it seems, stairs are present, lifting through the darkness hopefully, to who knows where. Frequently we have a slightly elevated three-quarter view, which offers a privileged angle on these city spaces and shows them to be smoky and desperate MC Eschers, cold impossible geometries which our pair nonetheless pass through. Diagrams freshly-built, but anciently anatomical. As soon as one man spots another, his body stiffening ecstatically out of his fatigue for a moment, his actions are quick and decisive. Often, looking up from a doorway, or down from a bridge over a river, where he rests for a moment, Jainet will spot, seconds after the viewer has, that the hunter approaches; he jumps up and runs, leaving the screen moments before he is caught. The next shot, the next scene, is in another location entirely. We cannot tell how much time has passed. Tension is never relieved, as every escape is followed by a wipe and a new scene. Sometimes, Jainet leaves the scene through an impressive stairway or a promising door; but he only ever escapes to the next screen, to begin again.[61]

---

[61] *to begin again:* Even though most of the film was shot on indoor studio sets, the Eziots were keen to shoot only during the golden hours just after sunrise and just before sunset. The studio, naturally, thought that this was a huge waste of time, leaving a cast and crew idle for most of the day. But the Eziots insisted, claiming it gave the production a sense of urgency when they did shoot. *We wanted our cast and crew to be like caged tigers*, Françoise said (Michel Dutonc: *"Interview with the Eziots", Cahiers Du Cinéma.* February 1964). My own golden hours were between the end of school at three thirty-five and getting home, a time without a clock. The obvious way for me to walk home was to head up Ambleside Way, or to cut through the alley behind the Chase Hotel (where we had lived for a few months when we first moved to Nuneaton when I was eight) and across the college grounds. But instead I'd started walking the long way with Jo and the Gavins (who didn't seem to mind), to the bottom of Higham Lane, where I'd turn left along Hinckley Road and they'd turn right towards town and go under the bridge. I'd learned a lot about L in a short time, and knew that she walked this way with Vicki. If my group happened to be ahead I'd stop to tie my shoe or pretend I'd forgotten something, and if we were behind I'd start a game to speed us up, like goading Big Gavin to steal Little Gavin's bag and run ahead. As the days went on, our groups merged until we'd all wait for each other at the gate. Jo was often keen to get going if L and Vicki were late, and would stand with her arms folded, but she'd still walk with us. L and Vicki would talk loudly about tough boys they knew from the other side of town and about parties they'd been to. They were showing off, clearly, but their experiences were beyond the rest of us, so we listened. They'd talk about films they'd seen that we hadn't. *Wayne's World. Parallelograms. Prayer of the Rollerboys. Society. Pump Up The Volume. Ten Spot.* Films they'd been to see with older siblings. (My sister and I had seen the end credits of *Wayne's World* when we arrived early to see *Medicine Man.* We immediately realised the mistake of our choice.) *Party on Garth*, L would say, and Vicki, enjoying the fact that she knew what came next and we didn't, would say *Party on, Wayne.* If (having heard this routine more than a few times after a couple of days) one us did interject, Vicki would say *You still haven't seen it though.* She'd stop and stare at us, smiling. She'd say *A sphincter says what?* Little Gavin would say *Don't say what,*

it's a trap, and Big Gavin would say, *Ha you said what*, and Little Gavin would say, *Ha so did you*, and they'd chase each other, wrestling onto the grass. Sometimes Little Gav would run down to the brook where the concrete pipe carried the water below the road. You could run through it if you kept your momentum up and leapt from side to side all the way along the cylinder. At the far end was a green abandoned area where a kid was once beaten up and left, like the body in *Brick* (Rian Johnson, 2005), except not dead. Once Little Gav escaped from Big Gav by running through the tunnel and coming out the other side, popping up across the road from us. We laughed.

I'd walk further and further with them each day before breaking off to go home, and soon I was turning right under the bridge towards town with them, and walking through the small industrial estate, further and further each day, one day turning back by the cemetery, the next walking as far as Jo's house, the next going all the way to the end of her road, where we stopped and hung around by the entrance to the subway under the tracks. We stayed there, encouraging Little Gav to stay later and later to get the train after the train he should catch back to Coventry, where he lived over a pub where he said he played endless games of pool when the pub was closed in the afternoons, stuffing towels in the pockets like the kids in *The Farmer of the City* (Jo Balance, 1965).

One day Vicki wasn't at school. Without her intertwining in-jokes and secret languages, I found room to hear more of L. I made her laugh once with an impression of Mr Price. I repeated it quickly, making it bigger, but her laugh was smaller. Wary of diminishing returns, I asked her to repeat some lines from films—lines none of us understood out of context, laughing only with recognition because L had said them several times before. I timed my laughs well, not overdoing it, making a variety of sounds indicating surprise, realisation, connection, warmth, admiration. The Wyld Stallyns introduction from *Bill and Ted's Excellent Adventure*. The Balthazar Getty speech from *Death and Emily*. The Gavins laughed too, while Jo lagged behind. Finally, as everyone else peeled away in the direction of their homes, it was just L and me.

I'll see you tomorrow Mark, she said, and turned away.

Can't wait, I said.

I walked home alone. In my room I wrote *I'll see you tomorrow* in my notebook. Wrote it again, the letters in a circle. Took out the vowels, put them back. Wrote the words backwards, as one whole word. Anagrams, like *Anagrams* (Chip Powell, 1945. Tagline: *If An Anagram*

might only see the pursuer *or* the pursued searching eagerly, or hiding, or even, on occasion, relaxing, putting the danger aside for a moment. This last type of scene is the most affecting, as when Jainet stops to drink from a stream and listen to the birds, or when the hunter stops in a bar and drinks a beer. Each looks tired. Each looks around, smiles, and then moves on. In at least one scene, the men pass each other without noticing. Every time the screen refreshes, we scan for those faces. The twitchy, hopeful Jainet, played by Serge Reggiani, the popular French-Italian singer. The lumbering, never-tiring perhaps-a-Nazi played by Gaston Modot, who played an angry German in Jean Renoir's *La Regle du Jeu* (1939).

At first, this theatrical espionage seems like a game for the viewer. Each scene is a mystery puzzle, a *Where's Wally?* in frosty greys and blacks. But soon, the beautiful complexity of an ever-repeating screen, with the water-torture tension of an eternal game of Pong, affects us. The knowledge that when Jainet ricochets himself beyond the edge of the screen that that is only the end of it for brief seconds is exciting, then annoying, then inevitable.

They depend on each other for meaning. This is their own private battlefield, a psychic chess, and it knows no international law or politic. The roles of pursuer and pursued could be reversed, and they

Uses All The Letters, It Can Never Be A Lie). I'll See You Tomorrow, Mark: *Yo, A Kilometre Slow Rumor. A Troll your work memories. Ow, A Murky Loiterer Looms.* Hidden meanings must be squeezed out. Smuggled ideas broken free. Suggestions understood.

would behave in the same manner. Like Japanese soldiers lost in the jungle, a mutual suicide, keeping alive only to spite the other, clueless as to what death to either would mean. Spy chases Spy.

The Eziots tinkered repeatedly with the film, and the most widely seen cut from 1949 is by no means the most definitive. In 1972, they toured a 72-hour version entitled *M. Jainet's Eternal Zigzag '72*, with reels replayed in random order: a stiffening, endless campaign of Zen warfare, fuelled by perpetual fear that the film would end, or would never end.

François Truffaut wrote about the experience of watching this version:

> In the theatre the fans celebrated this event in various ways. Their commitment made it like a sporting event or a festival. There were poetry recitals in the back rows, and a drinking game near the front that fell away by the halfway point of the film. One performance artist dressed as a bookie took bets on how many minutes it would be before Jainet was caught, knowing that he never would be. One group began to cheer the maybe-Nazi, perhaps finding in him the perennial despair of Wile E. Coyote, perhaps just yearning for a conclusion. Near me, a couple slept in each other's arms for the entire weekend, not looking up once. At one point, I became convinced

that the roles had been reversed, and that Jainet was

tracking his pursuer; the Eziots had hypnotized me, or

perhaps Jainet had realized that the best way to avoid

capture was to follow. Despite the singular, metronomic,

repetitive pacing of the film, the overall mood ebbed

and flowed throughout: at one point, almost everybody

cheered each carefully created scene, at another they

were slow-clapping, and at others it seemed like it didn't

matter what we were watching...after about eighteen

hours, the backgrounds through which the two men

move become less like Vichy France and more like other

wartime outposts—Morocco, Stalingrad, Cyprus. By

the fiftieth hour, I recognized nowhere. The longer one

watched, the further away from the original place we

were. I came to feel that if I were to watch Jainet running

for several weeks, he might end up leading his pursuer

into the sun, or the outer rings of heaven; similarly, the

viewer would leave the cinema to find themselves in a

completely different city, on another planet, or in another

body entirely.[62]

---

[62] François Truffaut, *"Cinéma Détente" Cahiers Du Cinéma*, November 1973. Truffaut's viewings of the film, like for most of France, did not happen until quite some time after the war: *It could be said that some of us were indulging in a retread of our escape fantasies and fears by watching this, I'm sure.*

The film was paid homage to in Rick Marving's home computer games for the ZX Spectrum during the glorious early-1980s years of quick inspiration, bedroom programming, and whimsical in-jokes.[63] Marving's *Monsieur Janney's Eternal Zig-Zag '82* and *Monsieur Janney's Still Running* were both famous for being never-ending, self-generating puzzles, with no *Game Over* or prize screen. Fans played them knowing

---

[63] *the film was paid homage to:* A 1981 episode of the television show *Blake's Seven,* titled *Zig-Zag,* contained many references to the Eziots' film. Comrades Kerr Avon and Del Tarrant are forced to duel against each other in a labyrinth, and rather than fight to the death as their captors wish, they conspire to bore their audience to sleep with an endless chase. Bobby, a kid in the year above us at school appeared in another episode of *Blake's Seven* when he was a baby, and subsequently had an acting career. He had been in a chocolate bar advert when he was eight. He had come to school wearing new trainers and with sweets to give out. He had earned a year's supply. In our unofficial list of famous people from our town he was third, behind George Eliot, novelist, and Trevor Peake, FA Cup winner with Coventry City in 1987. One summer he went to London to film roles in *Batman* (Tim Burton, 1989) and *Little Dorritt* (Len Shape, 1989). He came back with pictures of himself with both Michael Keaton and Miranda Richardson, but his parts were cut out of both films. He carried around the photos of his invisible summer, evidence that he had been in something that he wasn't, and twice. When he hit puberty his skin broke out, his skeleton stretched awkwardly, and his bright TV smile disappeared. He became sensitive to reminders of his showbiz past, and turned into a sullen bully. One day behind the science blocks he tried to sell me a book I didn't want. Jo pointed out the library label. *You saying I stole it*, Bobby said. *It's valid merchandise and I'm selling it for a good price. Give me the money*, he said. He came in close, eyeball to eyeball. *I don't want the book*, I said, backing up against the wall. *I-I don't need it.* Just then L and Vicki and the Gavins came around the corner. Little Gavin started humming the theme song from the chocolate bar commercial. Everyone else joined in. *Sod you lot*, Bobby said, and stormed off. We all laughed, like the gang at the end of *Losers Don't* (Petra Kystra, 1955).

Good job we showed up, Big Gavin said.

Yeah, Mark was just about to beat Bobby up, L said. She punched my arm, laughing. Contact.

they could never win. The game ended when you got caught. But in the Eziots' film, Jainet is always free, and never free too. The same goes for his pursuer.

M. Jainet's Eternal Zigzag

Directed by François Lepin Eziot and Françoise Lepin Eziot. Produced by Jean Eziot. Written by François Lepin Eziot and Françoise Lepin Eziot. Starring Serge Reggiani, Gaston Modot DisCina Films. Release Date: March 1941 (Fra). 99 mins. Tagline: How long can you run?

THE LIBRARY AT QUEEN OF ALL SOULS

SOULS

Leo McCarey, 1943

Once you permit those who are convinced of their own superior morality to censor and silence and suppress those who hold contrary opinions, the citadel has been surrendered.

Archibald MacLeish[64]

To admit authorities, however heavily furred and gowned, into our libraries and let them tell us how to read, what to read, what value to place upon what we read, is to destroy the spirit of freedom which is the breath of those sanctuaries.

Virginia Woolf [65]

I have always imagined that Paradise will be a kind of library.

Jorge Luis Borges[66]

---

[64] *A Book of Books: Quotes, Aphorisms and Sayings From The World of Literature* (Norton 1985).

[65] *A Book of Books: Quotes, Aphorisms and Sayings From The World of Literature* (Norton 1985).

[66] *A Book of Books: Quotes, Aphorisms and Sayings From The World of Literature* (Norton 1985). We used this book as a doorstop to keep the living room door open. I referenced it when my homework needed some extra juice. The more tired or distracted I was, the quicker I turned to it. In April 1993 Mrs White pointed out that *while quotations should be ornamental rather than bearing the brunt of your story, lately yours have been bordering on the superfluous. It feels as if you've been shoehorning them into your essays where they are not needed.* I nodded. *Many a poem is marred by a superfluous word,* I said. (Henry Wordsworth Longfellow, as quoted in *A Book of Books: Quotes, Aphorisms and Sayings From The World of Literature* (Norton 1985)).

123

Josie Werner (Barbara Stanwyck) dedicates her life to a library in a small town called Queen of All Souls, Texas. This charmingly ramshackle establishment operates from a barn, and due to donations, help from volunteers, and the commitment of Miss Werner, it flourishes. It even begins to get state-wide attention for its esoteric and uncensored selection of books. When a group of businessmen come to Queen of All Souls and start making promises about what they can bring, the townsfolk are curious. A new school, a hotel, and more trade are all promised. All they ask is for certain landowners to sell, at a good price. Miss Werner, suspicious of the motives of these men, refuses to listen to any offers for her land. *I am content with my calling as a caretaker of this bastion of learning, sirs,* she says.[67]

Mrs White smiled. *Mark, being...intelligent isn't just....how do I say this. Being smart isn't just being able to remember stuff word for word. It's being able to make reasonable arguments, pick up on social cues, things like that.* I nodded again. *Where all is dream, reasoning and arguments are of no use, truth and knowledge nothing.* Mrs White looked at me squarely. *I hope there are other kids in this school who appreciate a John Locke quote,* she said. *I really do.* But to me the words were Edward G Robinson's in *At Bosworth Field* (Bert Fisher, 1965).

[67] *bastion of learning: Knowledge isn't just a list of Kings of England or the words of the constitution,* Werner points out to a local dignitary in a town meeting. *Knowledge is knowing how to ask the right question, and of whom, and why, and when. And when* (at this point Stanwyck takes a delicious pause, sticks out her jaw, and offers a characteristically contemptuous half-smile), *to say nothing at all.*

I didn't, for example, need L to tell me to meet by the fountain Saturdays at 11. She knew I knew. Subliminal communication. I read the runes thrown down by a glance or an overheard half-message. Saturday routines: get up early – watch cartoons with sis – get dressed – smart black jeans – best trainers – band t-shirt. Soap and water to slick my hair back at the sides.

The efforts to persuade Werner step up. Many townsfolk can't

Walk into town, feel the energies begin to coalesce as I got nearer. Taking my time, so as not to expend the charge too quickly, brushing my hands along panelled fences, *brum-brum-brum*, a *ting* as my watch hits the railing. Bird calls to the left and the right as if they are witness to my curved path to the middle of town, the middle of the country, the country that invented the world, a bullseye with a fountain on it. Gaining power as I go, commentaries in my head: *Savage takes a painterly approach to his work, his deep care is evident in everything he does,* interviews with imagined journalists: *the notebook began as an idle distraction I never thought it would take me here,* or explaining the town, the lay of the land, to my Dad, who hadn't been here. Get to the pedestrianized centre at around nine-thirty. At around ten-thirty, Big Gavin would show up, rugby shirt collar flapping in the wind. *Wanna go to Our Price before Gav and Jo get here,* he said. I'd already been for a look, but went again. There were only two record shops in town (plus Woolworths which sold the chart stuff), so as long as we saved Risk-a-Disc until later, we hadn't exhausted the options. Our Price offered a good view of the fountain anyway. At about eleven, Little Gavin was there, talking to Vicki.

Fancy meeting you here, Vicki said to me when Big Gavin and I walked over. *Been to the George lately?* I couldn't decipher her tone. L arrived, shyly looking at me quickly before sitting down with Vicki. Jo walked up and looked pointedly at Little Gavin.

I thought you were helping me buy some new jeans today, she said to him. *I didn't know you'd invited half the school.*

L and I are going to do some shopping for her sister's birthday anyway, Vicki said, and stood up to leave. L gave us half a wave, and followed.

What was that all about, Big Gavin said as they walked away.

Someone can't take a hint, Jo said. But I had. I knew that the plan was that I was to lose Jo and the Gavins and meet L later. So I engineered a fight in *Risk-a-Disc.* When Jo said that she didn't like the new Fidgets single, *Gold-Rush At Wendy's,* I said that it was pretty good, even though I hadn't heard it. I quoted the *Melody Maker* review as if it were my own. It escalated from there, until Jo said she was going to Woolworths.

Coming, G, she said. I told them that I would catch up. I needed to go to the loo in the market. They shouldn't wait for me.

Fine, Jo said.

I explored town, tracking where L and Vicki might have gone. The market stall where they would buy bracelets, Claire's for earrings, the T-shirt shop, the park, the bandstand. I sat in the library for a while, as the window in the kids section gave a good view of the main road out of towards L's house. No Vicki, no L. After an hour I decided to head home slowly. If I went past the church and behind Sainsbury's I could take the long way round and pass L's house.

It started to rain, and my eyes stung as the soap from my hair was washed into them. I passed L's house, and saw her older brother cleaning the inside of his Ford Cortina, which was blue like the one in *Gristle* (Jim King, 1979). *I've heard more plausible tales from boys shouting about lupine invaders*, I wanted to shout, just like the titular hero, John Gristle. But I didn't. L's brother looked at me vacantly as I passed by. I enjoyed the frisson of excitement that came with realising that my anonymity to him would not last much longer. Like the hired killer chatting to his oblivious soon-to-be victims in *Little Gun* (Hadetori Ishoto, 2004), soon we would be intimate. But only I knew it for now. I pictured him inviting me to the pub, *just you and me tonight, Mark, eh? Just the boys*, and I would commiserate with him about his girlfriend troubles. *You're lucky you found someone like my sister*, he'd say, and I'd nod. *Luckiest man in the world*, I'd say. *And to think I'd never have known if she hadn't sent that card...*

Didn't see you in Woolworths, a voice behind me said. I turned around. It was Jo. Her shoulders were low; her dyed-red hair limp and wet.

I looked for you, I lied.

We waited for you for a while, and then went to Toppers for chips. I thought you'd dumped us for L and Vicki until we saw them there. They were at Toppers. Damn. *I would have bought you some chips if you'd come*, Jo said. *I had some money because I didn't find any jeans. They're all for skinny bitches.* We walked on, through the subway together. By the time we got to Jo's house on the other side, the rain had stopped and it was sunny. We stopped outside her door. She looked at her feet as she pulled her key out of her denim jacket pocket.

Do you still want to hang around with us, she said. *Me and the Gavs, I mean.*

Of course, I said. *Why do you say that?*

You only laugh at L's jokes when we're all together, and when she's not around you go quiet. And Vicki hates my guts.

That's ridiculous, I said. *We're all friends.*

She pushed wet strands out of her face and looked at me.

If you say so, she said.

land. The offers turn to threats. Anonymous poison-pen letters, vandalism, and attempts at arson. Then the businessmen get personal, digging
up any dirt in their efforts to turn public opinion against Miss Werner.
She is an unmarried woman with a history of personal relationships
with men, including an African American (Titus Chambers). Rumours
have always followed Miss Werner, we learn, but they were ignored, as
her bearing and hard work were so loved in Queen of All Souls. This is
where the casting of Stanwyck is perfect, because she has, in the knowing words of Fraser Campbell, *a look of experience*.[68] She seems plau-
sibly guilty of any activity she is accused of (not that a contemporary
viewer is likely to see any of it as a crime). McCarey certainly sympathises with her. Even to the pious god-fearing folk of Queen of All Souls
her alleged crimes are slim, so the businessmen step up their moral
assault and present an offer to the local priest for a new church building
if, in return, the priest suggests that the library has many books that *are
lacking in Christian merit*. The priest (Ray Milland) does so reluctantly.
Confident of her intellectual standing and rights, Werner offers to de-
fend the books in a public court.

It seems like we might know where the film is going: defiant
entrances into town halls, impassioned speeches in courtroom settings,
and a climactic ensnaring of a key witness in a terrible lie. But then a
plot twist sets the film on its head. The *deus ex machina* here being an

---

[68] *Hollywood Notes*, Paradox Books, 1963.

actual act of God, an apocalyptic storm. Suddenly, all recriminations are deemed petty, and as the businessmen scurry to the hills to safely, the town pulls together to begin the evacuation from a hurricane. *It's an act of* God, says one citizen. *It's a flash-flood!* The film folds back on itself and breaks at the middle. The second half of the film bears little relation to the first. As convoys leave the town, heading for mountains and bunkers, Miss Werner refuses to go. She shows no panic, but slips into a quiet silence as she organizes her books. When asked why, she doesn't explain. Weeping cousins come to try and persuade her to join them as they head to higher ground. She refuses, saying that someone must tidy the books. Miss Werner and her bloody-mindedness are the only constant. Stanwyck's natural defiance here rings like huge deep bell, no trace of trebly spite, just true and low.

If Josie Werner's reasons are unclear to us, they seem to be to her too; indeed, McCarey seems to be attempting to figure out the meaning of a life's work during these slow minutes, in the increasingly empty town and near-silent library. Josie walks around her carefully curated room, dusting a corner here, straightening a title there. She takes a book out to look at. *The Collected Works of William Shakespeare.* She reads to herself. *Good stuff, Bill. Good stuff,* she says. She looks out of the window. The storm approaches. Here we might be drawn to think about McCarey himself, whose own position as a credible and brilliant artist might have been secure (he had already directed several hits and two masterpieces, *Duck Soup* and *The Awful Truth*) but because of a health scare he wasn't sure how much time he had left. And being a maker of sublime films is not a karmic get-out-of-jail-free card. Leo McCarey will die. And so will Josie.

Nearing the end, Josie writes a letter:

I don't believe that good people make the world bet-
ter. And oftentimes they make the world worse, despite
themselves. But they should still try. One bad person can
do so much damage that it takes generations to repair.
But all the good people in the world I think keep the
world afloat. And they shouldn't have ever worried about
betterment or evolution because—what's changed? In
10,000 years? Textural things. That's all.

The music swells as if she has struck on something profound, but then it dies, and Josie screws up the page. A tear-jerking ending is offered, then revoked. The letter might have given the audience a retrospective explanation for Josie's decision to stay in the library, but McCarey trusts that we don't need one. Because there is none. *What can anyone say, anyway? It's all just words,* Josie says. She turns to look at the books. *Words,* she says, and smiles. McCarey pulls the camera away from Stanwyck, and away from the library, until the building seems tiny. The storm closes in.

The Library At The Queen Of All Souls

Directed by Leo McCarey. Produced by Leo McCarey, Jerry Wald. Written by Mildred Cram, Leo McCarey. Starring Barbara Stanwyck, Titus Chambers, Ray Milland. 20th-Century Fox. Release Date: March 1943 (US). 102 mins. Tagline: Just Because You Can't See It Coming Doesn't Mean It Won't Arrive.

DONNA, OR THE POWER OF CONSTANT THOUGHT

Hermoso Equipo, 1951

You know, if we really wish it, everything will be as we

want it to be. The bad things will be forgotten, the good

things will be everywhere, and nothing will be able to

hurt us. We just have to pray for it, more than we've ever

prayed before.

Debs, *Donna, Or The Power of Constant Thought*

Y ou've seen it. Or you've seen something like it, another version. The same anonymous actors, same colours, endless variations on the same trembling themes of sex and murder. In a wonderful opening scene, you'll remember Nick and Debs, or a similar young betrothed couple, stopping at a bar after a dinner date.[69] They like it here because it is usually quiet but tonight they walk into the middle of a big party. Employees of a local office are saying goodbye to a colleague, a secretary called Donna. The low energy in the room tells them that she isn't there yet, or maybe she has already gone. The place is covered in written testimonials, gifts, and pictures of her. Nick and Debs look at a picture of Donna in a bikini and sunglasses on a beach. Debs runs a finger over Donna's tan lines.

She's pretty isn't she, Debs says.

Do you think so, Nick says.

Oh come on, Debs says. *You'd be heartbroken to see her leave*

---

[69] *...you'll remember Nick and Debs...*: L's Mum was called Debs. So is mine. I had an uncle called Nick, she a cousin. The coincidences just stacked up. I could go on, I really could.

your office. She laughs.

Maybe, Nick says. He winks. She smiles. He pokes out his tongue. She punches him playfully. They laugh. A man with a garland around his neck asks them to sign Donna's card. They protest. *We didn't know her. We're just here on a date.* The man drunkenly persists. Eventually, to be polite, Debs takes the pen. When she looks at the card she sees a message:

Donna. Simply heartbroken to see you leave. Regards, Nick.

This is Nick's handwriting. *Did you sign the card before?*, Debs says. *Did you know her? Are you playing a trick?* Nick appears stunned. She keeps asking him questions, he keeps shaking his head. *I have no idea what is going on,* he says. The date drifts into confusion and anxiety. They go home. When they get there, there is a postcard in their mailbox:

Nick, I wish I could have gotten to know you before I left, D. x

Nick and Deb take a long holiday, during which they see glimpses of Donna lookalikes everywhere. Debs doubts Nick's fidelity. Nick doubts his own memory. They postpone their wedding. Their future is threatened by the ghostly Donna, who they may have never even met. The couple are haunted.

***

Producer Jimmy Jensen was part of the Danewood scene (a brief post-war Copenhagen group of state-supported filmmakers), until he left to start an off-the-radar operation in Mexico City. There he found a group already churning out copies of Hollywood thrillers, and with them he'd make over five hundred films between 1948 and 1956. They were filmed in a mixture of English and Spanish, and starred American nobodies, European never-weres, and young Hispanic talent. These pictures were largely shot with Mexico City standing in for LA, Chicago, or New York, and with their pulpy concentration of crime and lust became known as *Sexy Mexys* or *Sexiguns*. The group made several films simultaneously, with as many as thirty in production at once. Sometimes the cast and crew did not know which film they were working on, and some films are clearly a collage of several others, causing their plots to be a hash of tangled clichés and narrative *non sequiturs*. No matter who acted as director (and as many as twenty might serve the role on any one film) the films are attributed to a fictional director, Hermoso Equipo (inverted Spanish for *beautiful team*). The group found strength in this approach, with Jensen even believing that *the more different films we get in one film, the more authors involved, the more plots we refer to... the closer to the centre of fiction and humanity we get.* These quotes were originally attributed to Hermoso Equipo, as if he were a real person, in an interview with the LA Times in 1961.[70]

---

[70] Smith, Thomas "*Mexican Hollywood With European Flavor*" LA Times, December 2nd, 1961. This led to a story of a possibly apocryphal incident in 1963 when Fidel Castro invited *the genius who offers gorgeous satire of the evil empire, Hermoso Equipo* to visit Cuba. Castro, being a Spanish speaker, surely would not be confused by such an obvious ruse, but the story lives on.

American Chiffon Fahey and Englishman Martin Bastion, never stars anywhere else, made several Sexiguns together, notably *Bone Ring* (1952), *Sterling Silver Hallmark* (1953), and this. *Donna, Or The Power Of Constant Thought* also stars the Latina bombshell Luisa Teresa Caracas, better known as *Pipi,* a popular singer of overwrought ballads in her homeland, Peru. Here she is Donna, a gossamer image of charged sexuality who flickers on the edge of the grey screen, threatening to burst through Nick and Debs' idea of themselves with Technicolor vigour, and further, on through the fourth wall completely, covering the audience with gorgeous neon plasma. Such is her beauty. Fahey and Bastion as Nick and Debs, who, bothered by the suppressed memory/exposed id/vibrating chaotic alternative that is Donna, perfectly portray a milk-white and gaunt near-marriage, affectionate but drifting to tepid. This being Hermoso Equipo, footage from the same shoot is combined with new music and used to perfectly represent unsure newly-weds on the lam and kissing cousins in *Young Marrieds* (1951) and *Against God's Will* (1951) respectively.[71]

---

[71] *footage from the same shoot:* Nicolas Roeg said that watching the same sequence from the three films would teach anyone *anything they might want to know about how editing and post-production can change a film* (*"Roeg: Film Style," Film Comment,* Spring 1984). The differing music, background Foley, overdubbed dialogue, and the way the scene sits against those around it in each film combine to affect the feel of the footage. In one sequence that is reused several times, the pair sit at the bar talking and laughing. In *Against God's Will* they seem excited by each other, but scared to be seen together. In *Young Marrieds* the same footage is used, but now they seem more confident in their love, almost declaring it with every gesture. In *Donna,* they are comfortable to the point of complacency. *If you watch the sequences in this order, it tells the story of a*

good marriage, Gilbert Adair said in his book *Wreckages. Watch them in reverse, and it tells the story of a happy one.*

Similarly, a local DJ named Mark Keen who was on every night between ten and midnight used to play records backwards and try to sing the lyrics forwards over the top, but with the sentiment inverted: *I wouldn't do anything for love, but I would do that. I won't always love you. Don't kiss me.* I'd listen in bed with my battery-powered radio under my pillow. He'd play requests too, and often I'd hear classmates call in. I'd have my hi-fi ready with a blank tape recording the show in case he played something I liked. He made many jingles and songs about local businesses, and he'd parody hits of the day with new lyrics. He often sang *Beautiful Girl* by INXS, and instead of the refrain *Beautiful Girl/Stay with me* he'd sing *Beautiful Girl/Stay with Marky* to encourage us to keep listening after an advertising break. Once on the way to science class Vicki, walking ahead of me with L, turned to look at L and sang *beautiful girl stay with Marky* before turning and looking at me and laughing. L didn't turn around but I felt a sense of belonging all through the lesson, like the montage scene in *Top Class* (Jeff Minton, 1986) when the previously unruly group of kids use their street nous to team up and, against all odds, make a brilliant project, win a competition, and save the school.

In the last half-hour of his show Keeny would open the lines to anyone who wanted to call about anything. Sometimes the calls were serious, and Keeny would dish out advice or sympathy. More often callers did silly voices just to hear themselves on the radio. Once Little Gavin called and argued with Keeny about his repeated jokes about redheads. *Let me guess. You'd prefer to be called strawberry blonde*, Keeny said. We all laughed about it the next day, and after that there was someone from our school on the radio most nights, in character or otherwise.

One night L's sister rang up, pretending to be their Mum, complaining about the double entendres in the show. I only knew it was her because I'd heard L do an impression of her sister doing an impression of her Mum saying exactly this. *You've just got a dirty mind, ma'am*, Keeny said, imitating a comedian in a film I couldn't place, which annoyed me for a second, but then L's sister, (or was it Vicki, I now thought, or could it even be L herself?) carried on, still in the role of Mum, saying that she was thinking of leaving her daughter home alone for her fifteenth birthday in a few weeks. I sat up in bed to listen harder. L's fifteenth birthday was in a few weeks.

I might let her have some friends stay over to watch a video or two, and get them a piz-za, L's sister, or whoever it was, said, still pretending to be L's Mum. *What do you think Keeny?*

a young homeless boy with a bag of gold wanders across the screen, and Pipi sings a stinging ballad, apropos of nothing. These diversions, perhaps sections from other Sexiguns edited into the *Donna* mixture, actually serve to efficiently embody the protagonists' confusion about this strange girl; indeed, the constant dissonance of overlapping energies can at times be so potent that this hurried B-production transcends mere pastiche and becomes something more ephemeral and spectacular. *It is as if the actors are trapped in the screen, awaiting the cruel mercies afforded by sudden editing.*[72]

Think that's wise? She's a fan of the show.

    I wouldn't trust anyone who listened to me, Keeny said, before modifying: *Just don't let her watch videos that will give her ideas.* Then Vicki's voice (and it was definitely Vicki's voice, I listened to the tape back several times to clarify) said, clear and loud: *You're boring, Mark!*

    For a second I thought she was talking directly to me and not Keeny. But while he moved on to the next caller I composed myself, I realised I now knew my role at L's party: Entertainment manager. I must provide videos that will give her ideas.

    I had a tape in my bag from David H that might be good, but I hadn't seen it yet. He'd given it to me in the library with a grin. *Stick this in yer machine.* The previous tape I'd borrowed had half of *Amarcord* (Federico Fellini, 1972) on it. *It's wound right to the start of the sex scene,* he'd said. On the end of the tape was *Rooms* (Aziza Kartoskya, 1970, reviewed on page 251). I was spellbound from the beginning. When I gave it back the next day, he asked me what I thought. I went into a lengthy account of what I felt about the strange world of *Rooms. I was asking about the Italian woman's tits, but yeah, I know what you mean,* he said.

    Maybe *Amarcord* would be the thing. L hadn't seen it. It was funny, so the subtitles wouldn't be too much of a hindrance. It might get L's mind in the kind of sophisticated romantic mood that would be perfect for one of us to make a move and break our delicious detente.

[72] *sudden editing:* So says film critic Jean-Luc Sofie, whose book *Sexie* (Paragon Books, 1997)

Hermoso Equipo lost focus by the early sixties, and their pace began to slacken. By 1968 the Sexiguns were no more, but American producers were now keen to head south to make their own cheap B-movie homages to what were cheap B-movie homages to successful American films.[73] The Hermoso Equipo achievements are impressive: in fifteen years, as many as five hundred films were released, and an estimated thousand more jumpy hybrids were made. Most are lost, but some still surface at film festivals, on obscure cable channels, or on the internet.[74] Noteworthy Sexiguns *This Seems Like It's Real* (1952), *Pretty Worn Down, Whatever We Do Don't Tell Bill, 14 Carat Gold With A Very Sadly Shattered Amethyst* (all 1954), *Too Smoky To Be Emerald* (1955), *Turpentine Lipstick* (1956), and *The Dark Underbelly* (1959) are widely available.

---

was a crucial factor in directing critical attention towards the Sexiguns many years after the fact.

[73] *American films:* Gore Vidal: *The insecurity of American culture is such that it needs outside verification at all times.* (*The City and the Pillar,* E.P. Dutton & Co., 1948). Robert Christgau: *the literati went to Paris. Hendrix went to England. The most absolute presentation of American rock'n'roll to Americans came from The Beatles.* (*"Patriot Rock," The Village Voice,* March 1987).

[74] *or on the internet:* The online archivists Free Fantastic (www.freefantastic.co.uk) have made available over 200 Sexigun films. Their site also hosts a fun editing tool. By selecting scenes from thousands of hours of Sexy Mexy footage, the visitor can make their own pulpy classic of the genre, complete with a title generated (like many Sexiguns) from the mangled names of Hollywood noirs. Add a release date and the director, and the films seem eerily genuine: *Out of the Hat* (Hermoso Equipo, 1955), *In A Lonely Falcon* (Hermoso Equipo, 1949), *Indemnity City* (Hermoso Equipo, 1958).

***

The American-Korean bodybuilder Wi Fit was perhaps the most famous breakout star of the Sexiguns. His charismatically monosyllabic performances in *This Woman Is Amazing* (1953), *Very Of Their Time, Very Unique (1953),* and *The Crazy Folk Who Think This Is All Junk* (1954) led to a role in Vicente Minnelli's Hollywood musical biopic of Mussolini, *Il Duce* (1959) and subsequent roles in US television shows *Knife and Dork, Mister Probs 'n' Sister Probs* and *The Love Fund.* But picking out stars from such a collective endeavour seems beside the point somehow.

Near the climax of *Donna...,* Debs and Nick enter a gift shop in a seaside town. Debs scans a display of souvenirs. Nick, walking deeper into the store, sees a series of tiny carved wooden figurines. Cheap keepsakes that, looked at a certain way, might appear to be likenesses of Donna. Nick touches one, before turning back towards Debs. She is now wearing a large sun hat and some sunglasses and is posing for him, hands on hips.

Sometimes I think I'm dreaming, Debs says, grinning.

Me too, Nick says, quietly. Debs steps forward and embraces him. The hat hits his head, and they laugh. She squeezes him tight.

What did you dream about last night? Debs says. He looks out of the window over her shoulder.

I don't remember, he says.

Donna, Or The Power Of Constant Thought

Directed/Produced/Written by Hermoso Equipo. Starring Luisa Teresa Caracas, Chiffon Fahey,[75] Martin Bastion. Hermoso Equipo Films. Release Date: 1951 (Mex). 87 mins. Tagline: Can You Forget Her If You Never Knew Her?

---

[75] *Chiffon Fahey:* This actress shared a birthday with L.

DYSLEXIC FRENCH RED; NE'ER DO WELL (5)

Simone Tzerkovska, 1954

My friend at work says that he used to think if he said

all the right words in the right order, without making a

mistake, that he'd make his wife happy. Aren't you glad

we're not like that, my dear? Sweetheart? (silence) Can

you hear me? (muffled reply) I thought you were in the

room, I was talking to you. (muffled reply) Nothing.

Don't worry.

Husband, *Dyslexic French Red; Ne'er Do Well (5)*

The awkward title of *Dyslexic French Red; Ne'er Do Well (5)* is a cryptic crossword clue that stumps our heroine at a crucial point in this broody drama. That she can't answer it immediately is a surprise to her, as she finishes the crossword every day. And she doesn't just finish it: she can read the black and white shapes on the puzzle page of a paper left on a train carriage seat and know if she's seen it before. She can pass her hand over the clues like Braille and collect half of the answers in one sweep, returning to fill in enjoyable details subsequently (her husband thinks this gesture is an affectation, a flourish, but it helps her concentrate). She likes to picture the word grid as a house that she has to clean and illuminate, and each answer, despite being in black or blue ink, is actually removing dark dust from the far-flung corners. Large words please her; but more rewarding are the three-letter nuggets to be dug out, the tricky acronyms and abbreviations, little globs of adhesive that make the word house stand upright. She lives in an endless soup of computation and superstition. *It keeps her calm*, her husband says.

Off the page her movements are dreamy and vague. Cars honk at her as she wanders across busy Prague streets, chasing code in her head, rearranging alphabets. Her husband calls it *taking inventory,* as it looks like she is internally tallying wherever she goes.[76] He laughs about

---

[76] *tallying wherever she goes*: Just like the protagonist in *Mr Superstition* (Ben Sahar, 2001), I always counted the number of letters in words. For Mr Superstition (described by Kim Newman in *Sight & Sound* February 2002 as *Acid Rain Man*) it is crippling, for me less so. I would attempt to construct symmetrical sentences, made up of words of equal letters in each half, either in a repeating pattern (*'I Will If /I Have To* is 1-4-2/1-4-2) or in a mirror image fashion *(It Seems Like /That Would Be* is 2-5-4/4-5-2). I would sometimes try to make sentences to fit people's phone numbers (our number in Nuneaton was 329892, or *Can We Encourage Thinking Regarding Me?*). That Spring I was walking through the subway at the end of L's road when I saw Chris P coming towards me. *Alright,* he said. *Visiting your girlfriend again?* I buried my thrill at his use of that word and shook my head. *I'm going to town,* I said. *I'll come with you,* he said. *No, I've got to do something for my Mum,* I said. *If you say so,* he said, and walked on. I thought about what he'd said (*If You/ Say So)* and stopped at the end of the tunnel, on the ramp which led up to L's road.

I walked slowly past the end of the road, spying down the street. Then I walked back ten minutes later, this time congratulating myself for *not* turning my head to the right and looking towards her house, imagining that at that exact moment she was coming out of her front door, and she would see me passing by, without even slowing down, and she would suppose that I had so much going on in my life that the fact that I was near her house hadn't even entered my head. I headed back to the subway tunnel and sat on the railings at the top of the ramp.

Taking Chris as a sign, I took the five letters of his name and assigned them a minute each. If after five minutes I hadn't seen L, I'd go home. If I did see her, I'd walk up to her, kiss her, and walk away without saying anything. Such a simple decision-making device relaxed me. I swung my legs. A couple of kids from another school walked by. After five minutes were nearly

it with her by day, and visits other women at night.

One night they make a date to see a film, just like they used to.

The effort it takes to dress and have fun saddens them both, but they try

---

up, I realised the flawed science of my method. Chris' name was *Christopher*. Eleven letters. I gave myself an extra six minutes. A man walked by with shopping bags. The streetlight above me glowed brighter as the sky turned darker blue. *Christopher Michael Peterson* was his full name. Twenty-six minutes in total. After they were nearly up I heard noises through the tunnel. Shouting, laughing. I sat still on the railing. My legs were cold from the metal. The noise grew closer. I became convinced that it would be L, with some friends, having fun. The twenty-six minutes were the exact amount of time I was supposed to be there. I checked the zip on my jeans was up and the laces on my shoes were tight, and patted my hair. Then I did it all again. The noise grew closer. A school bag came skidding out of the tunnel and stopped at the bottom of the ramp. Laughter. A crumpled kid from the year below came running out of the tunnel and picked up the bag. Some boys followed. Five kids, all from the year below. *Pick Up Your Bag/ Dave Is Well Sad,* two voices said at the same time. They saw me. They went quiet as they walked past. *Alright mate,* said one kid. He had a shaved head and an earring. I nodded. They walked on. Then the earring kid turned and pushed me. I fell backwards off the railing. *Be careful,* the kid said. *You might fall.* They all ran away laughing. I looked up at the streetlight from the ground. The sky was black now. *Are you ok,* an old-lady voice said. I got up and ran down the tunnel, and all the way home.

When I got in, I went straight to bed. I turned the light off and the TV on. On Channel 4 a film was beginning. A rich man in a castle was getting dressed with the help of his servants. In the next scene the servants were talking about the strange behaviour of the master. The head butler told them to stop gossiping. *The master is just lonely since the lady passed. We're to take care of his wishes,* he said. When the commercial break came, the title card came up: *The Count* (1973). I watched on. It turned out that the Count never left the castle. He promised his family he would marry when, and only when, he had taken proper inventory of his estate. He counted his sheep. He counted his money. He counted the number of bricks in the walls and the daisies in the meadow. A greedy cousin attempted to claim the castle on the grounds of the Count's insanity. The film ended with the Count on a ladder counting the tiles on the roof of the barn. *Be careful sir,* the butler says. *You might fall.*

Echoes, signals, signs. I was on the right track.

not to show it. *We used to do this all the time. It used to be so easy.* They take a cab, line up for tickets, and smile at one another. He holds the door for her, and she almost laughs. They imitate themselves so well. They hold hands, even when it becomes uncomfortable. They check each other's reactions to the film, and then settle in. She is pleased at the neatness with which the protagonist's dilemma is set-up on screen, and the elegant movements of the implausible, but fun, plot. She likes Ernest Borgnine's face (or is it Humphrey Bogart or Hal Halloway or Robert Ryan? She finds it hard to tell the American men apart sometimes). But soon this pleasure recedes, and an uneasy quiet grows in her. Her husband is engrossed, so, giving his arm a kiss, she gently unhooks herself and heads to the bathroom to calm herself with a crossword.[77]

She knows, at the moment that the word *ROGUE* evades her for several minutes (and it is an easy one, an open goal), that something is wrong. She looks up at the cubicle door and listens. Nothing. She leaves, washes her hands, and looks in the mirror. Her face is hers, but a look in the eyes seems to serve as a warning that she cannot quite deci-

---

[77] *with a crossword:* The crosswords in the film are in English and are taken from the *Times* of London. Writer Victor Joi was in England during the war, when, even as an advanced English speaker, he found himself flummoxed by the perverse and often obtuse wordplay of these puzzles. Once back in Prague he had the crosswords sent to him, and over time he mastered their techniques and started to write a screenplay around them. As translation into Czech would be impossible, the puzzles, much of the screenplay, and the title were written in English. Director Simone Tzerkovska spoke very little English and understood few of the clues in the film. *I was as distant from the lead character's intelligence as her husband was,* Tzerkovska said. (*"Simone Speaks,"* Graeme Dodds, *Sight & Sound,* April 1970.)

pher. She recites clues in her head (*4 down: Sunken female?: THE LADY IN THE LAKE. 13 across: [it is intersecting so the third letter must be D] Repetitive ritualistic behaviours: OCD*), and the look fades. But she still suspects her reflection is tricking her.

She wants to head back to the film, but can't. Her husband, handsome and sensitive tonight, horrifies her. Minutes pass. She looks at the next clue, one that pivots across from *THE LADY IN THE LAKE* (from the tip of *LADY*, ending at the *L*, like a scissor open to a right angle): *Very sad unfinished story about rising smoke.* She knows, instantly, that *very sad* yields the definition; that the word will be sombre. *Unfinished story* suggests, obviously, an incomplete word which houses the *rising smoke* part. But here her brain follows the clue and itself seems to move upwards, rising from the empty bottom corners of her puzzle to the top, and then further, off the page and into the middle distance. It hovers in mid-air, vaguely aware of an alarm bell somewhere, in another room.

Her face looks reversed in the mirror; she thinks of the lopsided weather vane on the roof of her house whose arrow always points down towards their bedroom, accusingly. A new knowledge evades her slightly, but she searches for it. But there it is: she realizes she is going to leave the cinema and go home. And then she is, walking across the lobby with purpose. But something stops her at the door: the answer. *TRAGICAL.* Of course. The obvious solution makes her laugh: the rising smoke is a cigar, and it runs backwards up the page, clothed in *TAL*; which is almost *TALE*, and thus an unfinished story. It takes minutes, but order is restored. She decides to return to her seat, hold his hand, and pay attention to the film.

But he is gone. He vanished in the interim, already in a cab across town, dreaming of flights to carefree territories. (Tzerkovska's decision to show us this removes tension about his whereabouts, but allows us to, as critic Vikram Paul says *wallow in a certain misery that the leading lady can only suspect.*[78])

The last third of the film follows her as she walks around town, looking for him. She explores bars, restaurants, and parks. When she finally returns home the sun is coming up, and with some kind of awareness dawning, she finds a house cleaned of every sign that he was ever there. His drawers are empty, his closet too. The photo albums of their time together are blank. She sits on a couch, lights a cigarette, and in David Thomson's words, *has perhaps cinema's most concisely agitated brood* on the previous events.[79] She chews a nail, lights a second cigarette, and very slowly, her expression relaxes. A boy selling newspapers can be heard in the street. She smiles.

---

[78] *"Lost Classics No.321," The Times*, February 1996.

[79] *Have You Seen...?* Knopf, 2008.

Dyslexic French Red; Ne'er Do Well (5)

Directed by Simone Tzerkovska. Produced by Dexter Hunstler. Written by Victor Joi. Starring Elizabeth Tizla, Hanz Janck. Czech Film/CBK. 104 mins Release Date: Oct 1956 (Cze/Fra). Running Time: 102 mins. Tagline: The Clues Are Under Her Nose.

LE BOTOX

Jeanne Champi, 1957

The past it is a magic word/Too beautiful to last.

John Clare, *Childhood*

In the half-century it has taken to officially arrive in a credible DVD release, *Le Botox* hasn't aged a day.[80] Its joy is as infectious as ever, its anarchy still as cutting, and its cutting still as anarchic as that of any number of far more celebrated Godard films, and Jeanne Champi's free-and-easy filmmaking techniques, once described by Andrew Sarris as *of very mixed quality,* look not only resolutely masterly but distinctly modern.[81]

Le Botox follows the meandering lives of a group of young people in an average town in the middle of France. These kids are not hip and hypnotic like Jean-Paul Belmondo and Jean Seberg in Godard's iconic *À bout de souffle* (1960). They are small and plain, especially Suzette (Maria Lucho), who is so diminutive that we only really notice her emerging as the central character in the last third of the film. But this ordinary world is filmed with real panache. There is a long shot following Pierre (Vincent Carrieré) along the street, past the market and crowds that makes a similar sequence in *À bout de souffle* look flashy and contrived. And during the scene in which Paolo (Michele Abbruz-

---

[80] Le 'Botox' is a Medieval French word for a *hearty appetite* or *eager young boy*, according to Merriam-Webster, or *hungry young cocksmith* according to Mary M. Webster (citation needed).

[81] *"Oh, Jeanne" NY Film Bulletin,* August 1967.

zo) works as a waiter at the Rivière restaurant, the elegant complication of Champi's tracking shots, weaving like slick ghosts through a staged bustle, couldn't have been guided any more perfectly, or with more zip, by anyone else, not without drawing attention to their own genius. A later sequence, following a family's departure from Tours and out into the Loire Valley, is studded with such quiet gold as to render the need for such gimmickry as colour, smell and 3-D almost superfluous. All this without modern lightweight cameras too.

***

That Champi is not thought of as one of the French directors who *turned the 20th century about-face*[82] in the fifties and sixties is the kind of quietly cruel turn of events that the director herself constructs in her films. *True pioneers get lost in the wilderness years before civilization even knows they're gone*, contemporary Agnes Varda said at Cannes in 1972, when a campaign to have a new cut of *Le Botox* shown at the festival failed. *My friends like my films more than the public do,* Champi said. *That is just okay.*[83]

Her last two films, *Paris dans L'Ombre* (1973) and *La Fiction*

---

[82] Andrew Sarris' famous phrase included the core group of Truffaut, Godard, Rohmer, Chabrol, and Rivette. Like any group of outsiders, this collection was pretty exclusive. I thought that our group that walked home together each day should have a name. I tried a few: The Posse, Home Gang, L's Bells, Loop Group (named after the titular group of scientists stuck in a slice of repeating time in *Loop Group* [Sandra Schwartz, 1981]) but none stuck. A name is only a name if someone uses it.

[83] *"Jeanne, Champi of the World"* Betty Jones, *Sight & Sound*, February 1985.

est Fiction (1976) are failures because by then Champi had long abandoned her more subtle techniques. The latter in particular feels like an attempt to appeal to critics who were by now taken with the more assertive styles of Fassbinder and Scorsese, but the fast pace doesn't suit Champi. In comparison, the quieter *Le Botox* floats confidently in its own universe, its influences unclear. A touch of Ozu, perhaps, Bresson, certainly, but what else? It feels like it doesn't need to shout, that it knows exactly how good it is.

In *Paris dans L'Ombre*, the elderly Catherine (Valerie Gignal), when asked to settle a political argument among her sons says:

> *You always need to win. But have you thought about*
> *not playing the same old game? About playing a new*
> *one? With new rules? No. You just go on with the same*
> *arguments that will never end. Winning is so important*
> *to you, but no-one can ever get to the finish line, you pull*
> *each other back into the mud.*

The sons stop. They look at her for a second, and then tumble right back into their animated discussion, where they are apparently happy. It is hard not to think of this and other later films as Champi's attempts to join in the conversation, or the game, of commercial cinema. But as attempts they lack any real conviction. It is as if she knew when she was making it that *Le Botox* would be her masterpiece, never to be bettered. Such suspicions so early in life (Champi was twenty-four when she made *Le Botox*) seem to have inhibited Champi; if the wider world could not recognize the strength of her best work, what was she to do next?

What is striking upon watching and re-watching *Le Botox* is Champi's unflinching commitment to her central character's ignorance. Suzette is surrounded by men who display varying degrees of selfishness and aggression. Her brother leaves his chores to Suzette so he can go on a date.[84] Her father is a bully to the family, and has criminal connections outside it. Suzette's world is distinctly unfair, but she never quite realizes how put-upon she is. This creates a brilliant tension in the viewer: we expect Suzette's naive optimism to be damaged, or worse, to place her in danger. That is the path a film like this *should* take, we might think. We might hope that Suzette learns and grows wiser and smarter. We might fear that she is too fragile to survive her world. But Champi manages to put us in a position where we are rooting for Su-

---

[84] *so he can go on a date*: Aware of the need to build up good credit at home and at school, so as not to put any parental roadblocks in the way of L's party, I conscientiously did my chores and homework over the next few weeks. I exercised, wrote in my *Fictional Film Club* journal, and did my laundry. I washed and ironed my best outfits, folded them, and carefully put them away, vowing to not touch any of them until the big day. I was ready, like the small robot in *B.E.E.P. Repaired* (Mitch Pastis, 1986).

What's got into you lately, Mum said.

Nothing, I said.

Well, it's good to see you taking responsibility for yourself, she said.

Thanks.

It's nice to see you engaged rather than daydreaming, she said.

zette to both learn (because we care about her), and to remain ignorant (because we love her as she is).[85] When a new boy, Pierre (Carrieré), comes into her life, we know that he is the man who stole her bag from her locker at the beginning of the film (causing her to get beaten by her father). We want her to know this piece of information, so as to better make a judgement about him. Our expectations of storytelling demand that she finds out (at a narratively perfect time, of course: perhaps when she is truly in love with Pierre, she would discover her stolen belongings in his room, or he might confess on their wedding day). But she doesn't, and by withholding this information from Suzette while giving it to the viewer, the apprehension of their courtship is shifted. We now doubt the type of story we are being told.

Parts of Le Botox can be seen in the contemporary cinematic landscape, broken into more easily chewable pieces: the sub-plot in which Paolo, prompted by a writing class exercise, follows and becomes obsessed with a woman is blown up to fill the narrative in both David Thewlis' skinny and grim Lecher (2008), in which the director himself plays the man who ends up murdering the girl, and Neil Burger's Exercise (2001) in which Christian Bale follows a girl, only to discover that his wife is paying her to drive him insane by acting out a repertoire of his fantasies. The restaurant dynamics were borrowed wholesale

[85] *remain ignorant:* Writing about *Le Botox* in *The Independent on Sunday* (March 1997), Gilbert Adair said *Champi manages to hide several guns in the opening act that are never seen again. In stories, secrets come out. In* Le Botox, *as in life, they do not necessarily.*

for Christian Merc's *River Street* (1990). Vincent Carrieré also became famous in France playing versions of the idealistic, boyish Pierre, an escape from the hoodlum roles he'd been restricted to before.

Champi was never as caustic as Chabrol, nor as aggressive as Godard. She couldn't keep as cool as Rohmer, and lacked the consistent energy of Truffaut. She could match none of them for stamina. But filmmaker and friend Varda knew Champi's worth. She described *Le Botox* as...*the forgotten sixth vowel of the French cinematic language. If we could only remember it, and remember how to fashion its form on our page and in our mouths, we could complete perfect new secret sentences.*[86]

Le Botox

Directed by Jeanne Champi. Produced by Jeanne Champi, Michael Ravelle. Written by Thomas Brix. Starring Vincent Carrieré, Michele Abruzzo, Maria Lucho. SRV Films. Release Date: Oct 1957 (Fra) 119 mins. Tagline: Too Rich, Too Poor, Too Hungry For More.

---

[86] *"The Big Interview: Agnes Varda,"* Nick Pinkerton, *Sight & Sound,* September 2005.

FUTUR

Piotr Janas, 1958

Forty years and I have learned nothing, nothing useful,

about the people, factories, politics and personalities of

Hackney. The name has declined to a brand identity. A

chart-topper: worst services, best crime, dump of dumps.

A map that is a boast on a public signboard, a borough

outline like a parody of England. My ignorance of the

area in which I have made my life, watched my children

grow up, is shameful. I've walked over much of it, on

a daily basis, taken thousands of photographs, kept an

8mm film diary for seven years: what does it amount

to? Strategies for avoiding engagement, elective amnesia,

dream-paths that keep me submerged in the dream.

Iain Sinclair, *Hackney, That Rose Red Empire*

I n 1947, Piotr Janas moved from Gdansk in Poland to Hackney in London and immediately started work on his only film. His script revolved around a young man in wartime Poland who slipped forwards and backwards in time. But when he began shooting in the streets of post-war London, the problem of the setting was evident. *I didn't know if London was big enough to stage my memories of my bombed and oc-cupied home town. Even though it dwarfs Gdansk, the intensity of my destroyed home looms large.*[87]

---

[87] *Twin City Decade: Thoughts Toward A Futur* (Futur Books). This was Janas' complete and

Janas never planned much beyond making this one artefact, a nine-hour compendium of his every thought—waking, sleeping, and the delicious ether-world in between. He shot hundreds of hours of footage in London between 1947 and 1953, and became intrigued by the way that the narratives of his homeland could echo there. He filmed so much, imprinting his memories of a long ago past on his new home, that the effect was dizzying:

> *I began to see doppelgängers of childhood girlfriends*
> *in the windows of London buses and outlines of dead*
> *schoolmasters in café doorways. A turn down a calm*
> *street in Dalston one day drew me to my childhood road*
> *completely, even though they bear few similarities except*
> *for my own presence at one time, and then another.*[88]

unedited dream diary from 1940-1950, which he self-published in 1958 to accompany the film.

[88] *Twin City Decade:* Nuneaton is twinned with Roanne in France, Guadalajara, Spain, and Cottbus, Germany. (The road around Nuneaton is called *Roanne Ringway,* and the signs are traditionally defaced so they say *Poanne Pingway* as soon as the council replaces them.) We were all given a pen-pal in Roanne to write to in French, and they'd respond in English. Mine was Pierre. I confessed my love for L: *ma copine est la plus belle fille de mon école. Je lance une fête surprise pour son anniversaire où nous nous disons que nous nous aimons.* I wrote three pages of fairly competent French. Pierre's reply referenced none of my points and answered none of my questions about the film industry in Roanne. It was a brief letter made up of short and brutal boasts:

Mark, I have 15 years. I have baseball. I have National France Final Baseball. I have medal gold. I have burgers. I have TV. I have sex 12 girl. Your friend Pierre.

I read it to the Gavs and Jo and showed them the picture Pierre had enclosed. He was wearing shorts and sunglasses and held a trophy.

The French are so arrogant, Big Gav said.

In 1958 the film was released under the name *Futur* (Janas dropped the final 'e' to acknowledge the unfinished quality of even an exhaustive work like this). It is largely a science-fiction narrative following a man named Jan as he jumps between occupied Poland and a dreamy future. Jan is played by Robert Colt but his inner monologue is voiced by Janas himself. Jan walks around the city, but for long periods disappears from the screen. While we can imagine the footage we are seeing as Jan's viewpoint, it is as if our hero is gone, vanished from the text, lost amid documentary footage of Piccadilly Circus, Hyde Park, or Hackney's Mare Street. During many sequences, Janas' voice walks with us. His words are a jumble of his story and that of his character:

> *The future is made up of versions of the past. I think my brain makes links to make the distortions more palatable. When I am in the future, I have memories of the present, and feel nostalgia for a variety of pasts. Walking down a London street, I know this is the near-future, so I scan the surroundings for clues, and tread carefully. It is busy. There are lots of people and cars. A girl loading furniture into a van wears a face mask. A passing cyclist*

Does he think he looks good, Little Gav said.

You told him L was your girlfriend didn't you, Jo said.

No, I said.

Show me your original then, Jo said.

I sent it to him, didn't I?

Convenient. Jo said. *Very convenient.*

does the same. Other faces in the crowd wear them too,

but not everyone.

Jan attempts to prove to himself that he is *not* in Poland by doing something he never did there: commit a serious crime. He surmises that the visceral immediacy of this act will bring him into the present. After some deliberation, he decides to break into his neighbour's house. He does so, and steals a china plate which he vows to keep by the side of his bed as a solid physical reminder of where he is. This burglary itself is shot in near silence, without voice-over. When Jan/Janas talks again, he describes what he is seeing. At first Poland seems absent, but it slowly resurfaces:

> *The trees bend in the wind. I pass a row of shops. Outside*
> *the pavement is filled with flat trolleys, the kind used*
> *to carry large amounts of milk or bottles of water. This*
> *makes the pathway hard to get through, so I step up onto*
> *one of the trolleys to let walkers pass in the other direc-*
> *tion. A dark-eyed woman smiles from under a furry Rus-*
> *sian-style hat and fur coat. She is the only person making*
> *eye contact. Others move in and out of the supermarket*
> *with a grim calm that I recognize –*

Janas stops talking, and the screen freezes on an image of a pair of old women in headscarves carrying shopping bags. The freeze-frame holds for a full minute as Janas keeps talking:

...I realized immediately that I knew—that I knew them

from Gdansk. I'd seen these expressions before, on the

faces of Poles when the Nazis approached, and when

after the initial fear, we realized that panic stations

cannot be manned permanently. But more than those

expressions, I recognized the faces. This pair of strangers

in London was a pair of strangers I knew in Gdansk.

Jan keeps walking, upset that he can never leave his past behind. But by
the time he gets home, he seems to have arrived in a madness in which
his past and present truly overlap.

He describes the small flat that we have seen him living in as if
it is his childhood bedroom. But his bed is just like the one he slept on
in the army, and his neighbour's plate is the same one that his grandmother would use to serve him cake. He describes people entering and
leaving, but we only see him sitting alone, holding the plate.

Home, at mother's. Except it is different. I reason that

she has moved. It can't be too far into the future, but

something has happened. This is a big, gorgeous house.

I eat the bread with cheese, tomato, and cucumber. My

mother-in-law comes downstairs, and I remember that

she and my father-in-law are staying here. My mother is

out. My mother-in-law is carrying the vacuum—she has

just done the upstairs bedroom, I guess, typically keeping busy. I show her the bread, and she is suddenly very hun-

gry too. I cut more for her. I scan her face and the room

for clues, something to bring me back to my present, but

I see none.[89] *I am a time-traveller who never quite finds*

[89] *but I see none:* Jo took me aside after maths one day.

I got my invite to L's party today, she said. *I was surprised. I didn't think she wanted me to go.*

She's probably giving to me mine after school, I said. *In person.*

I heard from Little Gav that L is only allowed four people over. Dad's orders.

So?

Well the two Gavs got their invites yesterday, Jo said.

And?

Mark, can't you add up? Me, Vicki, the Gavs. That's four.

Maybe Vicki isn't invited.

She raised an eyebrow.

L and I have an understanding, I said.

Why are you wasting your time on her? She...

What?

Well –

Well what?

She's not even... that special.

L?

Yes, L, she said. She folded her arms.

I get it, I said. *Some Kind of Wonderful. Howard Deutch. Nineteen eighty-seven.*

What?

I'm Eric Stoltz. L is Lea Thompson. You're Mary Stuart Masterson.

What?

You're jealous.

She laughed hard.

Mark. You're an idiot. I just care about you, as much as you annoy me every day.

And anyway, Eric Stoltz ends up realising that the girl he likes, that one who was in Back To The

what I need in either time. My gifts of foresight are use-

less to me. The slivers of future I encounter contain little

to carry back to the past for profit or nourishment.

Jan stands, and drops the plate. It smashes. He begins to forget what his

grandmother's face looks like. The final sequence, a long, uncut shot

of men entering an adult cinema in Soho, is overlaid with Janas listing

the names of his classmates from school like a litany. Past and present

thrown together, and both more distant than ever.

Futur

Directed by Piotr Janas. Produced by Thomas Standish. Written by Piotr
Janas, Tomas Lewandolski, Richard Smith. Starring Robert Colt, Louise
Mather. Rabbit Films/CKF. Release Date: March 1958 (UK) 552 mins.
Tagline: The Futur Is A Robbr.

Future –

    – Lea Thompson

    – yeah her. He realises that she is a bitch. Look it up in your notebook.

GLITTERED SHOULDERS

Douglas Sirk, 1961

To know inauthenticity is not the same as to be
authentic.

Paul de Man

To appreciate a film like Glittered Shoulders *probably*
takes more sophistication than it takes to understand
one of Ingmar Bergman's masterpieces, because Berg-
man's themes are visible and underlined, while Sirk's style
conceals his message.

Roger Ebert

In 1963, Pierre Imperius, known best as the publisher of the short-lived *Insouciance '55* magazine and for his collaborations with Lawrence Ferlinghetti, penned a poem that was published in the *New Yorker* in its entirety. The 32,000-line effort, *If I Had A Suburban Cruise Missile* was a beat-freak assault on American values, and Hollywood and television in particular:

> *If dubious intent is the barometer*
> *Of febrile justice*
> *And judging by the nixed reactions to the Testament*
> *Of Offshore leaking*
> *And Korea*
> *The State of the United States*

Or not

Then tensions must surely rise upon the fluid release

From this hellish discharger:

Don't smirk with Sirk

He may purport to report on vanities that are to be
mocked

But he is decadence itself

And and and

Pictures of women not revolutionaries girls in white
dresses

Self-indulgence worthy of crucifixion, no chance of resur-
rection.

It was further evidence of what Douglas Sirk himself knew: cool young people did not regard his work as worthwhile. They thought it mannered, melodramatic, and unintentionally hilarious.[90] History hasn't

---

[90] *mannered, melodramatic, and unintentionally hilarious:* There have always been counter-arguments, of course. One comes from an unlikely source. In his erudite examination of road movies *Gas, Food and Longing* (1986), shabby philosopher Milo Holodex makes a pit-stop (sunny vista, near a large villa, walled gardens) and lingers on Sirk briefly, suggesting that, in his repeated examination of lovers and haters in situ (a house, a stage, a house as a stage) Sirk *tackles American displacement from within; his characters are eating their hearts out, whereas the Easy Riders and Kowalskis are just eating out, heartlessly.* Holodex makes another claim worth repeating: *The sixties represent the beginning of the end not because of drugs or sexual deviancy or civil rights or Vietnam, but because it was the first time that a huge minority of Americans became aware of the mass illusion that there is a joke that they have to be in on; this is what is loosely known as cool; it poisons the waters of the most benign offerings, and does so endlessly, so much*

necessarily been kind either, for while he is regarded as a great director, many put him firmly in the camp camp, holding him up as a representative of studio conservatism, or dimly praising him as a *stylist*.

But with *Glittered Shoulders* Sirk successfully constructed a Trojan Horse critique of Hollywood from within that later films like *Beyond The Valley of the Dolls* (Russ Meyer, 1970) *or Shampoo* (Hal Ashby, 1975) would make attempts to copy, if with less subtlety. Those films, enjoyable as they may be, wear their satire on their sleeves. Sirk's sleights-of-hand might occasionally be *too* clever, as some of his jibes can slip under the radar of an inattentive viewer. *Glittered Shoulders* is housed in Sirk's usual quietly queasy pastel colours, the backgrounds are filled with blandly beautiful starlets and walnut-coloured men, and this leads the viewer to expect an overwrought and earnest romance fashioned from his usual playbook. But as Pauline Kael observed, *the elephant in the room, with its irony tusks, is obscured.*[91]

Anita Ekberg plays a bombshell with an LSD addiction. Rich-

---

so that instead of admiring great achievements, we spend longer avoiding great embarrassments.

Most post-1965 ideas of cool directly reject the Sirkian. If they do evoke him, they do it from a distance: Todd Haynes' *Far From Heaven* (2002) and Betty Denny's *Flying To Yesterday* (2010) both clearly revere Sirk as a stylist, but can't remove the post-modern lens of the 21st century from their work. Sirk himself said *the great artists... have always thought with the heart*. He also said, (regarding *Glittered Shoulders'* relative box-office failure) *I could suggest a thousand reasons why nobody wanted this. But they would all be incorrect. Motives are always confused, always, if they are honest. And by honest I do not know what I mean* ("*Sirk by Bogdanovitch*" *Interview*, May 1980). These two statements need not be seen as contradictory.

[91] *Kiss Kiss Bang Bang, Film Writings 1965-1967*

ard Widmark is a producer from a storied Hollywood family who seeks to live up to his name with on-screen success and off-screen destruction. Groucho Marx has a flinty cameo as a cynical party[92] host with an

---

[92] *party:* Any mention of the party got me excited, but we all felt that way. It was going to be great, but with a little planning it would be special. The week before her birthday was Whitsun week, and L was to go on holiday with her family. She'd never been abroad except to Scotland and Minorca and was excited. She was coming home on the Friday, the day before she turned fifteen. This gave me time to prepare. I made a Birthday Book, a small booklet containing facts about her birthday in history. I included celebrity birthdays with notes: *Clint Eastwood is 63 today, have you seen* Bobby Hundreds (1986) *which he directed in which he plays a country star making an MTV comeback... Walt Whitman 174 today, is Whitsun Week named after him do you know?* There were other facts about the day that she might not know. *On this day in 455, Emperor Petronius Maximus is stoned to death in Rome...in 526 an earthquake strikes Antioch* (as portrayed in the film *Shook!* (Ted Lowen, 1971) starring TV actor Jim Norton, *whose birthday is spookily also today!)* I drew pictures and coloured them myself, and included several sketches of penguins, because I knew L liked them. *The hull of the Titanic was launched on this day in 1911, so it's not all good news! (ha!).* I ended on a positive note with a detail about how on this day in 1578, King Henry III laid the first stone of the Pont Neuf, the oldest bridge in Paris: *I'd love to see it one day. Wouldn't you?*

The Jim Norton detail was potent. He was born on L's birthday, and died on mine. Watching a Jim Norton film on her birthday would cast some kind of spell, underline the link between us. The action comedy *Hammer Blow* (Walter Hill, 1984) would be a good choice. David H stole it from the video shop for me in return for a bottle of vodka that I took from Mum's alcohol cabinet. I gathered several other videos to bring, just in case L felt differently. *Pump Up The Volume* (Allan Moyle, 1990) would be good as L looked like the female protagonist in the film, and Mum had once said I had Christian Slater's hair, but the pirated copy David H had got me (in exchange for doing science homework and mowing his Nan's lawn) had a soundtrack that was a second behind the action.

I tried on several outfits that week, before settling on the perfect choice. For the party I would wear my smart blue jeans and a new black t-shirt and my black leather jacket. My black boots. My red scarf would set it all off. I cut the tasselled ends to make it look more like the one

impenetrable hold on the tastemakers. Lana Turner, in a curious series

of wigs and eyelashes is Baroness Barba Gabrielle Gastoni (or *Lady*

Baba Gaga for short, and boy is she short with everyone, Marx says), the

that Marcello Mastroianni wore everywhere, even the sauna, in Elio Petri's *Jazz Caldo* (1977). My hair would only behave itself three days after it was washed, so I bathed on Wednesday, which got Mum's attention, as Sunday was my normal day.

    I would have to carry lots of provisions to the party but I didn't want to show up carrying a plastic bag, or worse, my schoolbag. I wanted to walk in to L's carrying two videos and a *Happy Birthday* balloon with hearts on (they had them at the card shop in town), nothing more. I'd have to plan logistics, maybe stash a bag somewhere close to L's house. I timed the walk from my house to L's. Not because I didn't know how long it would take, for I knew exactly now. I was hoping to strike up a frisson of juju by walking the path, a practice of success, an envisioning, a future quest played out through these preparatory repetitions.

    I did the walk in the outfit I would wear, being careful not to scuff the polish job on my boots. I thought of how many actors I'd read about who stayed in character when they weren't filming, and wore their costumes and insisted the crew call them by their character name at all times. I got soaked coming home on Thursday and had to force my jeans through the wash. This made me realise that I might need extra supplies nearer to L's house, just in case. On the night before she got home I packed a bag (a white shirt and smart jacket in case it was a dressier affair, pyjamas and underwear in case it was a sleepover, two pairs of socks, a toothbrush, deodorant, old trainers, a condom, hair gel, a comb, a pack of cards (to show off a couple of tricks I'd learned after watching *F For Fake* [Orson Welles, 1975]), the VHS copies of *Pump Up The Volume, Hammer Blow* and *Amarcord,* and unmarked copies of *Vixx* (D.L. Ujpesti, 1984) and *Flesh Gordon* (Howard Ziehm, 1974), just in case L wanted to watch something a little bit racier. I put in the booklet of birthday facts and a small *Welcome Home* sign I had made. I had coloured in the letters on the sign alternately in Ferrari red (L's favourite colour) and olive drab (an in-joke calling back to an art lesson earlier in the term when a kid challenged the army outfits I had drawn in my depiction of a firefight on a bridge in Arnhem inspired by the film *A Bridge Too Far* (Richard Attenborough, 1977). *Why are they wearing diarrhoea colours,* he said. *That's olive drab, the official colour of British Army fatigues in 1944,* I said. He shook his head in defeat. L laughed from across the room. She'd get the reference, I was sure.).

lost lead around who the film spins. She enters, she leaves, she sighs, and endless orchestral variations of Henry Mancini's *Theme From Glittered Shoulders* follow and follow and follow, until it feels like this elegiac drift is less of an announcement of her beauty and presence, and more of an uncertain query as to whether she actually exists.[93] As she says at one point to no-one in particular: *If I think I'm at a party, and the newspaper says I'm at a party, and someone is handing me a drink, then I must be at a party, correct?*

All of the characters speak with apparent wisdom (of goings on, of what to do, of who does who, and how they do), and yet every quick remark screams of sadness. Marx is particularly effective in this regard; his familiar smart-aleck persona is rendered, with a slight shifting of mirrors, unlovable and desperate. The difference is minor (Groucho Marx is, after all, *always* Groucho Marx), and many critics see here only a shallow imitation of his best performances. But might this be a Sirk masterstroke? By restraining a genius he frustrates both the audience and the performer, and by doing this perhaps finds something else, something deeper. Sirk performs a dramatic castration, an orchestrated self-sabotage in epic and lushly toned surroundings.

Paul de Man said: *Irony divides the flow of temporal experience into a past that is pure mystification and a future that remains harassed*

---

[93] *actually exists:* The main theme song was sung by Ricky Nelson, composed by Henry Mancini, with lyrics by Mack Discant: *When you rub shoulders with the stars, you might get glittered limbs/You compose wild hymns/In your pseudonym, she swims/And other synonyms.*

forever by a relapse within the inauthentic. It can only restate and repeat it on an increasingly conscious level.[94] Sirk's skill is that he manages to unite these two separate time zones so delicately that it took viewers and critics years to discover that his breadcrumb trail led somewhere. If they followed it at all.

Glittered Shoulders

Directed by Douglas Sirk. Produced by Ross Hunter. Written by Allan Scott. Starring Lana Turner, Richard Widmark, Anita Ekberg, Groucho Marx. Universal Pictures. Release Date: June 1961 (US) 113 mins. Tagline: Come! Rub Shoulders With The Stars.

---

[94] *Blindness and Insight: Essays in the Rhetoric of Contemporary Criticism,* University of Minnesota Press, 1983.

SCALA QUARANTA

Beppe Nona, 1963

The second half of Scala Quaranta *is a really wonderfully*

desolate examination of what happens to a family home

when someone important—and anyone in a family is

important—is absent. It's about the complete weirdness

that can creep in to fill that vacuum.

Mark Kermode

This cannot be approached like other Nona films. It beguiled Gilbert Adair, who said *as if sensing our critical apparatus even when our advance is silent,* Scala Quaranta *hastily retreats into the undergrowth. It has rarely been seen in captivity (underwhelming audiences in early screenings, it shrank from view), and a firm description of its confusing silhouette proves elusive.*[95] Critics throw it in with Nona's *Casa* stage, the period of domestic films made before his entry into the global bloodstream with the Bond/Barthes/bebop melange of *Sigh Your Name* (1966) and the subsequent theft of international hearts with *Wine For Song* (1967). But really, *Scala Quaranta* stands alone. At first it seems set to be the kind of Old Country whimsy that delights outsiders, the Italy that never was, for people who have never been: a god-fearing family work, eat, and play in a small rustic town.[96]

---

[95] *Movies,* Penguin, 1999.

[96] *rustic town:* L's Whitsun week holiday was in Rimini, Italy. I rented *Rimini* (Al Signori, 1983) to research so I could ask pertinent questions when she got back, but the film was filmed in

In a delightful opening, their routine is established. The chil-

California. The night before she got home I finished my preparations. I sneaked out just after dark and set off over the back fence and through the allotments. From here I cut through the Horeston Grange estate. I walked down the hill, past the Little Park, and through the Big Park. Once the path got to the cricket pitch on the edge of the estate, the streetlights dropped down to one every fifty yards or so, and were whiter than the usual yellow. So rather than being bathed orange, I was walking with the empty black grass to my left and the dark houses on my right, from cold spotlight to cold spotlight all the way down to the bottom corner of the estate, where the river cuts through.

I followed my own specific geography, a swift and deliberate path down tracks and shortcuts. Brash Dylon (William Katt) has a monologue at the kids' playground in *Teenage* (Chris Styler, 1974) that I recited as I walked: *Who are we? Who are we? You shouldn't be asking that. You can tell who we are by where we are. Look around you. We're too big to be pushed on these swings by our folks, but here we are. But we're too young to get into bars. We're stuck in between ages, so we go to the in-between places, the basements, the alleys, the fire-escapes, the grave-yards, the reservoir...anywhere that is not here and not there. That's who we are.* I didn't know all of the road names on the map, but I knew every tree that kept the rain out, every loose fence panel, every unlit corner to hide, watch, write. The river and its banks were ripe with treasure if you knew how to look. That night I saw a stack of home interior magazines with the covers ripped off, left in the long weeds where the path meets the bridge. I looked with interest for the progress of a bag of clothes that, as the days passed, had been rummaged through and strewn across the bushes and grass. A bright yellow t-shirt like the one the kid wore on the poster for *Elephant* (Gus Van Sant, 2003) getting damp then muddy then dried then dusty and diminished then one day gone. Gone into a hermit nest in the bushes or burned by some kids on the AstroTurf of the cricket pitch, a tired bonfire that's been burning on and off for decades. A used condom/dead jellyfish hung from a branch, left as a tribute, or a claim.

I walked over the wooden bridge, then up the short hill past the Portakabin graffitied with the slogan *BOZ*. This building had interior blinds pulled down and long grasses growing out from under the sandbags that skirted its edges. It managed to appear both temporary and abandoned, as if it had been built by an army to act as a planning centre for an advance that never came, because the retreat was sounded at short notice and the men left with only what they could carry. I crossed the train track, my shoes sounding heavy and solid on the wooden platform. I once

---

saw David H tell some kids to put pennies on the tracks here because when the trains come they flatten them to a disc the size of a frisbee. He didn't tell them the tracks were unused. He persuaded them to leave the coins and watch. Every time they said they were going home he leaned low and put his finger on his lips, touched the track carefully, and said *do you feel that... vibration?* It was a long-con joke at their expense and his own, as he stayed for hours with them. At mine too, because I stayed and waited for nothing, a joke without a punchline, as no train would ever come, although the commitment of his performance caused even me to doubt. After that day, I always hurried across that track a bit quicker.

I walked into the small industrial estate at the end of Jo's road. A feeling of certainty, like I was on a mission. *I never had purpose before*, the dying soldier says with a smile in *Vichy Guns* (Terry Leibniz, 1956), and I knew what he meant now. Past the cemetery, past Jo's house (her bedroom light was on, so I stayed in the shadows under the trees across the street), down through the subway, where I could hear the wind in a way that I'd never heard before. It was a high-pitched whistle, and I slowed to hear it properly. It died and came back stronger, a flute switching up in pitch, backed by the distant brushed cymbal of the trees moving, all correct sounds, but closer than seemed likely, higher in the mix on the soundtrack. Then, as I came out the tunnel, the wind dropped, and the sounds fell away, as if the mute button had been hit. I was holding my breath.

I chose to walk round and approach L's house from the path that entered the cul-de-sac from the far end. Her house was the last in a row of terraced houses. There were no bushes there that seemed convenient for my stash. I'd have to try the back garden. Checking for nosy neighbours, I climbed up her back fence and into the tree. From here, I dropped down into L's back garden. There was a weedy bush there that would be perfect for my bay. I bent down in the small paved backyard area and dug around in my bag, doing one last check. There was one last thing. I pulled out the *Welcome Home* banner that I'd finished colouring earlier that night. It was slightly crumpled. I smoothed it out and decided that the best place to put it was on the front door. But then I realised I didn't have any tape or pins. I briefly considered putting it through the letterbox but that would diminish its effect, surely. I suspected that they'd have tape inside the house, and I knew that there was a key under the flowerpot in the alley. I'd seen L's brother come home drunk enough times as I'd walked past over the last few months. I decided that the commitment to the romantic gesture required me to go inside the house. I'd be quick. It was worth it to do the job

Pappa tastes the vegetables and opens the wine. Each family member

properly. *She'll be so surprised.* I slipped back into the alley, found the key as expected, and I was inside the house in seconds.

I was in the kitchen. I stood for a second, adjusting to the new interior atmosphere. The stillness inside was different to the stillness outside, muffled, thicker, like the air was heavier. It smelled like overripe bananas. I was Seymour Cassel taking off his helmet and realising he can breathe on the alien planet in *First Howl* (Hal Mintz, 1977), or Ben Gazzara walking through the mirror into an alternate version of his own apartment in *The Other Side of the Room* (Su Spink, 1995): sniffing for minuscule differences, eyes adapting to the blue dark, and noticing the tiny ways that I knew that L was lower than me in the class food chain, if not actually poorer. Struck, if anything, by how *familiar* everything was. I'd imagined this kitchen so many times, and here I was. I took it in for a few seconds, and then refocused: *Tape.* There were several drawers in the kitchen, like any kitchen, and I tried the one that I hoped would be the miscellaneous junk drawer, the one nearest the back door, away from the sink. Jackpot. Old bills, batteries, broken pencils, eraser, *tape.* It was if I had written the details of the kitchen in myself, as if I was inventing L's house as I was going along. I started to laugh. I guessed which drawer might be cutlery, and heard the familiar shaking rattle of stainless steel as I pulled it open. A feeling of calm confidence fell onto me. Now I was inside it was obvious that rather than taping the banner to the outside of the door I should put it in L's room.

She'll be so surprised.

I walked into the hall, which was just where I'd just imagined it, the stairs terraforming in front of my eyes, growing from the gloom like the backgrounds that materialise on the horizon and clue Samantha Mathis to the fact that she is living in an alternate reality in *Video Game* (Issey Noki, 1993). *Samantha Mathis, the female protagonist in* Pump Up The Volume, *even my idle thoughts are connected, linked up to a larger purpose.* I drifted silently up the stairs, the lush carpet muting every sound, turned past the parents' bedroom, then two more, until I came to the small front bedroom that I'd looked up at many times from the other side of the street.

L's room was simple, austere even. The bed took up most of the room, and there was a dressing table with a mirror that reflected the streetlights. I stood still and held my hands together, not as a prayer as such, but more as a respectful nod to the moment. A standard bedside table, a made bed, nothing exceptional except the heavy curtains that I'd heard L talk about. Her dad had taken them from the old theatre when he helped to knock it down, and they were the first curtains

takes a turn to lean out of the window to shout *Beppe!* The rising alarm
I'd ever seen in a real house that would be large enough for someone to hide behind like in so many films. I knew they were purple with a gold trim, although in the gloom they looked brown and light brown.

I didn't want to linger for an inappropriate amount of time. I taped the banner to the door. I put the Birthday Book under her pillow, and then thought better of it, and put it in her underwear drawer, making sure to not touch any of L's garments myself. I turned to leave, but then stopped, and thinking again I decided that under the pillow would be the best place for the book: intimate, but not too suggestive. I looked at it: *Samuel Pepys records the last event in his diary on this day in 1669, citing poor eyesight,* then carefully slipped it into place under her pillow, sticking out slightly. I touched the wall above the bed, as I stood, and wondered if she'd ever placed her hand exactly there where mine was now. I closed my eyes and breathed deeply, trying to suck some juju out through my fingertips and exchange it for some of my own. Our essences were intermingling glacially, and I wanted to watch and notice every step. The big night was a cocktail of potential in my mind. I wanted her to come up to her room after a great birthday party, after saying goodbye to me on the doorstep, and find it, a quiet and chaste end to the night. Perhaps I'd be outside, under the lamppost, and she'd look outside, down at me, holding the booklet, and I'd look up at her, and then walk away, our narrative sealed, our future very much *on.*

I wish I could see her face when she comes home.

Time to go. Leaving the room, and thinking about leaving the house, and heading home, it was as if my radar had shifted, as for the first time I noticed a noise that I suspected I may have been hearing for a while. I stood still and the sound grew, from a distant ambient fuzz to something more rhythmic and urgent, until I identified it exactly as a patio door being slid back and forth, but I didn't see a patio door. It was too far away to be in the street, but too close to be inside the house. An image popped up in my head of a shadowy figure pushing the glass door along its tracks then pulling it back, *hoo-hugh, hoo-hugh, hoo-hugh,* like a large-backed lumberjack bending over a saw. I stood dead still, my eyes everywhere, imagining new exits from the house. The sound stopped. I was still. I was still still. A boiler noise clicked behind me, then nothing. I exhaled, slowly, and it was only then that I realised that the sounds were coming from me, that the great booming whizz was coming from my mouth, as I breathed into the red scarf: *hoo-hugh, hoo-hugh, hoo-hugh.*

I quickly left. Shaken, I struggled my way over the back fence, falling into the dirt as I landed. I sprinted round the corner onto the adjoining road, skidding into a quick walk when I got under the streetlights. I slowed down, attempting an impression of an innocent kid on a late night wander, when a car rolled up next to me. A woman in a business suit leaned across and rolled her window down.

Excuse me, do you know the way to the A5, she said. Her voice throaty and old, not matching the youthful, if tired, face. She had been translated into another language and dubbed back. I examined the question for tricks and traps before answering.

Take a left, then follow the signs, I said. I hadn't spoken for hours, and my voice croaked out high and weak like I'd borrowed it. She looked dubiously ahead, thanked me, and drove off.

I took the long way home, sticking to the lighted main road over the Leicester Road Bridge then onto Hinckley Road. I didn't want to go under the subway, or past Jo's house. I'd spooked myself, I suppose. It was cold and very late, and I was suddenly tired. I wanted to be at home. But with each step I felt the dream recede, and I was returned to solid ground. I had legs, boots, a scarf, a brain. I'd managed to leave carefully made gifts for L. The hard work was done. All I had to do now was go to the party tomorrow, enjoy myself, and let what would happen happen. I'd felt like I'd done all the training I could. I pulled my scarf up tight, put my hands in my pockets, and marched on. That's when I found the cold hard object in my left pocket. I passed it between my fingers to identify it. The key to L's back door. I hadn't put it back under the flowerpot.

I debated my options for a second or two, and then did what was obvious. At the roundabout at the beginning of Hinckley Road I took a right down the grassy path that ran down towards the wooden bridge that I'd crossed on my way to L's a couple of hours earlier. I climbed down to the water's edge, kicking sods of grassy earth down with me. The water line was low, and I was able to skip along the bank easily enough until I reached the opening of the large concrete overflow tunnel that ran north. The pipe was about five feet high. I entered it with my legs splayed and pinned against the curve either side of the water. I took out the key and threw it underarm as far as I could, hearing it clang, tinkle, and skid to a stop with a splash. They'd never find it. They'd never find me. I was strong. I was quick. I knew every shortcut. I was the town, I was a continuation of every cul-de-sac, and I was the point beyond every dead end, the thread in the stitching. I was underground, below everyone, able to move unseen, cover my mistakes with

his name, Beppe (the delightfully podgy Paolo Rossi) is clumsily rushing up the street, ready to sit in the last space at the end of the table.

At dinner they talk about their day and plan for tomorrow, the chores to be completed, the shopping to be done. The details of their lives are worked out exactly, and yet they enjoy petty squabbles and jolly arguments as if every day is an improvised chaos.

After dinner they play cards. Mamma says this is her favourite time of day, the only time she can relax, but she bustles around them as they play, tidying, cleaning, serving dessert. The family gamble for small amounts, laughing, fighting, cajoling, as Mamma brings out chocolates. *I love how we always do this, Mamma,* says an older child. *Drink your milk,* she says.

When asked to cut the deck, youngest son Beppe turns over a joker. This is seen as good luck. The family laughs, calling the boy fortunate. He denies this, suggesting that he has a special skill. When given a second opportunity, he again pulls another joker. The family teases and hugs him all the more. Pappa (Giancarlo Bianchi) bets him a week of chores that he can't do it again; but once more, Beppe cuts the deck and finds a joker. The family erupts. Amid the laughter, Mamma stops, and tells Pappa to shuffle the deck properly. He does so, at length, as the other brothers and sisters lean in. When Beppe cuts the deck

---

more mistakes, able to divert and subvert. I was the future of the town, its present, its past; I was a Saxon burial mound, I was a Roman suffix, I was the dead centre of England, a bullseye. And tomorrow was L's birthday.

and finds a joker once more, Mamma screams and crosses herself. She shakes Beppe, asking him how he is performing this trick, and accuses Pappa of fashioning a cheat. But they deny it vehemently, and Beppe, now upset, sits silently. When Mamma thrusts the deck in front of him once more, he at first refuses to cut. But under a barrage of shouts, he sullenly does so, drawing a joker again. There is no laughter now. *This just does not happen.* The family argue the significance. They borrow a neighbour's deck, and ask them to shuffle it, before offering it to Beppe. When he cuts, he finds a joker every time. After twenty-five consecutive jokers, they stop. This is no quirk. Meaning must be found. A priest, a doctor, a professor are all visited, and all react differently. But none can satisfy the family, especially Mamma. She works herself into a frenzy over the next few weeks. She begins to clean ecstatically. She throws out belongings like offerings for a domestic sacrifice. She spends money in tears, buying new decorations and trinkets to hang around Beppe's bed, his door, his neck. *Are we saving the child from Fate,* Pappa says. *Or is Fate the child*, Mamma says. Neighbours close their doors. But are they superstitious and afraid of intertwining with Kismet, or are they hiding from Mamma's apocalyptic euphoria? The family give generously one Sunday, and stay home the next. The correct course is yet to be found.

Throughout, Nona never allows the viewer to completely sympathize with or against anyone. And the whole affair seems simultaneously ridiculous and staggeringly significant. Beppe might be an evil presence, a proto-Damien, but he might also be a victim of abuse. Is Mamma a superstitious sadist, a brave matriarch, both, or neither? Only Pappa is the same in most readings, emasculated and pale, haunted by his own inability to act. The central mystery about whether the jokers are a clever trick or a supernatural sign is never explained, and the family drifts into the shell-shock of a self-imposed exile, not remembering what the question ever was, but searching the walls for an answer.

The final sequence is a dinner preparation scene, echoing the one very early in the film, and each step of dinner is lovingly showed in slow detail, as before: the children set the table, Mamma stirs the sauce, and Pappa tastes the vegetables and opens the wine. But this time each family member doesn't take a turn leaning out of the window to shout for Beppe. The shutters on the window stay closed, and the room is lit by candle instead of sunlight. Beppe doesn't run up the street, and at the table there is only an empty place. As the family sits to eat, in silence, the noise of cutlery on plates carries on as the camera pulls back to show the exterior of the house, just as it had done at the beginning. But now we see the differences: barbed wire on the fence. No toys carelessly left in the yard. No laughter.

Scala Quaranta

Directed by Beppe Nona. Produced by Gilberto Moretti. Written by Beppe Nona, Astrid Luna. Starring Alberta D'Agostini, Paolo Rossi, Giancarlo Bianchi, Rosa Bianchi. Cino Del Duca/Janus Films. 144 mins. Release Date: Oct 1963 (Ita/UK). Tagline: None.

RUBICON

Rupi and Sunil Singh, 1966

My only intention is to love. Is that really so terrible?

Emmess, *Rubicon*

The final scene of Rupi and Sunil Singh's *Rubicon* lasts barely thirty seconds. It is a two-shot of siblings Rupi and Sunil Singh (who also co-direct), sitting in a markedly fake space shuttle prop. A painted backdrop of stars shakes gently behind them. No words are spoken, and the two actors do very little as Isa Tomita's chintzy synth soundtrack beeps and bloops out an arrangement of a Mozart sonata. So simple, it's almost nothing, and yet so many of the techniques that make *Rubicon* a nuanced portrayal of human desperation are present here. The high camera, the still actors, the desolate poses all combine to somehow conjure an Edward Hopper loneliness on a cheap set in a Tulsa warehouse. The nervous expectation of the early part of the film has capsized into resigned fatigue. As Donald Ritchie said when talking about the way Yasujirō Ozu's shot composition showed the despair in the everyday: *Rearrange a still life and a green banana can look overripe.*[97]

Stills from the film might suggest a camp romp, but this is an inverse *Barbarella:* no flash, no polish, all ideas. The sets are cheap, the uniforms worn by the actors playing henchmen G I and G II are clearly made of foil and wood. The script dabbles in B-movie tropes

---

[97] *Ozu: His Life and Films,* University of California Press, 1977.

but with complexity. Twenty-four planets (collectively known as the Archipelago) on the outer rim of the solar system have banded together for trade and security purposes. They are far weaker than many other entities in the galaxy, but while a tentative peace holds, as a bloc they have a notable minority voice in the universal government. Each year one of the planets in the Archipelago hosts a gathering to celebrate their bonds. Most of the human and humanoid residents of the twenty-four planets are clones, a fact that means they are taken less seriously by the universal government. Most of the clones in the Archipelago are clones of clones. While having reproductive organs and being able to reproduce, these humanoids are considered to be genderless, and all the characters in *Rubicon* are presented with a pointed androgyny. The actors are shaved hairless, and masculine and feminine linguistic kinks are removed. Instead of *he* and *she* they use the word *vu*.

Contemporaneous television series *Star Trek,* with its miniskirts and interracial kisses, was sexy and modern, but was still recognisably *American.* A progressive, tolerant, multi-ethnic America, an optimistic, dreamy America even, but still an expansionist, imperialist America. And the crew of the USS Enterprise are the (mostly) human lens through which we meet alien cultures and ideas. But in *Rubicon* everyone is an alien, and the rites and rituals of the cultures are not clearly explained, leaving the viewer deliciously adrift, unmoored from a safe orbit.

The paltry budget meant that convincing action set-pieces were a challenge, but the Singh siblings had other aims anyway. *We wanted to make social satire, or at least a critique of suburban values,* Sunil Singh said.[98] *We loved Godard. I wanted to call the film* Weekend in Space. *But if you ask Rupi, she'll tell you that we were trying to remake something more classic, Renoir's* La Règle de Jeu. *We remade that large mansion setting and the class issues, the theatrical performance, and used it all in the intergalactic palace. For all this celebration, we're talking about the small successes and failures of comfortable but lonely people.*

Whereas so much science fiction of the sixties is shot through with an imperial optimism, *Rubicon* is about frustration; in many scenes the dialogue overlaps, causing what we think of as the primary narrative—the pursuit of the hostess princelet Elle by a suitor—to be bathed in background noise. *Failure must always be an option,* one character says to another early in this film. *That isn't how the saying goes,* another replies. These characters are Javanelle and Emmess, played by the Singhs. They are representatives of the planet Locus on their way to planet Rubicon. This exchange is a throwaway during their preparations to land their ship, but it serves as cute foreplay for a central dynamic at play in the narrative: Javanelle, who sees possible failure everywhere, posits that this is not a fearful position, but quite the opposite. Emmess can only imagine success, and so is blind to the pitfalls. Emmess, after

[98] *"Double Singh,"* Tom Bond, *Shock Cinema* 9, Fall/Winter 1996.

all, has not been invited to the gathering, and hopes to charm a way to Elle's side. Javanelle, concerned that Emmess' presence may cause an incident, tries to protect the mission.

But it soon goes awry. Emmess is discovered, and is revealed to have not only faked credentials to get into the gathering, but also to have broken into Elle's private sleeping chamber to plant gifts for Elle to find. Deceived by the royal purple and gold curtains, Emmess breaks into the wrong chamber, and instead leaves the presents under the pillow of Elle's sibling, the Questor, or King/Queen. When discovered, these acts threaten the careful diplomacy of the whole region. The highly anticipated festivities are suspended, and the guests are apprehended by the royal guards. After a confession, Emmess is allowed to leave the planet without charge, but must never return. Javanelle, in an act of loyalty, goes too.

The film's action is divided into two sections: the hopeful build-up, where Emmess, in particular, speculates at the fun that they will have, and the regretful second part after the gathering has been cancelled. As Rupi Singh says: *As teenagers it always felt like most parties we went to were not as good as we'd hoped they would be, and that's if we were invited.*[99] *But also, more deeply, we wanted to capture that teenage feeling of always feeling like you're looking forward to something better in*

---

[99] *invited:* I mean, I wasn't explicitly *uninvited.* It was reasonable to presume that, being part of the group, the correct etiquette would have been to make it clear to me that I couldn't go to the party. And why. The alleged break-in (it was hardly that, I'm sure you'll agree) is a separate issue.

the future, and sad for something in the past. It's like you're slowly finding
out that life will disappoint you in some way, especially if you're proactive.

As Emmess and Javanelle wait for their ship to pick them up
and take them home, they talk. Javanelle, exasperated at their friend's
lack of self-awareness, tries some home truths:

Never mind the various threats to peace caused by any number
of broken protocols, never mind how you managed in the first place to
breach royal security... I can't believe that you thought breaking into the
consort's sleeping area was a good idea.

I never went in that room Emmes says.

Only because you got the wrong one.

I never went in that room.[100]

That's not really the point.

It was meant to be a surprise.

It's aberrant. It's threatening.

It's not like I stole undergarments or anything.[101]

Emmess are you even listening to me? This is an intergalac-
tic incident. Treaties are threatened. You may have started a war. Our
diplomats won't be welcome here for the foreseeable future. You can never

---

[100] *I never went in that room:* I repeated this several times over the next few days. To Mum, my
stepdad, the police. It seemed important that people knew. The room I'd stared at from the street,
the one I'd imagined being in, the one I'd finally entered with the most personal but chaste gifts,
wasn't L's, but L's sister's. I made a mistake. *That's not the mistake,* Mum said.

[101] *it's not like I stole undergarments or anything:* Fact.

return. They're rebuilding their security system at great cost. You're lucky that they didn't imprison you.

That was at Elle's bidding, Emmess says.

Only because they wanted an end to it. You destroyed the festival.

Perhaps Elle saved me for a reason.

Emmess, you're a fool.

Perhaps she likes me.[102]

At this point, the soundtrack rises, and the music threatens to muffle the conversation (playing Mahler in reverse, credited to *Relham).* This has the effect of creating a feeling that this conversation has gone on before, and will again, beyond the fade out.

Emmess. You can never approach her planet again. Javanelle says. *Do you even understand?*

They could have tried me and kept me. Put me in prison or termination. They didn't. To me it's a sign, Emmess says.

You're unbelievable, Emmess.

Why?

Elle was so uncomfortable around you. I'm so embarrassed for you that you can't see it.

I thought we had a rapport.[103]

You have no idea, do you, Emmess. She thinks you're weird. Everyone does. Even me, and you're my best friend.

---

[102] *perhaps she likes me:* Perhaps.

[103] *I thought we had a rapport:* Of course we did. We do, of course we do.

If only you didn't try so hard. If only you listened to me. I've been trying to tell you.[104]

Emmess says nothing.

Things will never be the same after Rubicon, Javanelle says. And so the set-up of the final shot: small, patient, nothing. We know that Javanelle will continue to tolerate Emmess, but will Emmess ever see himself the way others do?

Rubicon is a film about the corrosive aspects of obsession, and the ways in which romantic obsession with another are really a form of narcissism. Emmess, as if grasping for our attention, for a place as a protagonist in the film, is driven to more and more desperate acts. Emmess's fear of not being spectacular is increasingly pronounced.

The making of this film walked the line between commitment and obsession too, taking several years to complete as teenage siblings Rupi and Sunil Singh borrowed a camera from their father and shot their ambitious science fiction concept in an empty warehouse in Tulsa (and on visits to their parents' home town of Mumbai) with money from friends and family. Lack of funds meant the production took five years, which brought its own problems. Most of the cast were teenagers and some went to college, or moved away for work before their parts had been filmed completely. Some aged visibly within scenes. Rather than hiding this, the Singhs wrote it into the script, suggesting that the

---

[104] *I've been trying to tell you:* I know, I know.

ageing was caused by the atmosphere of Rubicon. But this gave them problems with their ending, as the final shot is a repeat of the first shot. Rupi Singh once more:

> *Sunil looked like he was younger at the end than he had been just minutes before,* Rupi said. *But if anything, it adds poignancy, and makes a dramatic kind of sense. It's like the character he plays, Emmess, will never learn, and is doomed to always return to the same place. We couldn't write that in. We didn't have time. But that's how I explain it to myself: Emmess is stuck in a loop of ignorance.*[105]

Rubicon

Directed by Rupi and Sunil Singh. Produced by Rick Kevan, Sachin Singh, Rupi Singh, Sunil Singh Written by Rupi Singh, Sunil Singh, Lou Ross. Homespun Films/CEO. Release date: May 1966 (US) 99 mins. Tagline: Appointment With Destiny.[106]

---

[105] *Double Singh.* Ignorant? Mrs White says I'm perceptive. I've read more books than anyone in school.

[106] *appointment with destiny:* I had appointments to see a police liaison officer, a court-appointed psychologist, a school counsellor, Mum's friend who was a social worker/psychic and *you know, knows about things,* and the head teacher to discuss the ramifications of my behaviour. It turned out that going into L's house and *not* stealing was more troubling than stealing. Thieving, while frowned upon, is a crime that is generally understood. I was perverse, or worse. At points I considered admitting to stealing some cash, or a video or two, just to get an easier life. I felt like the girl who falsely confesses to being a witch in *Worship* (L. Lee, 1969) and is spared the dunking test which kills her equally innocent friend.

MATHEMATISCHE (GEOMETRIES)

Cecil Franck, 1966

It is possible to remake any piece of film into any new

story that you want. It is possible to make someone think

that they are watching a different film to one they've seen

before when they aren't. I can hide in a film and forget

the truth of my situation. Film-makers are conjurers. All

my films are the same and none of them are.

Cecil Franck

This hypnotic film is part of a larger exercise in what Franck called *narrative mind-mapping*, a project that he returned to throughout his career. Essentially an internal monologue over the top of images of a boy walking the streets of suburban Stuttgart, it hints at the melancholy of Albert Lamorisse's *Le Ballon Rouge* (1956) or Dani Silva's *Girl of Five* (2001). Franck shot the footage, featuring his nephew Jens, in 1955, and subsequently reused it in more than 100 films (including *Mathematische*[107] and *Mathematische II, III* and *IV*), re-cut and com-

---

[107] *mathematische: I didn't do my maths homework,* I said. We were in the car sitting outside school. The Monday after. We had a 9am appointment with the Head.

That's the least of your worries now, Mum said. Then she looked at me, her face softening. *I just feel...*

Disappointed in me?

No... I just feel... are you acting up? To try and tell us something? Mum said.

It's nothing to do with you, Mum, I said. I was trying to let her off the hook but it came out harsher than I meant.

I mean it's not your fault, Mum, I said. She sighed. She tidied the cowlick of hair that

bined with different voice-overs and swathes of music, an ever-evolving

never sat straight on my forehead.

You can always talk to me, she said. I nodded. She pulled down the mirror flap and checked her eye make up. She'd been crying over the weekend and looked tired.

About anything, she said.

You look nice, I said. She pushed the mirror up, clutched her car keys and held her jaw high.

Let's get this over with, shall we?

The school secretary gave Mum one of those sympathetic smiles with a crumpled chin that only parents know how to give, and showed us to a seat. The Head smiled warmly when he popped his head out of his office, and invited us in. We sat in his office. He stood with his back against his desk rather than sitting behind it, an informal gesture. But he still started on a sombre monologue, and as he spoke I thought of the *The Head* (Anton Vernon, 1975) and I squinted, trying to imagine his disembodied head floating around the corridors eating pupils.

Do you understand what I'm saying, Mark, he said. Mum looked at me. I nodded.

Good, he said. He explained to us that the *pupil in question's parents* were very upset, as was the *pupil in question.* They had requested that I was to be moved from classes that contained the *pupil in question.* I was to stay away from *the pupil in question* at school. I was not to talk to *the pupil in question.*

There's no official restraining order, Mum said.

No. The parents of the pupil in question have been, ahem, uh... restrained, pardon the pun, in their handling of this. You've to thank their generosity in not seeking further police action against you for your transgression. They understand that you did not mean to cause distress.

They've already... the police have spoken to Mark, Mum said.

That's what I understand, the Head said. He paused for a moment.

And anyway, he's a minor, Mum said.

Yes, yes... the problem I have is that the governors at this school have been able to maintain high standards largely because of a firm, but fair, disciplinary policy. I will meet with them this afternoon, and offer them my recommendation. But I have to warn you that, in light of Mark's attendance record-

-Mark had some medical issues when he was younger, but he's been at school regularly since, haven't you Mark? Haven't you?

experiment in film. From 1955's *Light Line* to 1984's *Lazer*, Franck's

-uh yes, well, my notes don't correlate with that exactly, the Head continued, *and uh…*
that's a matter we'll be discussing, but, with that in mind, every kind of action, uh… everything
will be on the table.

He's never been in any kind of trouble before, Mum said. I immediately saw the
gang leader on the roof in *He's Never Been In Any Kind Of Trouble Before* (Mae Susann, 1959),
shouting to the city of Paris: *You'll never catch me, I could take all of you.* That film was shot in
Burbank, the Paris skyline was a projection, and the anti-hero was stabbed by an underling in the
next scene.

Do you understand, Mark, the Head said. Mum looked at me, nodding slowly. I nodded. The Head's eyebrows raised.

Yes, I said. Mum was crying.

Expelled, Mum said.

Like I said, it is only one possibility. Mum cried more. The head held out a tissue. I did
a quick mental scan of other schools in the area. Etone wouldn't be so bad, as they are less than
a mile away, and finish five minutes earlier than we do. I could be able to leave there and get to
the gates here in time to meet everyone every day. We could still walk home together. It would be
fine. Other schools might be a problem. I could make it work though, I knew it. Extra effort. I'd
be fine. Just fine. I took the tissue and handed it to Mum, who was looking at her lap.

I'll be alright, Mum. This made her cry more. She held out her arm, as if to say to the
Head *see, he's a good boy.*

That would be on his record wouldn't it, Mum said. The Head winced. Mum sniffed
and wiped her face. St Thomas More wouldn't be so bad, I thought, but I doubt they'd take
expelled kids. Mum sat up straight. She looked directly at the head. Nicholas Chamberlain was in
Bedworth. Too far. Where else?

Maybe none of that will be necessary, Mum said. *There's… something that even Mark*
doesn't know yet that… she turned to look at me *and I'm sorry you're finding out like this, Mark…*
but… my husband has been… relocated at work, and it looks like we're going to have to move.
Away. The details are not all there yet, but it looks like the summer holidays might be the time.

Where, I said.

To the South Coast, and like I said, I'm sorry that it's coming up now, it's just that she
turned back to the Head *it's just that, it seems to me that as there's only a month or so of term*

manipulation of just an hour of the same visuals, over and over, is an

endless working towards answers to, what were to him, the central

---

left...

    Well, the Head said. *That does change things somewhat –*

    The South Coast, Mum said, looking at me.

    I, well, um, I'll talk to the governors this afternoon –

    Why do we have to move, I said.

    Mark, we'll talk about it in the car –

    Um... I'm sure we can arrange an unofficial suspension until then, um –

    I can't move. I won't. I can't.

    – nothing too drastic, we can send work home for Mark until –

    – it's not happening.

    – Mark, let's talk –

    – No –

    – until the end of term, judging by Mark's record, when he is present, uh, he's capable
of self-discipline –

    I stood up and left. Mum, apologising to the Head, tried to follow, but I moved quickly, running down the corridor, out the fire escape by the back playground and out of the back gate. I kept going, jogging erratically through Weddington until I was on a road I didn't recognise. It wasn't new, just anonymous, a slight variation of the other roads. I felt hidden here, as if on a street I didn't know I couldn't be known. Like closing my eyes to make the monster vanish. It was as if these houses had been generated for my own camouflage, as if the only way to hide was to be lost.

    I walked all the way up to Higham-on-the-Hill. I sat in the middle of the field, right by the spot where our art class had sat months earlier to sketch some of the old buildings. I'd drawn an effective charcoal likeness of the church and the old oak tree next to it. L had told me it was a pretty good cow. That was L, always seeing what I could not. God, I'd miss that. And her sense of humour. I sat in the exact same spot, to see if I could conjure up that feeling, that effective flashback, a touch of emotional time-travel. But the wind came up, buffeted the trees, making the union jack outside the closed pub whip, and I felt nothing. I did sense a dull ache from the electrical pylon nearby, but no gravitational pull. It felt like the middle of nowhere.

questions of art and meaning(lessness).[108]

[108] *art and meaning(lessness):* The next morning I got up early and walked around to the shops on the estate. I went into the newsagents. I looked at the comics and magazines for a while, until I noticed the owner leaning on his till to look at me, some *this-isn't-a-library* remark imminent. The bell rang as a customer came in. An older man. The newsagent straightened.

> *20 B&H, as usual, Jim?*

> *Yup. Any news?*

The newsagent pointed to a copy of the Tribune open on his counter.

> *The councillor got the sack. Boro's stand is crumbling. Young father killed by a lorry on the Long Shoot.*

> *Normal week then,* Jim said, pulling out some coins.

> *New survey says Fenny Drayton is the dead centre of England.*

> *Really? Higham-on-the-Hill won't be happy.*

> *That's what they're saying. I myself thought the marker was in the middle of town. On the roundabout. Turns out that was very old information.*

> *News to me.*

> *Me too.*

> *I don't get it. Did the country move?*

> *Bloody Fenny Drayton didn't.*

> *Too right. Nothin's moved there for years.*

> *It's the coasts, isn't it?*

> *What's that, Rob?*

> *Erosion, longshore drift, global warming. Tides. The moon. And the new computers measure better, I suppose,* the newsagent said.

> *Bloody computers.*

> *Too right.* The newsagent noticed me listening.

> *Buying anything, son,* he asked. He looked at Jim, and they exchanged a shake of heads that said *Bloody kids.* I grabbed a box of nice letter paper and envelopes and walked up to the counter. Jim took his cigarettes and left.

> *It was me that did it,* I said.

> *Did what,* the newsagent said.

> *Shifted the country. Made it move.*

Mathematische opens with a boy stepping out of a house. He turns and reaches up to close the door behind him, before jumping off the porch onto a path and rushing to the front gate. He stops and looks left, right, and left again. A boy's voice-over begins and we might

---

He looked at me for several seconds, his patience already evaporated.

Anything else?

I focussed too hard. Made the poles vibrate. Got too close.

Aye, and I suppose you robbed the jewellers and won the pools and scored for Boro on Saturday too didn't you?

No, I said. I wasn't sure why he was angry. *That was someone else.*

That it? he said. Even more annoyed now.

A packet of stickers, please.

He threw them on the counter, gave me my change, and looked back to his paper. I stood for a few seconds. He looked up again.

Yes? he said, through his teeth.

Do you have any nice pens, I said.

He didn't give any flinch of recognition at this direct quote from *Shots* (Finlay Cooper, 1973), uttered by the deranged musician (David Hemmings) during his breakdown at a rural hotel where he is trying to compose a masterpiece but instead murders the staff. Maybe he didn't know it. Maybe he did (the quote's fame, such as it is, is larger than the film it is from) and didn't want to talk to me. Either way, it felt like I was scoring a small moral victory in a week of defeats.

At home I wrote a letter with my new stationery. I ruined several sheets before I decided brevity was best:

Dear L,

I'm sorry if I upset you by breaking into your house. I've had a hard time lately because my Mum is terminally ill, and we have to move away so she can be looked after. It doesn't look good for her but I'll be ok.

Regards,

Mark

I tucked the letter into an envelope and wrote L's name on it.

assume it is his. But it is disembodied both by not coming directly from his mouth and by the words themselves, which seem to be the words of a man talking about a time long ago:

When I was a child I would love to make games out of
everyday activities. Any walk was a race with imaginary
opponents. Or I might consider cars to be my enemy, and
attempt to pass a lamppost before they did. This worked
fine on quieter streets, where the noise of the car in the
distance would serve as a challenge; I'd pick a marker
ahead, one that seemed to be far enough away to not be
too easy for me to reach before the car.

The boy opens the gate and hurries across the street. He walks along the pavement, watching the traffic, speeding up for a few steps, slowing down for a few steps.

A truly satisfying judgement would result in me dipping
slightly to take the tape mere feet before the car passed
unknowingly. On busier streets it would be harder to pick
out individual cars in the hubbub, so I would change
the game. For example, I might designate the sections of
grass between the pavement and the street as safe zones,
behind which passing cars were no threat. In this case, I
could not pass between them across a driveway entrance
at the same time as a car went by. Again, I could not run

or stop, but by adjusting the pace of my stride, I'd hope to
navigate an entire street without being 'hit' by a passing
car.

Close-up of the boy's face, time-lapse of him looking off-camera, blinking.

I would spend a lot of time imagining lines, running
from the edges of the grass through perpendicular angles
across the road and across the pavement. I'd also imagine
similar lines across the front and rear bumpers of cars
fizzing at 90-degree angles across the pavement, shots
of invisible laser or light that would be repelled by the
grass but would otherwise continue across the unguarded
pavements, burning everything in their path. Imagining
these lines became second nature; they'd spin out from
parked cars (also designated as cover sometimes) and
benches, walls and any vehicle. Geometric prettiness
from unseen shapes, dealt with by checked strides and
sudden spurts.

As late as 2005, with the release of *Luxuriant Jay,* Franck was still making films with the same pieces of footage he had shot of Jens in 1955.

I have not lifted a camera or been on a set in fifty years,
he said, *for the images I collected then contain endless*

possibility. There are a million films to be made from

those sequences of Jens, and I will never be finished. I am

like a musician composing using only one chord, on one

instrument, and through this repetition I discover new

things that I could not with a wider palette.[109]

Jens Franck died in the year 2000, aged fifty-one. His uncle continues to remake his image, combining it, in various constellations, with various music (self-composed minimalist electronics, or commissioned/borrowed works from [among many others] Klaus Schulze, Holger Czukay, Robert Wyatt, Françoise Hardy, and Die Krupps) and snippets of broken words.

Now Jens is gone, I feel like my mission has sharpened,

my idea more correct. I can reflect on his life, his family,

his loves, his passions, through the way in which I edit

a small section of his life as a boy. It is all in there, his

entire existence, if only I can reframe it, highlight it, show

it. For him.[110]

Mathematische
Directed by Cecil Franck. Produced by Cecil Franck, Tomas Duhbyoose.
Written by Cecil Franck. Starring Jens Franck. Franck Filmproduktion.
Release Date: Nov 1966 (Ger TV) 55 mins. Tagline: Still Here.

---

[109] *Sight & Sound* interview, May 2005

[110] *Sight & Sound* interview, May 2005

TOM KEEPS SCORE

Barry Bishopsfield, 1967

...Of course, I wanted to call it Statistical Breakdown,
but that seems too clever, too arch...but sometimes I do
still like it, and go to screenings of Tom Keeps Score *and*
shout out I should have called it Statistical Breakdown!
over the credits.

Barry Bishopsfield

A long with Tony Richardson, Lindsay Anderson, and Karel Reisz, Barry Bishopsfield was part of the Free Cinema movement that invigorated British film in the early sixties. These directors wanted to make modern films that dragged the country out of its post-war hangover by putting characters on-screen that hadn't been there before: class-conscious juvenile delinquents who knew that there are *them* and there are *us*. Labourers toiling all week for the glory of Saturday night on the booze. Fathers dying before sixty after repeated exposure to toxic chemicals in factories, and their families who spent the insurance payouts on fur coats and alcohol. Small-time robbers who couldn't keep quiet about their take. Widowed landladies extinguishing cigarettes in kitchen sinks. Pregnant teenagers with dreams of college, London, and the world, or even just the next town along. These films were shot in new ways, on location in unglamorous places. Places that, frozen since the war, would have still been black and white even if the films were shot in colour: Morecambe. Derby. Deptford. Claygate. Battersea. Wakefield.

Barry Bishopsfield followed the tone of the Free Cinema movement with his first film, *Radio Play* (1961). But by the time of *Tom Keeps Score* he had moved away from the quasi-realist style that the group generally employed, towards something completely his own. Initially, the visual grammar and subject matter appear very much to be in the Free Cinema vein. The central character, Tom, is a newly-orphaned working-class boy whose story catches the eye of a local rich family that pays for him to attend an elite boarding school. As the film opens we see Tom (played by Richard Jones, in his only film appearance) get on a bus with his grandmother in a grey corner of Manchester. Their journey, across town, through the more affluent suburbs, into the countryside, and finally to the lush acres that house the ancient school seems to, in ordinary film language, show us the distance from Tom's old life to his new one.[111] But then something different starts to happen.

---

[111] *Tom's old life to his new one:* In a way my new situation on suspension wasn't that different from my old one of months earlier, before L. Back then, I'd spent more time out of school than in it, doing homework in the library. Now I stayed at home and did work sent to me. The only difference was I now had a desperate longing. And a certain notoriety. The Gavs brought me homework and told me what was being said at school. The rumours about what I had done to L had an outsized glamour. Is it true that I jumped off L's roof? Did I get in a drunken fight with a policeman? Did I really threaten to run across the tracks because L wouldn't love me? I was happy to be part of the school gossip, particularly if the story involved myself and L. Even if the words were unflattering.

Jo's been asking about you, Big Gav said.

As the bus moves, music plays, and the opening credits roll. Voices can be heard on the soundtrack, which at first seem like background chatter from the bus passengers. But the volume rises, lines can be picked out... *Hold it Richard... now look at Gran...yes...look away again...out the window, remember he's never been this far away from home...there'll be music...the titles will pop up here...the font's not right...less Gothic... less Gothic...plain...good...* This is the voice of the director Barry Bishopsfield, and his instructions, both on-set and in the editing suite, are left in the final mix. This continues throughout the film. When Tom is

Said she knocked for you a few times, but your Mum said you weren't in, Little Gav said.

I'll give her a ring at some point, I said.

It hurt that the finely calibrated routine that I'd built since February had been ripped away. My punishment was perfectly designed for me. I'd have handled detentions, chores, or repetitive work easily. But removal from my focused world, the one whose movements I understood like the inside of a clock, was torture. *I don't want diamonds, or a fast car, I just want to see you at the break-time snack bar,* I sang, like Sooz in the single *See You At School.* (Used on the closing credits to *Into The Nite* [D. Shoeberg, 1991]). I had deciphered a mess of signs (the way L dug around in her bag near the end of science, for example, told me that she would stop at the bathrooms with Vicki before the walk home), learned patterns (L's preferred paths around school, her speeds, who'd she'd stop to talk to), and manoeuvred carefully to maximise my time. All gone.

But when they stopped me going to school they said nothing about youth club. It was Wednesdays. It was on school property, but wasn't run by any teachers. Volunteers manned the counter in a hut on the edge of the playground. There was pool, table football, table tennis, a TV, a Nintendo. I used to go there, but hadn't been since I heard Vicki say it was for sad sacks and L laugh and agree. With only two weeks of school left, I decided to make my move. I stuck a note through Jo's door the night before saying I'd be there and I wanted to talk.

Youth club opened at 7 and I showed up around 7:15. As I hoped, Jo was there. She was eating popcorn and watching some lads play pool when I walked up. She didn't move.

shown his new lodgings by a gangly prefect, Jones stammers over his line. He looks towards the camera for a direction, perhaps to return to his mark for another take. Bishopsfield's voice cuts in: *don't worry son... that's good...the stammer works right here...just look around the room with curiosity...and a bit of fear...nice.*

So far, so Godard. But Bishopsfield developed idiosyncrasies all of his own: *Tom Keeps Score* is overlaid with an audio track not just of these captured on-set directions and mistakes, but of extra words added in post-production. These are a collection of thoughts, ideas for ways to re-shoot, explanations, and exclamations, often about the shortcomings of the film. This approach is remarkably similar to the commentaries that have come as a special feature on DVDs since the late 1990s. Of course, on the DVD, this is an easily ignored optional extra, but it is central to *Tom Keeps Score* and there is no option to remove it. Instead of the measured, wry tone most modern commentaries seem to hit, with anecdotal background, praise for an actor's choice, or an account of a piece of serendipitous luck in a particular shot, in *Tom Keeps Score* we hear a panicky Bishopsfield despairing about his vision falling apart before his eyes. Increasingly, his frustration at the impossibility of recreating on film the confusion in his head coincides with the subject of the film: as Tom struggles to make sense of his world, so too does Bishopsfield. Tom, newly alone and in an alien environment, is prompted to note things down in a book by a kindly headmaster. *Good idea* says

Bishopsfield on the soundtrack. Then *Bad idea.* Then *It's just an idea.*

Tom begins by copying maps from atlases. He doesn't trace them, but sketches careful and accurate versions. He notes down pertinent facts about countries, states, and counties: populations, land areas, relevant dates, languages spoken, currencies. Here Bishopsfield interrupts to reflect on how *when I was a child I collected coins and had some from India, Canada, and Poland that I wanted to use in this shoot. I could not find them. I feel that this is important to state.*

Tom starts plotting a map of his new school. He paces out his room, the corridors, the halls where they have assemblies and supper, the high-ceilinged classrooms, the narrow boiler room, the athletic fields. Seeing Tom sketching at the edge of the cricket field one day, the games master mistakes his interest for a love of the game, and shows him the official record book of the school cricket eleven.[112] Tom says he

---

[112] *the school cricket eleven: Can we talk on the cricket square,* I said.

I'm not sure you're supposed to be on school property, but yes, she said. I didn't say anything until we got out into the middle of the field. The sun was setting orange and purple, the clouds were inverted bluer than the sky. I stared up at it and put my hand on my hip.

I'm going to start talking and I don't want you to say anything until I'm finished, I said. She said nothing. I kept staring at the colours in the sky. *I've received some news that while not necessarily bad in the long run, is fairly devastating to me right now. By telling you I'm hoping to –*

– *Share your burden,* she said.

...yes... if you don't mind... these words aren't easy for me to say

Share Your Burden, she said. She pulled her bag of popcorn from her pocket and started to eat.

I'm trying to tell you something, I said.

likes cricket ok, and Bishopsfield interjects here to say that *I do not like*

Am I right, she said. *Share Your Burden. Directed by Jeff Somoneorother. Nineteen Eighty One, or whenever.* I turned.

What now?

You were doing the scene when the tough cowboy has to tell his family that he's going back to the war.

Huh?

My memory's not as good as yours, but I think that was word for word.

No, Jo... I'm trying to tell you something.

Carry on. She chomped more popcorn. *I've missed this. All your film trivia stuff.*

I wasn't doing a scene, I said. *I have some news...*

Oh. Ok, she said. She looked at me sadly. *I'm sorry to interrupt. It's just that sometimes... I mean, it did sound like a scene...*

– it's not, I said.

– but then you know how I feel! Sometimes... it's hard to take you seriously. I mean. I love you, you're my friend. But sometimes, your rich fantasy life is too much, you know? You're always in your head in some heroic story... it's like you think you're not interesting enough so you have to make stuff up all the time. If you could just relax, you might see that people like you as you are.

I know that, I said. My voice sounded shaky and petulant.

Look Mark, Jo said. *I'm glad we're talking. I've felt uncomfortable for months about a few things. The whole valentine's card charade, I know it was innocent and no-one got hurt, but it got to the point where it seems like you forgot that you wrote it yourself –*

– oh come on Jo, this isn't what I want to talk about...

– I mean, I get it, I was happy to help you get a card, make a show of delivering it... and I even understand you pretending to try and decipher it for a while, keep up the story, pretend you didn't send it to yourself... I thought it was pretty funny that you'd written it in code... thought it was clever, even, that way you'd not have to reveal who it was from. I was happy to try and help boost your ego a little bit. That's what friends do for each other. But it made me angry to hear you tell the Gavs that L sent the card –

– I did not

– well they seemed to think that, and as much as I don't like her, well I don't like Vicki,

222

cricket, but I do find its slowness and endless statistics to be perfect for

but L doesn't like me –

> *– she does like you!*

> *– well anyway, it wasn't fair to pretend it was from her. It wasn't cool. And at times it was even like you'd convinced yourself that she did send it...*

> *I don't know what you're trying to say –*

> *Mark. You're unbelievable. You wrote a card to yourself and said it was from L. Then you seemed to believe that it actually was.*

> *It's not like that...*

> *And I'm cast as the grumpy handbrake on your flyaway fantasy. That's how you see me isn't it? The nagging girl. Except you don't see me as a girl.*

> *Steady on –*

> *No, Mark. I love you to bits and I'm gutted that you're moving, but it will be a bloody relief too, if I'm honest. You manage to turn any conversation about anything into her.* She screwed up her popcorn bag and put it in her pocket. She crossed her arms. She did this when she was pretending to be annoyed, but I could see this was real.

> *You know I'm moving,* I said.

> *Of course.*

> *Oh.*

> *You thought you had a big secret, didn't you? You were looking forward to stunning me with it.*

> *No. Yes. I suppose.*

She came over to me and leaned her head on my shoulder.

> *Your dad got a job down South. You really are Sam Two,* she said.

> *No. It was my stepdad who got a job. Get it right,* I said.

> *Not like you to get bogged down in facts,* she said. She laughed. After a beat I did too.

> *Do you think you could do me a favour,* I said. Jo yanked out a handful of grass by her knees and let it fall.

> *I'm not sure,* she said. I pulled the letter for L out of my pocket and smoothed it in my hands.

> *If you could let L know that I'm moving I'd appreciate it--*

> *Mark, listen –*

my metaphor, and as Mark Twain said (or perhaps he did not, I should

check) 'allow the poet his metaphor.' Tom, with no interest in actually

playing, agrees to the task. The games master (played by Roger Livesey,

who it must be noted, Bishopsfield interjects, *bears an uncanny resem-*

blance to the games master who beat me thrice weekly at school, and as

such bears an uncanny resemblance to the vision of Lucifer in my head,

---

I mean, discreetly, of course, no fuss.

Mark –

Just take her to one side over the next few days and give her this –

Jo looked me in the eye.

I shouldn't do this. You're not supposed to have any contact.

I'm not contacting her. It's just a... goodbye.

Jo sighed and took the letter.

As long as there's no crap in here about you having won the lottery. Or going to work
for *NASA. Or that you're dying or something.*

Why would I say that?

She gave me a knowing look.

Ok, I said. *I swear. There's no crap in there about me winning the lottery. Or working*
for *NASA. Or that I... that I'm dying.*

Ok, she said. *I'll see what I can do.*

She stood up, and slipped the letter into the back pocket of her jeans.

Wait, I said. *Maybe I'll just post it to her,* I said, holding out my hand. Jo looked into
my eyes and then gave me back the letter.

Maybe that's better, she said.

Yeah.

I should get back, she said. She opened her arms wide. I stepped into her hug. Then
she stepped back to look at me.

By the way, I said. Share Your Burden *was directed by Jeff Peacock. And it came out in*
1983.

I hate you, she said.

and is thus more perfectly cast than anyone could ever suspect apart from his height) notes Tom's eye for detail, and taking pity on him, gives him the important job of being the official scorer for all of the school's matches in every sport: not just cricket, but rugby, track and field, boxing, hockey, and lacrosse.

Here Bishopsfield interrupts again with some statistics:

The film is 73 mins and 32.21 seconds. This is 4412.21 seconds. The film has 490 shots. The longest shot lasts for 12.43 seconds (the whirling pan when Tom is confronted by the big city). Of the 490 shots, 201 are stationary. The other 289 involve camera movements. Number of people that appear on screen: 164. Number of people that speak: 17. Number of people that tell Tom that he needs to 'stop writing in that bloody book': 7. Number of words Tom speaks: 121. Number of words Tom speaks inside his head: 1207. Most common word: 'I' (heard 97 times). Number of times Tom writes something down in his notebook: 54. Number of minutes Tom is on-screen: 52 mins and 56.21 seconds. Amount of perspiration: immeasurable.

Problems arise when Tom's obsessive scoring holds up the game. He asks the umpires to pause while he notes down not only the important details of the last piece of action, but the minor ones too. The crowd begin to boo him. Bishopsfield's insertions and interruptions mirror Tom's: both want the perfect sequence of events recorded perfectly, but both find that their study overwhelms their subjects. When the ball is hit in Tom's direction, he holds on to it and refuses to return it, buying himself precious seconds to catch up. But then he realises he has inserted himself into the action; his commentary must include his own behaviour, and describe not only the feel of the ball in his hand and which pocket he places it in, but the details of the scuffle as some older boys shake him and inspect him to retrieve the ball. Pausing the narrative only pushes it in a new direction.

Similarly, Bishopsfield, with increasing frequency, pauses the film itself to explain his thoughts, lingering on a single frame to point out small details and nuances the viewer might not have noticed. A second of footage seems to contain a hundred riffs for him to chase. And he does.

But even this was not enough for the director. After the film was released, to mixed reviews and general confusion, Bishopsfield took to turning up at screenings of *Tom Keeps Score*, carrying with him a large piece of cardboard with which to cover portions of the screen at particular points, to better reveal the activity in other parts of the frame. He would also comment on his own commentaries, creating a loop of directorial uncertainty, an echo chamber of Barry, Barry, and more Barry. Cinema-goers in Morden, Brixton, and Wimbledon were especially likely to have their already over-directed fare interrupted by the director himself. In 2001, The Curzon in Soho had a special showing of the film, to which they invited Bishopsfield to recreate some of his interruptions. A BBC camera crew showed up to film what they expected to be another of Bishopsfield's performances. But he sat quietly through the whole film, listening carefully to his own voice as it ran over the actors' dialogue:

It wasn't Mark Twain that said that, as I incorrectly guessed on the soundtrack. Oh no, I cannot attribute it. There is another quote that I can correctly assign to GK Chesterton, however, that goes like this: The fatal metaphor of progress, which means leaving things behind us, has utterly obscured the real idea of growth, which means leaving things inside us. *I disagree of course, and hope to leave nothing inside me by completely expelling all energies, true or false, into public...*[113]

After the showing, Bishopsfield was asked why he didn't interrupt the film. Was it because the cameras were there?

No, he said. *I just realized that I'll never get it right.* Was this the first time he'd had that thought? *Yes, actually.* Does that trouble you? To feel that you'll never make it perfect? *No. It's actually quite a relief,* he

[113] *"Barry Keeps Score"* Anthony Wall, *BBC Arena.* 2005.

said.

Tom Keeps Score

Directed by Barry Bishopsfield. Produced by Barry Bishopsfield, Karel Reisz. Written by Tom Warne, Barry Bishopsfield. Starring Richard Jones, Benjamin Tot, Roger Livesey. Bryanston Films/ Continental Films. Release Date: June 1967 (UK). 74 mins. Tagline: Someone Must Always Keep Score.

LE JOUR NOUS AVONS PERDU

UN MOIS (THE DAY WE LOST A

MONTH)

Chris Marker, 1968

But time is the only thing we all have. How can it be

taken from us? Even prisoners get hours within which to

think and dream.

Unnamed man, *Le jour nous avons perdu un mois*

*L*e Jour Nous Avons Perdu un Mois or *The Day We Lost A Month*
was directed by the Frenchman Christian Hippolyte François
Georges Bouche-Villeneuve, known better as Chris Marker.[114] He
emerged internationally in 1962 with *La Jetée*, or *The Pier*, a seismic
short film composed of still photography and voice-over that tells the
tale of a post-nuclear time-travel experiment.[115] While *The Day We Lost
A Month* uses live footage rather than stills, like *La Jetée* it has a weary
narrator who tells a story over a sequence of images. They initially seem
unconnected:

An old lady feeds ducks. A couple stand under an umbrella. A
man eats a hot dog on the bed of his truck. Children listen to a story in
a classroom.

---

[114] *Chris Marker:* He used many other names including Chris Mayor, Marc Dornier, and Magic
Marker. *Magic Mark.* Vicki had called me that once. *So L and I can tell you apart from Mark
Jones*, she had said. *And because you always seemed a bit...* special *to us.*

But now I was in limbo at home and Mark Jones was the only Mark at school.

[115] *La Jetée* was later remade, by Terry Gilliam as *Twelve Monkeys* (1995), by Mamoru Oshii
as *The Red Spectacles* (1987), and by Jeff P. Ryde as *Time Bitch* (2001). *Le Jour Nous Avons...*was
crudely remade by Nick Cassavetes as *No Thanksgiving This Year* (2002), starring Nicolas Cage
and Madeline Stowe.

A female voice explains: *The Day We Lost A Month was in February. The governments of the world announced that they had made a discovery: the forthcoming November had vanished. They did not know how or why, or what it meant. Their projections going forward to July, August, and September were normal; for October, their numbers oscillated violently; and then, where November should be, there was nothing. Futurologists, meteorologists, astrologists, psychics, and analysts of the twitching codes of the markets all came to the same conclusion: November is gone, and we have eight months to make a plan.*[116]

---

[116] *November is gone:* June was a waste. School was nearly over, the homework dried up, and the Gavs didn't visit every day any more. It was still weeks before we would move. A few times I hung around at the bottom of Hinckley Road to see my friends walking home. Knowing that I might get in trouble if I spoke to L, I hid by the brook leading to the tunnel below the road and watched as different groups walked by. The Gavs and Jo walked together but not with L and Vicki. For the first few days I was there I didn't see L at all. Maybe she was ill, or maybe she was getting a lift home with her over-protective parents. The day I finally did see her she was walking with a group of older kids. I guessed that recent events had given her some playground gravitas, a sprinkling of schoolyard celebrity, and I was pleased that I had helped elevate her social status, however indirectly. I followed the group from a distance, under the railway bridge, towards town, until they splintered off towards their own houses. L stood talking to a boy who worked at the House of Laser. She'd always talked about trying to get a Saturday job there, and I figured their conversation was about that. They talked for a long time. After they separated I followed L down the subway tunnel towards her house. At one point I kicked a stone in the tunnel and she turned, but I knew she could only see my silhouette from where she was. She hurried on, and I watched from the end of her road as she walked away. Pink lines and numbers had been painted on the pavement on the corner, next to the fence I was hiding behind. At first I thought it was graffiti, but then I looked further. A precise blue line was below the pink, leading to an arrow that pointed off towards the street. At the end of the arrow were numbers, in yellow: *20:16*. A bible reference, a date, or instructions for someone with tools to dig up the street. Where to cut, where to avoid.

Now it is summer: A picnic on a roof in Paris. A woman tap dances in the street while a man plays a violin. Children kick a ball against a mural of Charles De Gaulle.

The voice goes on: *What can no November mean? Will we go to sleep for thirty days and wake up in December, rested and dreamless? Will it just be a bump in the road that we can look back on and smile? Will every year from now on jump from October to December? Can we just call December November, and move on? Or would this mean that one twelfth of our lives were to be stolen? That is at least six years to a healthy Westerner. Where would those years go? For most people, even these felt like optimistic scenarios. Others didn't buy any of it.*

The images continue: A dog on a leash but with no owner, sniffs around a car wheel. A man removes posters from a bus shelter. A market trader sells fruit.

Early government reports clearly designed to avoid panic were regarded as whitewashes. Television programs devoted segments to surviving the lack of November, or denying the lack of November. Newspaper

How long had this been here? What other things had been changing? I vowed to suck it all in, see it, note it. I watched L's back, the familiar bounce of her hair, until she turned into and disappeared safely into her house.

I repeated this for the next few days, seeing myself as a ghostly escort, a spirit guide. I was recording, making notes, honing my knowledge. I would be so familiar with the path L would be taking and the time it would take that after I moved I could be in both places at once. I vowed to imagine this walk home every day at 3:30 as I walked home from my new school in my new town, wherever it was. This lost month of not being at school was my apprenticeship as an invisible man, a flickering dot on the radar, an unseen presence on a light breeze.

editorials blamed our disregard for the environment, or Zionists, or it was Islamist rebels fighting for a free Algeria or Palestine. Or they said that only the Soviets have the technology to remove a month from our calendar and from our lives. Protest marches, against whomever, against whatever, for whatever reason, turned into riots. Deep down we suspected that the authorities were as clueless as we were.[117]

An empty stadium. A factory prints newspapers; headlines obscured. Birdsong at sunset.

We hoped that we would wake up on the first of November in our beds as normal, with nothing changed. But somehow this scared us too. That so much panicked energy could be devoted to such an anti-climax.[118]

---

[117] *the authorities were as clueless as we were:* One day when I got home Mum was waiting.

You haven't tried to contact this girl have you, she said.

No.

It's just that Sally said she saw you near the school yesterday.

Who is Sally, I said, knowing that Sally was probably made up by my Mum to make her point, just like the main character in *I Never Knew Sally* (Brit Exxon, 1984) who is blamed for destroying the livelihood of a Kansas town despite, it is revealed near the climax, never existing.

David H's Mum, she said. *You know Sally. But it doesn't matter. What matters is that you've been keeping the agreement.*

I have, I said.

[118] *to such an anti-climax:* I learned from Big Gav that on the last day of school a group of kids were going to see *Jurassic Park* at the big multiplex halfway to Coventry. They told me I should go and make it part of my goodbye. Big Gav's mum would give us a lift, and pick us up afterwards too. Jo too. Mum let me go on the understanding that I would finish packing up my room the following day. When I got in the car that Friday night, in the exact outfit I'd put on for L's birthday, I slid in next to Jo in the back seat. She took one look at my clothes and whispered *she's not going to be there.*

By September, there were as many parties as riots.

A man chops down a tree with an axe. A child watches cartoons and drinks milk from a bowl. Bugs Bunny is dressed as a girl.

The speculations were rife: what if November does arrive, and seems normal, but then, like a frozen lake with too many skaters, it caves in, leaving five billion people scrambling for the solid banks of October, or December? In which direction should we swim? Will the current flow forwards or backwards? Will the water be too cold? Do we even have any idea of what time is, and where it can go?

I know, I said, even though I didn't.

We arrived just as the film started. The other kids had already taken over the back few rows, and we couldn't get four seats together apart from right at the front.

After the film we stood on the steps, the three of us, waiting for Gav's mum. L never did show up. At one point I saw a girl with a similar jacket, and I know Jo thought the same thing because she spun to look at me, but I managed to not look like I was looking. Other kids were throwing popcorn at each other and running around, laughing. Jo got annoyed when one of the cool girls knocked her as she ran past.

What's your problem, the girl said.

You knocked my arm, Jo said.

Oh I'm sorry. No need to have a mardy.

The girl looked at me.

Oh you used to be in maths with me, didn't you? I nodded. *Didn't you get expelled or something?*

I wanted to say yes. I did. For robbing the tuck shop. For putting a knife to the throat of a teacher. For liberating the caretaker's cat.

That's crap, Jo said. *He has to move and it's not his fault.*

The girl looked at me.

Sorry to see you go, she said, quite politely really.

Rumours said that the very rich would attempt to escape in space shuttles. Or buy the services of quantum physicists who could provide them with a perpetual August to live in like an ageless gated community. This led to vandalism of mansions, and home-made bombs sent in elevators up to penthouse suites. The message was clear: if we're going, you're coming too.[119]

A line of people wait to vote outside a school. White clothes hang dripping on a line. A cat plays with a dead kingfisher.

A group of revolutionaries in France successfully captured a used May Day. What was their intention? Might they be able to hold onto this chunk of twenty-four hours, like a life raft? One speculative theory was that they hoped to cool it artificially into a likeness of a November day. If successful, they would kidnap other days too, stockpiling as much as a week's worth, to be spread thinly across the expanse of where November used to be, like stepping stones. If it worked, the same could be done next year, and by removing the occasional expired day at carefully selected intervals (and refitting them, with the correct weather, the correct ambi-

---

[119] *if we're going, you're coming too:* Finally Big Gav's Mum picked us up and took us home. When we stopped outside my house Big Gav's Mum turned around and smiled.

All the best at your new school, son, she said. *Keep focussed, eh. There's a good lad.* Big Gav and Jo got out to say goodbye, but we didn't really know what to say. We looked at each other.

I wish Little Gav could have made it, Big Gav said.

Yeah, I said. *Tell him I said bye.*

Will do, Big Gav said.

Jo hugged me, promised to write as soon as she had my address, and that was it.

ance, the correct poetry), we could eventually build a makeshift Novem-
ber, from leftover twenty-ninths of February and eighteenths of July and
twenty-sixths of October, and knit the two halves of the year together into
a navigable route. Each year we might do it with different days, so that no
one is left with a life of unbirthdays.

But the French government, backed by NATO and China and
with the quiet consent of the USSR, freed the May Day and killed the
revolutionaries in a daring televised raid. The May Day was displayed by
the French President. He stood behind a podium next to it as it wilted,
withered and died in the September air. Time was slipping away.

A car drives in the rainy countryside. A film plays to an empty
theatre. Judy Garland clutches Toto.

The American plan naturally involved a potentially suicidal act
of heroism: a small group of elite marines would be dropped by time-plane
into the day after October 31st to see what was there. This mission was
named The October 32nd Drop *and was deemed by many to be sure sui-*
cide. The men prepared in an intensive camp that filled their brains with
November residue: they showered in rainwater collected in Maine the
previous All Saint's Day, and they ate Thanksgiving dinners every night.
The theory seemed to be that if the men could arrive in the abyss with as
much November as possible on them and in them, they might be able to
survive in the void, even traverse it. But you can't water a desert, a man
on television said. They left a week ago, and no reports have come back.

Perhaps they have fixed the breach, and wait for us on the other side. We might not know until our clocks rotate enough times for us to catch them up.

Men in suits sit around a table. The aftermath of a street party. A soldier guards a gate with barbed wire across the top of it.

October. Hysteria built. It was just like a war had begun and no-one had fired a shot yet. A move in the general direction of the west occurred, as people all over the world felt that if November had gone, they might hide a little longer in the last strains of October as the sun dropped. Some headed east instead, towards oblivion. Some stockpiled food and drove to the hills. There was no suggestion that they would be any safer there.

On television, a respected intellectual of some fame sucked on a cigarette, and took questions from a studio audience. One said: maybe this is like the panic over the introduction of the Gregorian calendar. They thought they were losing thirteen days of their lives, but they were not. The author smoked his cigarette down to the filter. He said: you can save your childhood photos from the fire. You can't save your childhood from the fire. Yesterday you were a teenager in love on a mountaintop. Tomorrow you are not. There is no villain. No cure. No fight. Just death.

The last scene of the film takes place in the centre of Paris. The thirty-first of October. A crowd stands below the Arc de Triomphe, waiting. They wear hats and scarves or Halloween costumes. Some are a little drunk. Some sing along with a man who plays popular songs on guitar. He is dressed as a cat. A crying student is reassured by his friends. A man dressed as a soldier who might be a soldier starts a countdown. The crowd look at their watches, or tentatively embrace. The countdown hits zero. The screen goes black. A deep chord, a low D, is held, and somehow grows deeper and deeper without changing. The black screen somehow seems to grow even blacker.

Le Jour Nous Avons Perdu Un Mois

Directed by Chris Marker. Produced by Anatole Dauman. Written by Chris Marker, Jacques Sternberg. Music by Paul Misraki. Starring Helena Chamelaine, David Richard, Serene Vespa. Athos Films/Criterion. Release Date: June 1968 (Fra). 103 mins. Tagline: Where Were You Yesterday When Tomorrow Didn't Come?

Aa

Niko Hämäläinen, 1969

There is order in everything. We just choose not to see it.

Niko Hämäläinen

This is a review of *Aa,* and also of *Bb* (Niko Hämäläinen, 1979), *Cc* (Niko Hämäläinen, 1992), *Dd* (Niko Hämäläinen, 1999) *Ee* (Niko Hämäläinen, 2005), *Ff* (Niko Hämäläinen and Eva Hämäläinen, 2009) and another twenty planned sequels, which, even though they don't exist yet, can be imagined quite readily. Niko Hämäläinen's series will have no twist endings, as we know exactly where it is going, every step of the way through to *Zz.* The shooting script for every instalment can be bought in any bookshop and read, word for word.

Niko Hämäläinen's preoccupation was, is, and always will be, words. Not just what they mean, but what they look like, and what we think of when we say them and when we see them written down. He makes visuals to accompany them. All of them. His first film, *Aa,* is a series of images representing each word in the Oxford English Dictionary beginning with *A,* in alphabetical order. The sequels follow suit. So *Aa* begins with an image of the letter *a* itself, before we see some lava, up close. The word *aa* then appears and is defined as *lava that is of a rough surface.* Next we see an aardvark, and so on. Hämäläinen uses a combination of stock footage, found photographs and his own drawings to make his films. The challenges are clear: *to articulate both* argue *and then* arguing, *never mind* argument, *in interesting and not repetitive ways is perhaps the biggest difficulty I face. And of course, how to render abstracts such as* abstract *in images is an interesting problem.*[120]

Aa, the first film, was finished in 1969. When the BBC visited Hämäläinen in 1975, for a documentary called *Dictionary Man*, he was still four years away from completing *Bb*. When they made a follow-up documentary in 1999, called *Dictionary Man Forever*, the fourth film, *Dd*, was just being finished. In both documentaries, the interviewer asks the same question again and again:

Why, Niko?

Why what, he says.

Why this?

I don't know what you mean.

Why film the entire dictionary? It is an impossible undertaking.

Pause. Niko thinks, as if for the first time, about this.

Well, what else would you have me do?[121]

---

[120] *"A to Z: Niko's Quest"* Sandra Sidhu. *Sunday Times,* February 1999. This interview delivered a rare and deep probing of the man and his work. Most interviews, and Hämäläinen has given very few outside of Finland, approach him as if determined to make him admit that what he does is a joke.

[121] *what else would you have me do:* On the morning before we left in the lorry with all our things my stepdad went out to sell our old car. I left for one last walk. I had with me a cassette that I'd been making for L for months. I hadn't perfected it, but it was good enough. It would tell the story of our curious arc, from our initial meeting, through the frantic months of contact, to where we were now, apart. It was tailored to be a goodbye for now, an open-ended farewell. Within it, in the sentiments contained in the verses, the feelings of the riffs, the energies drilled down into the

The deeper questions, not explicitly asked in *Documentary Man,* might be: Do we see Niko Hämäläinen as a romantic spirit, and do we find his bloody-minded devotion admirable? Isn't his a foolhardy heroism in which no-one can win, for there can be no glory?[122] What

---

sounds, if L listened carefully enough, would be an inventory of everything we ever did. If anyone else heard it, however, it would just seem like a collection of contemporary music that I just happened to have access to. This seemed appropriate, as so much of the feeling in our relationship over the last few months had been unsaid, unseen, and unheard. Despite the difficulties along the way, we had been the resistance, sharing enemy movements with a series of blinks, and alerting one another to a change of plan with a scratch of the ear.

The tape opened with The Lemonheads' cover of *Different Drum,* a perfect bittersweet break-up/perhaps one day we'll make-up song. Then *She Kissed Me* by Terence Trent Darby, even though she didn't, technically. I ended up putting most of *Angel Dust* by Faith No More on there (because I knew she wanted it). Side B had *Wigwam* by Flu (because I knew she was getting into more indie stuff), *Little Lost Sometimes* by The Almighty, *Worthing* by Strut (even though I didn't like it very much, it fit thematically, as I was moving down south), *Twice As Hard* by The Black Crowes, *Follow Me* by Tense 'N' Nervous, *Get The Message* by Electronic, *Runaway Train* by Soul Asylum, and *Meet Me At The Station Tomorrow* by The Hu-Nos. Side B ended with a secret bonus track, *Beautiful Girl* by INXS, recorded off Keeny's show, naturally. I didn't even really like it very much. But art must transcend taste. On it went.

[122] *there can be no glory:* I put the tape in a plastic bag along with the packet of stickers and some treasures I'd found when I cleaned out my room: a figurine from a cereal box, a postcard for the film *Pounce* (Abby Tendor, 1991), some penny chews, and a still life I'd drawn in an art lesson last year of a bicycle tyre next to some bricks and wood. I heard that L had seen it when it was on the wall and said it was good. As I had resisted the urge to give the tape extensive sleeve notes, and had decided to forgo even a list of track titles (the sentiments of the songs would speak for me, for us), the picture would identify, if L needed it, that the gift was from me.

I headed towards L's house, walking slowly to take mental notes of any last unnoticed details: the angles of fences, the patterns of paving stones. When I got to the subway I headed straight through, climbed the ramp, and headed down L's road. *Can you feel the electricity?* Dick

would Hämäläinen's reaction be if he were to get close to completing his task? Would his knees buckle like a rookie serving for the championship at Wimbledon, having been fearless up until the very point that possibility is fast becoming probability? We cannot know, for time will beat the project. Surely. He is old, and not even close to halfway.

Animals are not chasers of lost causes. Humans are, says Hämäläinen at one point. *Wrong causes, maybe. Causes that are fuelled by self-interest and self-loathing. Causes, even, that are taken up against ourselves, against our wishes, against our better judgement. We get in our own way, and sabotage ourselves. That is what it is to be human. Why is what I do any more troubling to you?*

The documentary prompts more questions: is it a defeat for an

---

Turpin (Peter Wyngarde) had said to his horse, anachronistically, during his just-one-more-gig robbery in the period drama *The Highwayman* (Brian G. Hutton, 1971). Electricity was the only applicable word, I felt, for that exciting tingle. I looked around to see if anyone was watching as I approached L's house, and without breaking my stride I dropped the bag into the front bushes and moved on around the corner.

There is no reason to think she ever found it, or if she did, to know that it was from me. As time passed, the idea that there was something that I had made for her, hidden so close to her, grew powerful to me. I could imagine the tape there inside the bag, yards outside her front door. It was a totem, a secret. Perhaps, occasionally, she would find herself thinking of me when she passed those bushes, without knowing why. Her parents wanted to keep me away from her. Fine. But like a fish left in a radiator as a prank, my tape would leave an inexplicable psychic aroma that no-one could get rid of.

When I got home they were waiting for me by the moving van.

Ready son, my stepdad said. I nodded at the floor. We got in the van.

We got two hundred quid for the car, Mum said.

artist to die before his work is done? Don't all artists die before their work is done? Some, perhaps, are done long before they die. We know *exactly* how much further Hämäläinen has to go, of course. We have access to his shooting scripts. He was 74 when his latest, *Ff*, chapter six of twenty-six, was released. And while this chapter has a polish that *Aa* lacks, and more imagination in some of the transitions, the truth remains that his style and technique are largely the same, more than forty years on.

Gilbert Adair was quite taken with Hämäläinen's project:

Why are the letters of our alphabet in the order

they are? It would work just as well if they were

reversed, or thrown on the floor like scrabble

tiles and reassembled in a new way. What does

our order mean, besides sitting the Alexes and

Andrews on the sunny side of the classroom and

the Zacharys and Zoës in the dark? What does it

mean, beyond putting Springsteen, Bruce next to

Springfield, Dusty (but far, far away from Buffalo

Springfield) in the record store? What chiming mo-

ments does such a pervasive ordering of the world

reveal? Is our alphabet a key? Can it tell a story?

What Hämäläinen does, in not so many words (or

perhaps, in exactly so many words), is ask these

questions, with a direct action so bold and hopeless

that we question his sanity.[123]

Niko is a calm and sweet man on camera, quietly committed to his work. He also grows roses, and in *Documentary Man Forever* he is filmed tending to his impressive plants. *To keep a garden is to believe that tomorrow will come,* he says. He doesn't seem to fit the eccentric artist stereotype that the filmmakers might initially have laid out for him. But he has his demons, according to his daughter Eva who co-directed *Ff*:

> *My father is a man haunted by dreams of an over-*
> *sized alphabet forest, where rain falls and an l tips*
> *over, uprooted, or a k bends to offer a branch for a*
> *climber. Whether this is why he chose this project,*
> *or whether it is because of the project... well who*
> *can tell at this point?*[124]

Eva is unsure quite how far she will carry on her father's project after he is gone. At this point she is not short of helpful offers from other film-makers. But this would dilute the Sisyphean nature of the task somewhat, something that she feels might trouble her father. He hasn't expressed feelings either way, she says. *But he'd tell me that finishing is not the point,* she says.

Adair again:

[123] *Sight & Sound,* Feb 1996.

[124] *Helsinki Times* interview, August 2009.

The truth is that he could have chosen to make
films about his family, or his home, or something
else that was superficially more subjective. But the
small decisions he makes in his films express his
personality in ways other filmmakers fail to do over
countless confessional memoir-tinged fictions. The
skittering creature he chooses for the word bee, for
example, or the grey, ashy block for the word brick;
both articulate with precision the character of their
quiet curator.[125]

The latest in the Visualised Dictionary series, *Ff*, was released in 2009, a mere four years after the release of *Ee*, which itself was only seven years after *Dd*. *Digital video technology is helping us speed up,* Hämäläinen says, optimistically. *Besides, Xx and Qq won't take me long, they are short letters.*[126]

---

[125] *Sight & Sound*, Feb 1996.

[126] *they are short letters:* Niko Hämäläinen was hospitalized after a cardiac arrest in late 2017. He is stable, but complications after surgery mean he needs constant care and it appears unlikely that he will be able to return to filmmaking. He turns 90 in 2020. According to Eva, the films *Gg, Hh, Ii,* and *Jj* are completed, and *Kk* and *Ll* are almost done. Plans for their release are not known at this time. *Papa says that unfinished is okay. He enjoyed working while he could,* Eva said in a Twitter statement. *But who knows. Maybe he'll come back.*

  Who knows, Mum said as we pulled into traffic on the A road leading towards the motorway. *Maybe we'll come back.*

Aa

Directed by Niko Hämäläinen. Produced by Niko Hämäläinen. Venstock Films/Aqua Film Distribution. Release Date: August 1969 (Fin) 261 mins.

Tagline: A Complete History of Absolutely Everything, In Order.

NIE FÜR DEN BUS LAUFEN

(NEVER RUN FOR THE BUS)

Serge Grebiot, 1969

Your grandfather had three rules: Always eat breakfast.

Always wear the right jacket. And never run for the bus.

Or was it always run for the bus? I forget. The point is,

he had three rules, and he stuck to them.

Irma, Nie Für Den Bus Laufen

Serge Grebiot died in May 2011, to little fanfare. In contrast, the deaths of fellow French film-makers Eric Rohmer and Claude Chabrol the same year were rightly mourned and their lives celebrated. They were two men who produced worthy art right up to their deaths. Grebiot lacked their consistency, for sure, and perhaps more precisely, their *desire* to make films (his last completed effort was 1997's *How To Make An American Quit*, a lazy jingoistic comedy, displaying, finally, his complete loss of juju), but when his powers were firing, most notably between 1968 and 1973, the films he made could stand toe-to-toe with those of anyone.

One reason for his exclusion from the canon could be that he was a Frenchman who made films in Germany, thus falling between the cracks of two national cinemas at different stages of revolt and reform. Serge Grebiot, *Die Französisch Deutsch* (The French German), was born in Montpellier, joined the army as a teen to fight the Nazis, and was subsequently stationed in Frankfurt as a photographer when the

Allies occupied Germany. Grebiot fell in love with a German girl, and stayed, becoming a photojournalist then a filmmaker. It was a deeply unfashionable place to be making art in the late 50s; whereas Grebiot's countrymen were harvesting international acclaim with chic new-wave manoeuvres, Germany had yet to find her post-war feet, and as such much of the art produced was samey and fearful. *Remember; we could not sweep away all of the Nazis. Many perpetrators of atrocities were still in power. We still needed school teachers and policemen and judges after all. As such, most art tried to ignore the past quietly, and was thus beleaguered and anodyne,* said Uschi Obermaier, model, activist and member of free-form radicals Amon Düül.[127] Amon Düül were part of a generation of young Germans who, in the late sixties, wanted to depart from this Old Germany, but also didn't want to mimic the styles of American or British idioms such as rock'n'roll, pop, or the strong-armed glamour of Hollywood. Fassbinder, Herzog, Wenders, Kraftwerk, Can, and Neu!, all high on the rebellious fumes of '68, saw new future possibilities and built new roads that were distinctly German but distinctly *not* old Germany.

Grebiot was inspired by these figures, but being an outsider, didn't share their self-loathing with regard to their national identity. *I always felt like a tourist, and the things a tourist wants to see in a new country are the things that the locals never go to see,* he said. *Parisians*

---

[127] *Krautrock: The Rebirth of Germany,* BBC Films, 2009.

do not climb the Eiffel Tower.[128] In a way, his films can seem definitively German at times, much in the way that many of the films that defined America in the first half of the 20th Century were made by immigrant talent like von Sternberg, Chaplin, Garbo, Dietrich, Wilder, Lang, Ophüls, and Hitchcock.

Nie Für Den Bus Laufen[129] was dubbed *Hausfrau Noir* by Ca-

---

[128] *Film Comment, vol.* 4, no 11, April 2002. Little Gav went to Paris that summer and sent me a postcard at my new address. Its sentiment was kind but its lack of information and detail was typical. I read it many times in bed where, as a protest against my situation, I had faked glandular fever symptoms and stayed for several weeks as my family explored our new town. This seemed right and proper. Anything less would have felt a betrayal to Nuneaton and to L. Mum knew I wasn't really ill. I knew that she knew. She poked her head around the door a few times to check on me. On one occasion, her expression was the exact echo of the face on my tv screen at that exact moment (it was the mute girl in *4eva* [Sven Zimmer, 1965], at the point where she was nursing the wounded baby crocodile and wordlessly demonstrating sympathy for the distressed creature). As I lay there in my new bedroom with the curtains closed against the sun, I was struck by the feeling that sometimes films appear that directly comment on your situation. It is as if they didn't exist until you conjured them up with the depth of your emotions, even though they had been around for years. Just like the kid in *Hey Jood* (Larra Williams, 1991) who, having sung the Beatles' song *Hey Jude* for months after hearing his mother sing it, is aghast to hear the original on the radio. *They've stolen your song Mom,* he says.

[129] *Nie Für Den Bus Laufen*: The full title was *Immer für den Bus überfahren, Nein, Nie für den Bus laufen,* translated as *Always Run For The Bus, No, Never Run For The Bus,* apparently to reflect the protagonist Irma's indecisive nature, for there are no buses mentioned in the film. She betrays a confusion over the correct punishment for her children, or even whether they merit punishment, and speaks frequently with a muddled folksy wisdom. Even if we do not hear her say these words, we might imagine them in her voice.

The first week at my new school in Worthing was slow and quiet. I didn't talk to many people apart from teachers. *Try to focus on making new friends,* Mum said. I didn't. I watched films in the evening and wrote about them during lessons. During lunch I made long lists of films

hiers du Cinéma (the delicious collision of the two languages being a doff of the chapeau/kappe to Grebiot's dual nationality). The *noir* is there in the sharp silhouettes on-screen, which carry echoes of the Weimar gargoyle shapes that went on to inform so many American thrillers of the 1940s. The *Hausfrau* comes from the way that Grebiot returns these

---

I wanted to see. In Nuneaton I'd had a period of obsessing over the minutiae of my surroundings and certain people in it. Now I was removed again. In French a kid asked to borrow a pencil sharpener. He smiled. It seemed like a gambit to open a conversation. I closed him down quickly by telling him to go ahead and help himself to anything in my pencil case, and returned to my work He dug around.

Who is L, he said.

What? I looked up. He was reading a note.

Someone special? I snatched the note away.

Where was this, I said.

In your pencil case, he said. I took the note and looked at it. It said: *L loves U make a move on the lips silly. I know it will be OK when U do take it from me. Vicki.* I felt excited for a few seconds, then I remembered. I'd written it, in my best Vicki handwriting, with my best version of Vicki's poor diction, and hidden it. From myself. To surprise myself.

And it had worked. *Surprise.* There was a buzz in my stomach.

And who is Vicki, the kid said.

Old girlfriends, I said.

Both of them?

Yeah...

Bollocks, he said, but I could tell he wasn't sure whether to believe me or not.

At break-time I went to the toilets and opened the note in the cubicle. I read it again. L kept coming back. Even though I'd written it, I couldn't help but imagine that L was psychically alerting me any way she could. I pulled out a piece of paper from my bag, one that listed all of L's lessons. I had avoided looking at it for three days, and had congratulated myself, but now I had fallen back. I unfolded it and looked at my watch. 9:58. L would be in Maths.

The bell rang. English was next for her. Me too.

effects to Germany—these private dicks, morally ambiguous *femme fatales,* and promises of one last job—and shackles them, incredibly, to a one-room drama about a working-class household in Frankfurt. Instead of a weary but smart Sam Spade, we have a mother of four, Irma (Betty Schneider), whose tired demeanour betrays a tense household.[130] Her husband is absent, presumed dead, and the action (or lack thereof) centres on Irma's quiet inquisition of her children, who, it seems, are perpetrators of various minor misdeeds such as being messy, being loud

---

[130] Stanley Kaufmann riffed on the idea of a house falling apart in his *New Republic* review of the film (March 1971). He called it *a 'digs' in a hole, an abode of corrode, a crashed pad, a dwelling that dwells.* Picking up on the Hausfrau Noir style, he described the film as *Raymond Chandler in a kitchen-out-of-sync.* This particular review was given the *Pseud's Corner World-wide Trophy 1971* by *Private Eye* magazine, an award to recognise the *most excessive and forced journalism in the English Language.* Kaufmann, unlike most winners, showed up at the ceremony in London and gamely accepted his trophy, using his acceptance speech to read out some of the puns he deemed too poor to make it into his review.

His repetitive humour might be distracting, painful even, but it could be argued that it is in keeping with the film in question. As Irma grills the kids, she constantly clicks from accusation to apology and back, each time trying to cover her anger with humour, and her sadness with a joke. Her lines are filled with many desperate ironies that are meaningless to an English-speaking audience, but include in-jokes for the native speakers, and references to German Shibboleths used during wartime to oust non-native spies.

I made a list of in-jokes that L and the gang had that morning in English. I couldn't remember them all. Some of my favourites included Vicki pretending to be annoyed when she saw me by saying *you again* and the number of funny nicknames for me that came up, usually proposed by Vicki. Mark the Dark Park Barker, Mark the Creepy Park Lurker. How we all laughed. Once L came up with one that must have been pure gold based on Vicki's laughter when L whispered it to her, but they didn't share it with the group. An in-in-joke, I guess. I'd ask L about it at break time, I thought, until I remembered that I was now hundreds of miles away.

at the wrong times, and drinking the last of the milk.

Irma's obsessive pursuit of details seems both prosaic and insane. The way that Grebiot shoots the regular to make it seem irregular (the checkerboard territories of the tablecloth, the luminous whiteness of the plates, the endlessly held stares of the children) builds suspense like a suburban spin on *The Innocents* (1961), only with the horror motifs of the haunted house replaced by household chores and neighbourly gossip.[131]

Irma slowly strikes on clues and sniffs out hunches as the narrative spins out of control. She draws harsh conclusions about the slack moralities of her own generation, and the slovenly habits of the next, in a climactic lecture to the children on her street. She assembles them in her living room and paces in front of them, pontificating in the style of a brilliant detective. Even though she is clearly suffering from some kind of breakdown, Irma's words were taken at the time to be a harsh indictment of Grebiot's adopted country by some of the more sensitive German newspapers. But Grebiot refuted this, and always spoke fondly

---

[131] *neighbourly gossip: Totalitarianism is a stifling blanket stitched together by good behaviour and small talk,* said Grebiot (citation needed), and I did try to talk now and again, in an effort to blend in at my new school. But my repertoire of stories evaporated quickly and earned me little. A lengthy anecdote about my uncle's time in the RAF (augmented with details borrowed from the lesser-seen *Escape From Camp K* [Derek Bough, 1967]) that had once kept the Gavs entertained all the way from Big Gav's to the far end of town, got me nothing here except general indifference and a half-hearted punch from a mute and bored older kid. I thought of the struggling poker player in *The Wolf Who Cried Boy* (another Derek Bough effort, from 1975) who can't translate his hometown luck to the big time in Vegas: *Cards is cards, until it ain't,* he says, and so did I.

of his adopted homeland: *I am not, and will never be, big enough to speak of Germany. I can only speak of the world.*[132]

Immer für den Bus überfahren, Nein, Nie für den Bus laufen

Directed by Serge Grebiot. Produced by Karl Stuch. Written by Max Friedl, Serge Grebiot. Starring Betty Schneider, Patty Ernst, Lukas Fricker, Tomas Fricker, Roland Schneider. Futurefilm/Octocinema Productions. Release date: Jan 1969 (Swe/Ger). 88 mins. Tagline: Mother Knows Best.

---

[132] "Serge Grebiot," Mary Astor, *Positif,* May 2002.

ROOMS

Aziza Kartoskya, 1970

Kartoskya is a cartographer of the fears that are invisible to most men. There are thousands and thousands of them.

Christianne Metz, *Fear Factories*[133]

There's a point where you realise you're making it all up yourself. Your whole world is a lie.

Mariam, *Rooms*

There is a shot in *Rooms* where we might—if we're paying attention to the grammar of the film—notice that the protagonist has less self-awareness than we might have thought. It comes about an hour in. We have already seen Mariam (Mariam Fakhreddine) looking from her window several times at the children playing in the street below. Each time she sings an old folk song: *you angels don't know who you are, you have no idea what the world is.* This time, the camera takes the same perspective, from Mariam's window, to look down on Mariam talking to a boy, Karim, that she has befriended. On the soundtrack we hear an orchestral reprise of the melody that Mariam sang earlier. Now Mariam is not the observer, but the subject, suggesting gently perhaps that *she*

---

[133] *Gremlin Books,* 1987. No, *Gorgon,* 1985. Note to self: check the names and numbers of all footnotes.

has no idea what the world is.[134]

All of Aziza's films—the black and white rush of noise and image *Scissor* (1966), the psychedelic body-horrors *Shark* (1968) and *Burn* (1973), and the serene *Us* (2005)—share identifiable concerns. Her heroines wrestle with self-doubt, a lack of self-belief, and a variety of manias caused by the position of women in society. Men frequently appear as confident and self-assured, even when they have no reason to be so.

As an Egyptian woman of modest origins who married a Russian Jew and moved to France to be educated, Aziza had opportunities to witness prejudices in various places, high and low. She was Aziza Kartoskya when she made *Rooms*, arguably her masterpiece. Although she subsequently is listed as just *Aziza* in the credits of her films, the fact that she made this film as a wife felt relevant to her. *This was my marriage film. It is about the sadness of loving someone but knowing they are not right. And knowing that they know it too. And that that is ok.*

Aziza returned to Cairo after an amicable separation from her husband Aaron (who has acted as producer on many of Aziza's films)

---

[134] *she has no idea:* In clues I picked up from letters from Jo and the Gavs I ascertained that L wasn't doing well. Maybe she'd started smoking and spending time with a bad crowd. Maybe she found the school workload harder this year. The letters didn't say this, in fact they all went out of their way not to mention L, despite my questions. But this said more to me than if they'd said anything at all, just like the bland newspaper stories that actually send coded messages to rebel factions in occupied Prague in *Ticho hovoří nahlas* (*Silence Speaks Loudly*, Jan Jankulovski, 1988).

to make *Rooms*, which she called *my autobiography*. This initially seems curious, as the film is about a middle-aged widow (Fakhreddine was 37 at the time, but is playing a character who is supposed to be in her late forties) shot by Aziza when she was in her mid-twenties. The widow Mariam lives a life of quiet solitude, cleaning houses for rich families and returning home to a small neat apartment. She keeps herself to herself, and politely declines neighbours' invitations to dinner. She tends to a shrine to her late husband in her closet. It is adorned with a photograph of Miriam and her son (then a child) from whom she is estranged.

One day in the market she sees a boy who is a remarkable doppelgänger of her son. She runs back to her apartment, scared. It can't be him: the boy is eight or nine, and her son would be in his twenties now. But curious, she returns to the market the next day and befriends the boy. His name is Karim. He is there every day to sell anything he can scavenge to make money for his family. Mariam offers to pay Karim to help her clean some houses, and over the weeks they work together. Mariam even lies to one family that Karim is her son. *It's easier than explaining*, she says to the boy.

She lets him come and visit and play with the toys of her son that she has kept, even though the son has grown up and hasn't lived with her for years. Karim begins to ask questions about the son.

His father sent him away to school when he was your age, she says. *But after his father died, my boy blamed me. He wouldn't come home. He stayed with cousins and friends. I don't know where he is now.*

Don't you love him?

I do. Very much. But I don't know that he thinks of me very often.

That is sad.

Karim tells Mariam that he has dreams in which he is an old man in a huge building. All the rooms he has ever been in during his long life are in this building. He keeps moving through the rooms, seeing people he supposes that he vaguely remembers from his childhood, or from business. They are the detritus though, the props and extras from his life. What is really important must be in the next room, he supposes, so he keeps on searching.

Then what happens, Mariam says.

I'm thirsty, says the boy.

Critics of this scene find the boy's ability to articulate abstract feelings to place him far above his actual age. But in light of what we later suspect—that there is a supernatural link between the boy and her son, that the boy or the son may not exist, that Mariam is perhaps indirectly directing the action—the unlikelihood of his dialogue might be read as another clue: Mariam, driven by loneliness and grief into chasing something, is misinterpreting evidence to fit a hypothesis. Reading the film in this way makes us doubt what we see, as if it is not an objective rendering of events after all, but projected from Mariam's mind onto the screen. We can't, therefore, believe our eyes.

Mariam's sister Lara[135] comes to visit and witnesses Mariam's closeness to Karim. This is when we see the familiar shot from the window where previously Mariam had looked out on the world. Now it is Lara looking out and she watches Mariam talking with the boy and is now an active participant in the scene, not a viewer.[136] At first Mariam

[135] *Lara:* I was trying to distract myself from L, but she was everywhere, her name shouted down the corridors of every film. She was the subtext that swelled to swallow the story, the footnote that spilled over many pages. I buried myself in films and recorded everything in my film binder. She showed up everywhere. An above average number of characters shared her name, or her face shape, or her walk. I tried to write to her, but didn't know what to say. There were many abandoned efforts filled with jokes, stories, and confessions. The ones I actually finished were more careful and restrained, like a soldier's letters home that had been redacted by his government. *New school is fine. Not as good. Everything will be ok. Weather not bad. Write soon.* They were so below par I couldn't send them.

[136] *not a viewer: Actor not audience. On the stage, not in the crowd. Participant, not viewer. These are the decisions that Aziza's women seem to have to make. To be taken away by their destiny, or to wrestle with it.* (Metz. *Fear Factories, Gizzard Books, 1986*). Participant, not viewer. What if you could be both? During October half-term my stepdad took Mum away for a romantic break. They left food in the fridge and extra money for emergencies. After they went I scooped up the cash, my notebook, and a bottle of vermouth from the drinks cabinet, and headed for the train. I'd never drunk vermouth before, but was influenced, predictably, by the Mickey Rourke character in *Dry Vermouth* (Van Hill, 1988), who gives a lengthy and eloquent speech, about the titular drink, to what he later realises is an empty bar. Besides, it was from last Christmas and wouldn't be missed. My plan was to go to Brighton to buy some videos, but at the station I was soon asking how much a ticket to Nuneaton was. *Where?* I had enough for a return with the emergency funds. I knew that my friends would still be at school. Half-term was next week in their school district. I could be waiting outside the school gates, victorious in my leather jacket and black jeans, carrying a bottle of booze. *Sorry I didn't write, I've been* (enigmatic pause) *busy.* I took the train to Brighton, and made good time, because it only stopped at Shoreham and Hove. But my train from

denies noticing the similarity between Karim and her own boy Ali. The sisters argue, and Mariam cries. Lara reveals that she has been in touch with Ali for years. Ali had made her promise not to reveal the letters to Mariam. Mariam is upset. Lara says[137] that Ali is living in France, where

---

Brighton to Bedford was delayed, and we waited outside London for a long time, so I missed the connection at St Pancras. I had to wait for 45 minutes for an East Midlands train towards Sheffield, and that was when I opened the vermouth in the train toilets, which cost me 10p to get into. By the time I got off at Leicester it was past 3:00 and I was three-quarters of the way down my bottle of vermouth. I changed for to train towards Birmingham New Street stopping at South Wigston, Narborough, where there was a rail replacement bus to Hinckley where I got back on the train again to Nuneaton. Burrowing on towards the centre of the country, albeit circuitously. It took six hours, and was getting dark when I got to Nuneaton.

[137] *Lara says:* Lara says, Lara says, Lara says. Sometimes I couldn't remember the sound of her voice. Vicki's coarse syllables rattled around my head like tools in a tumble dryer (she only softened her volume to talk to boys she liked, or to deliver an especially vindictive kiss-off), and I could hear Jo's distinctive low deadpan and Little Gav's excitable giggle, and Big Gav's deep laugh, a few seconds behind everyone else. But L's voice was gone, if she ever even had one.

By the time the train pulled into Nuneaton, I knew I was too late. As I got off my train, I saw Little Gav in his red school uniform getting on the train on the other platform, the one going the other way, back to Coventry. I called his name. He didn't hear me. The train pulled away.

But did I call his name? Did I even see him? I'm not always sure. Like the girl in the *Rashomon* (Akira Kurosawa, 1950) rip-off *Bystander Apathy* (V. Bunce, 2012) says when review- ing her statement to the police: *As I read my words back they seem to make sense, even if I can't imagine saying them. If you believe me then I guess I must be telling the truth.* I'd imagined Little Gav's role in the tableau of my return hundreds of times: as I leaned against the school gate, the bell would ring. Kids would start to leave the buildings and file past, eyeballing me with vague confusion, unable to reconcile my somewhat familiar face. Little Gav would be the first of our gang to come down the drive. He'd run up to me, laughing. Then Big Gav would punch my arm. Vicki would grudgingly concede that my leather jacket was cool. Jo would say something smart and funny, and we'd laugh, even L, whose eyes would shyly meet mine across the group.

he has just finished a university course and is starting his own import business. He is married and his wife is pregnant.

Lara promises to forward Ali's letters to Mariam, as long as she doesn't try to contact him. Lara says she will write and ask Ali once more if he might consider writing to Mariam. She has seen a thawing in his tone in recent months, and suspects that his impending fatherhood might make him want to reach out to his mother.

When Mariam receives a letter from Ali with a picture of himself and his pregnant wife, she is overjoyed. He invites her to come and visit them in France. He will pay for her ticket. Mariam packs ready to go, and goes to the market to tell Karim about her trip. She can't find him. She delays travelling for days as she can't find him. She writes to Ali saying that she will come soon, there are things she has to tie up.

Upon investigation, Mariam finds out that Karim has died after a short illness. Mariam somehow feels responsible, like her attention was taken from him, and this caused his death. (His death is not foreshadowed by a cough or a faint. He is just gone.) In shock, she takes her bags and immediately starts on her journey to Paris.

When she gets to Ali's address, he is not there, and the landlady there has never heard of him. Mariam shows the photo, no-one knows

---

But I was too late for that now. I gently set the empty vermouth bottle on the platform edge like a statue tribute to who knows what. I'd try and pick up another to bring with me if I could get served. I started walking.

him. She goes to the university, and no-one recognises him. She takes his business card to the location of the business, and it is not there. She finally calls her sister.

He's gone.

Who is gone? Mariam, who are you talking about?

Elements of Mariam's own life drift in and out of a closing montage sequence, like memories and dreams fragmented and rebuilt. We see Mariam's husband's grave, then we see him in Mariam's house talking to Karim; we see Ali and Karim playing together in the square, then a doctor telling a young Mariam that she cannot conceive, followed by a sequence in which Aziza herself is told the same thing by the same doctor.

Aziza once more:

> *I suppose that* Rooms *is a film about my lack of a child, yes. It is also a film about someone who cannot see the truth about their situation. Someone who does not realise how desperate they are, how lonely they are, how wrong they are. This is the most common human feeling, I think.*[138]

Rooms

Directed by Aziza Kartoskya. Produced by Victor Garda and Aaron Kartosky. Written by Aziza Kartoskya, Mikel Kartosky. Starring Mariam Fakhreddine, Ahmed Omar. Release Date: Egypt: May 1970 (Egypt/Fra) 142 mins. Tagline: Nostalgia Is A Luxury.

---

[138] *I think:* (citation needed)

ANDY WARHOL PRESENTS

RYAZANTSEV

Paul Morrissey, 1970

ANDY WARHOL'S *RYAZANTSEV*

David Salle, 1976

"RYAZANTSEV"

Tanya Ryazantsev, 1978[139]

---

[139] *1978*: This last version, Tanya's own, was presented on May 15th, 1978, the same day that L was born at George Eliot Hospital in Nuneaton. Ryazantsev played Dorothea in a French TV version of Eliot's *Middlemarch* that was first shown on British television on Sept 6th, 1988, the week, give or take (the school's calendar that far back is not online), that L started at Middlemarch Middle School. The loop just winds tighter.

To truly tell my story, I might really make a book of

photographs, no words. The pictures would show all of

my body parts, in a specific sequence: the tight calves,

stretched as if about to snap; the protruding collarbone,

as distinct from my upper torso so as to look like, as

Andy said, a garland constructed, ceremonially, from

the braided tibias and fibulas of smaller mammals. My

eyelashes, thin and fair, invisible in the sun. Everyone

will say: Ryazantsev at times seems to be very exactly

the sum of her parts, not a gram more or less. I'm just

another girl. I'm not important in your life. Or any life.

Tanya Ryazantsev, "Ryazantsev"

*N*ever *has anyone made acting look so hard*, Gore Vidal said of Tanya Ryazantsev. *She's iconic as a statue and her acting is like one too*, said Orson Welles.[140] Critics of her performances find her

---

[140] or vice versa. I appreciate that my secretarial work is slipping as I get sucked into my own back story, for which I can only apologise, but just like the boy in *The Second Draft* (John Loose, 1999) my only way out is to go in, so to speak, even if the velocity of the narrative is slowing.

It was after five when I got to Nuneaton, so I started to run. I fell over taking a shortcut by the brook in Weddington and got mud on my jeans. By the time I got to school, giddy and breathless, the lights were on but the car park was nearly empty. I saw a cleaner through a class-room window, emptying a bin. I leaned into the gates. I was short of breath and felt vomit rising, but I swallowed it. For my whole journey I had been focused on the prize like Anthony Delon as the brilliant painter in *Absent All Doubt* (Kyra King, 1988), but I'd missed my cue, the stage

gauche, or bereft. Her husky voice and deadpan line readings earned her the nicknames *The Spy Who Came In With A Cold*, *The Undead Red*, and *Teak Tanya*. Her association with Andy Warhol only seemed to confirm, in many eyes, that she was not the real deal, but a posture, a face, a model more than an actor. But at home in the Soviet Union, and across Europe, she had a different profile as an able actress who performed in a wide array of credible productions. The feeling at home was that in America she was being woefully misused, like Mozart miming to

---

was empty, and the theatre was dark. Now what? I felt distinctly discombobulated, like I was experiencing the confusing side effects of time-travel. *You go away and come back, and folks look at you different, especially if you haven't changed*, Bob Cassidy (Robert Mitchum) says in *After A Fashion* (Mick Frazzo, 1979). I was back on a map that as recently as February, March, April, and May had been full of hot potential, when treasure might be around any corner, but now it was October and all I could see were empty holes that had been dug by someone who looked like me.

I was a couple of hours late, but it may as well have been twenty-five years. I could see, if I squinted, these gates still here in 2019, looking the same only with a layer of paint and other kids' memories all over them, like a video that gets taped over and still looks like the same plastic boxy object (only the information it carries is altered), or like the dementia-ridden eternal starchildren trying to jumpstart their ruined memory drives in *It Was Always The Future Even Then* (Beck Plenti, 2003). It hurt. This was *my* school, much more than the school I was now attending. Remember the couple fighting over the custody of their uploaded memories in *Nostalgia Ist Lux* (Freya Baumann, 1982)? Feeling that the sanctity of their own memory was poisoned by knowing that the other remembered it too? They don't want to share the good times, even from a distance. They're willing to yield property and money to each other, but will spend vast sums on having the other's memories wiped. They barter parts of their minds as if they're photo albums: *You can keep the Honeymoon memory. I want the Africa trip recollections. We'll alternate the kids' birthdays.*

a backing track on kids TV.[141]

[141] *like Mozart miming to a backing track on kids TV:* In 1985 Ryazantsev appeared on the Saturday morning show *Kidz* where, in full Wolfgang Amadeus Mozart drag she mimed to the songs *Rock Me Amadeus* by Falco and *I Heart Mozart* by Jenny Spinning. I knew nothing of Jenny Spinning's pop career (such as it was) when I first saw her in October 1994, when Channel 4 showed the previously banned *Toto* (Anna Kirsten, 1981), in which she plays the teenage prostitute trying to find her dog. October 19th, 1994 it would have been, one week before I turned sixteen, and I remember it because I was keeping a quite thorough diary at the time, and the next day was a red letter day: my parents would go away for the weekend, and I would make first and only return to Nuneaton.

On the night of October 19th, after *Toto* had finished, I had fallen into a fitful sleep, troubled by the recurring image of Jenny Spinning walking into bars and cafes in Dusseldorf with a photo of Toto from *The Wizard of Oz* (Victor Fleming, et al, 1939) asking *have you seen my dog?* In my dream I was in a future world in which it was possible to walk around my past like it was a kind of virtual reality. This power had limits. I could only go places I'd been before, and I wasn't allowed to see a younger version of myself. That would, I knew, be dangerous. I was also restricted to a street view. I could not enter buildings, or go off-road. I appreciate that this dream is nearly exactly the plot to the film *Learning and Growing with Gogol* (Jayne Wilson, 1994), in which a robot goddess from the future named Gogol Urth gives humanity this ability in order to encourage us to learn from our past mistakes and save ourselves from an impending environmental catastrophe (spoiler: we don't learn and grow, we just drift into navel-gazing nostalgia). But I didn't see this film until years later, I swear.

Anyway. That dream informed the trip to Nuneaton the next day, it coloured it, laid a thin gauze over the top of it. Never more so than when I had arrived at the school too late, and started to walk anywhere, nowhere, to, let's be honest, we know *exactly* where.

I headed south on the old after-school route. I walked past the Chase Hotel, named after the establishment in the farce *The Chase Hotel* (Basil Lloyd, 1931). We lived in the Chase when we first moved to town, before we found the house. *Hotel Boy*, I got called, for quite a while, and it wasn't because my peers had seen *enfant de l'hôtel* (Paul Cocard, 1971), it was because kids anywhere can turn any detail into an insult. I was the eight-year old new kid who lived in a hotel, so *oi, hotel boy* followed me down the corridors, across the playground, over the fields, and now I was a fifteen year-old new kid in another town, and I could see endless futures of being a new kid in new schools, new bedrooms, new jobs, forever *hotel boy.*

A group of kids I didn't recognise walked past. My local knowledge suddenly seemed out of date. Or, like Tommy New in *Newtown* (P.R. Jones, 1968), who becomes convinced that his family are imposters and his surroundings have been replaced, I felt like I was in a plausible dream reconstruction of Nuneaton, good enough for me not to notice, because I wanted to believe in it, but if I looked too closely at a bush or a drain or a crisp packet on the floor, the kind of thing that a few months ago I could have written a novel about, I'd see its lack of realistic detail and wake up. I started to doubt my certainties. Had my friends even been to school today? Yes, I'd seen Little Gav at the station. Or if it wasn't him, it was someone in the school uniform. Beyond that I knew little. Perhaps L was ill and hadn't been to school for some time, and that was the terrible thing that the letters from Jo and the Gavs had been avoiding saying.

I walked on, past a house on the corner where we had all sat once after school talking for hours, none of us wanting to be the first to leave, until, finally, L bravely stood up and said goodbye, way after dark, and I wondered *did that happen only once?* Looking closer I thought I must be confused in the drunk dark because the wall was six feet tall. But there was the cemetery opposite, where it always was, *the real dead centre of England*, I said to L once, and she snorted (did that exchange happen several times?). I looked closer at the wall and noticed that the brickwork up to about two feet off the ground was a different red than the bricks above. It *was* the same place: the wall had been built up since I left. As the only information I had about this house was that, firstly, we used to sit on the wall, and secondly, the wall had been made too tall to sit on at some point after this, I was drawn to the conclusion that the owners did it because of us. I imagined my friends continuing the old rituals after I left, a thought that was both reassuring and terrible. They couldn't sit on this wall again, but they'd have moved on, resourcefully slipping from inbetween space to inbetween space, drifting in and out of the nowheres that you might be able to film but they never show up on screen, they're such slick ghosts, like that small building next to the inactive train tracks, anonymous, graffitied, unnoticed. I know for a fact it's where David H lost his virginity, and probably dozens of other kids over the years too. But take a picture of it, and it would look like you were trying to shoot something else and you missed, its potencies untranslatable.

I walked on, passing Jo's house on the darker side of the street. I couldn't just knock on the door unannounced. Besides, we all know why I'm here (*We All Know Why I'm Here* [Peter

rial for a whole university course on notions of authorship, ownership,

Fitzgerald, 1956]). Anyway, I told myself, I could come back here in October 2000 or October 2020 and it will still be Jo's house. Her Mum would never move. So I walked on, towards the dead end at the end of the street where the active train tracks cut across. The railings had been painted, hadn't they? Maybe it was the boozy twilight playing tricks, or maybe I didn't really ever pay enough attention. And if I didn't notice, then who would bother? Like the teacher says about Tom in *Tom Keeps Score* (Barry Bishopsfield, 1967, reviewed on page 205), *If the Poet Laureate of Neither Here Nor There didn't write it in his book, it didn't happen. The lad sees everything.*

A container train trundled by, and it was still clattering and echoing overhead when I got down the ramp and into the tunnel, those large empty containers labelled with anonymous androgynous international names making it hard to imagine what the cargo was and where it was going. It felt like a prop train only there to make the dramatic rumbling metal thunder sound effect. I stood and breathed deeply, piss and mould, until the train had rattled away to nothing.

L's road was at the end of the tunnel. *Don't run*, I thought, don't hurry too much like the escapees in *Reich Tunnel* (Sedgewick Vance, 1971) who are caught at the last minute by the Nazis. I took a few steps, visualising what was ahead (the shock on L's face, my opening lines, etc), but a fuss ahead made me stop to listen. Footsteps were approaching the entrance to the tunnel ahead of me. They were up the ramp at the other end, so I couldn't see who it was.

First thought: It might be L.

No, she wouldn't be walking this way. What was this way? L wouldn't knock for Jo. They would have seen each other on the way home from school, if they'd wanted to. No, everything was in the other direction. L's gran's house, the House of Laser, the kebab shop. Town. Unless L had a new routine, new rituals, new friends. A new *friend.*

Second thought: It might be one of L's family. I didn't want to run into them. But what were the chances? Besides, it had been six months. *Surely no-one remembers my crimes now*, I thought, just like the heroic dissident Tammy in *Rebels Rebels* (Ari Hajsafi, 1990). He was shot in the back in the next scene by a bounty hunter who had pursued him for a decade. I cursed the lateness of the hour. A long shadow ahead of me started coming down the ramp, so just like Billy the Kid throwing the authorities off the trail by heading north to get to Mexico in *Young Guns II* (Geoff Murphy, 1990), I turned and headed back the way I came.

Hello, a voice shouted down the tunnel. I started to run but stumbled, cracking my kneecap into the concrete. The footsteps stopped, then started again, moving towards me quickly.

collaboration, the male gaze, and feminism. Warhol and director Paul Morrissey shot Super 8 footage of Ryazantsev in the Factory in 1966 and 1967, during her first stay in New York. This footage is reused in each of the three films to startlingly different ends.[142]

The Super 8 high-contrast black and white flattens Ryazantsev's cheekbones and renders her complexion as pallid as one of Warhol's own hairpieces.[143] Warhol was cruel to Ryazantsev during the shoot,

---

Are you alright? A voice asked. I scrambled to my feet and limped away as fast as I could. I didn't look back.

[142] *different ends:* I did a big loop to lose my pursuer, and by the time I stopped running I was on Poanne Pingway. I had to think. I couldn't just march up to L's front door. I had to be more methodical. I hiccupped into the damp air and rubbed my knee. Sticky blood showed through my jeans.

I'd work my way in slowly, peering in at the places L might be, if she wasn't at home. I'd minimise the chances of parental interference that way. *No-one understands the world better than teenagers,* someone says at one point in *Romy and Julian* (Valerie Starque, 1991), *adults know too much and they forget what's important.*

I walked past L's gran's house. All the lights were off. The swings in the small park behind L's gran's house, where I'd watched L and David H share a cigarette once, were empty. The House of Laser was round the corner from that. I hit the top of the high street and tried to gauge my reflection in a car window. I had mud and blood on me, but the darkness would help me there. My hair wasn't behaving, but it never did. *It's more about attitude than clothes,* cool kid Rick (Dexter Fletcher) says in *Bodies* (Chris Thompson, 1988). I sucked in my cheeks and nodded at myself.

[143] *flattens, pallid: We should have seen this coming,* one of the characters says in *Plot Twist* (Dav Burley, 1960). In the dark I thought I'd just turned a street too early. But I limped past where I thought I was going (my knee was throbbing now, and seizing up). I saw a familiar row of shops in the right place, walked back, and I then knew. *My soothsaying has proved, unfortunately, correct,* as the soothsayer (Nicol Williamson) says in *The Soothsayer* (Nigel Roberts, 1977). The

making her pose awkwardly for hours even when there was no camera

House of Laser was gone. It was now a supermarket. I'd foreseen it the last time I'd been inside those high black walls, but I was still shocked. *There's no surprise bigger than finding out something you already knew,* Bob says in *The Country According To Bob* (Bob Thommass, 1990).

The House of Laser had been in the shell of the old ballroom, and while you could argue that wasn't the most respectful use of the grand old place, at least it had still been upright. It was tatty and sad outside, but it was *there*. We'd run around inside like wartime kids in a bombed-out cinema, but there had always been the possibility of a resurrection. But now they'd knocked the whole thing down to put the supermarket up. In six months? Maybe I had been gone longer. When was I? How much time had I wasted? I had to move. I'd use the bathroom inside, fix my knee, steal a bottle of vermouth (as a protest against the building, and to replace the gift for L that I'd already consumed), and finish my mission.

I still had hiccups, and I held my breath as I went through the sliding doors. The teenage cashier was reading a magazine, and didn't look up. I wondered whether not breathing in this compromised reality rendered me invisible, like Donqui in *les enfants rouges dansants de la terre* (Sylvie Robert, 1981). But then an older lady employee with a broom said *we're closing in five minutes*, and when I didn't respond, she followed me to shout after me *five minutes*, which to me meant that I had five minutes, whatever that meant here and now, but her tone seemed to imply that I was supposed to turn around and leave immediately, but I walked on, deeper into the store. I found a bottle of vermouth, held it in the crook of my arm, slipped into a toilet with an illustration of a wheelchair on it, and closed the door

It was pitch black. I breathed deeply. Urine cake and bleach. Of all the things they could have put here. A supermarket. I couldn't find the light switch, and in the dark I imagined any number of rooms from different times and places that I might be in (a room as cavernous as the Vatican filled with children at a ball dancing in the black, or an orchard filled with hand carved wooden trees and felt grass, like *Opulence* (Josef von Sternberg, 1937), or a large theatre at the end of the 19th Century where a magician does a futuristic trick, like *The Mesmer* (Louis Grenier, 1894), or in a cabin at altitude (*Behold The Awesome Mountain,* Dexter Himmler, 1938), or a bar in Mexico City (*Donna, Or The Power Of Constant Thought,* Hermoso Equipo, 1951), or maybe it was Cairo in 1969 or Oklahoma in 1966 or Hollywood in 1961, or somewhere closer because there was a smell that reminded me of an old teacher, no, it was the boxy room with no window and a curtain for a door, I pictured playing cards with my Italian mother but she's not Italian (that's *Scala Quaranta,* Beppe Nona, 1963), then a kitchen with a German mother interrogating her children (that's… wait, it's on the tip of my tongue), then I could feel shouts through the floor, it must have been the warehouse part of the supermarket but it sounded like there was a sporting event or a war, a boxing match, no, I remember Big Gav telling me that there was wrestling in the seventies round here it throbbed in the walls and I could feel it, the shouts of smoking men, and I realised I was crying because I never believed Big Gav when he told me those stories about his Dad in the ring, *I'm so sorry Big Gav,* maybe, I thought, I could go and knock on his door, and his Mum would have fish and chips for us and we'd play a board game like it's 1991 or 1992 and I'd sleep on his bedroom floor and wake up and it would be 1991 or 1992, and I'd know that this particular sequence could be changed with different steps just like the basement time portal in *Different Steps* (Joseph Resnick, 1954), and I could save L and myself from this situation, when really what I needed was to be *there* in the toilet and *then* in the toilet, getting my head on straight. This was the moment before the moment of truth, the part where I looked hard in the mirror at myself, and then went and won the prize, defeated the dragon, saved the girl.

I groped for a light switch. Click. I was in a small room with a toilet, a handrail, a sink, a dryer.

No mirror.

I thought about Banshee in *Sinewave Trellis* (Whip Snyder, 1990) who keeps photos of every bathroom they've ever used in a photo album and I wondered how many I'd ever been in. Were any important? I felt that it was too late for me to start keeping a tally then (although now I'm older I would have appreciated if I had).

I don't want to recount the whole momentous trip, that would be a vanity, like the theatre director in *Synecdoche, New York* (Charlie Kaufman, 2008) who attempts to create a set to house a play of his entire life. I'll skip the prescient visions I had about how Nuneaton would change in the future (how, for example, did I know that they would build a large glass justice building in the early 21$_{st}$ century that looked just like the hotel in *Edifice 2020* [Juan Pavon, 1985]?), and fast-forward through the next minutes, when various time-lines seemed to converge in one space, and in my inspired state I could see a kind of double vision of 1994 and every other year, and I was escorted from the premises by a store detective and the older lady employee.

She said that if I wasn't planning on stealing the vermouth then why did I take it into the toilet, and anyway, I'd be committing a worse crime by trying to buy it, as I was underage and

I'd incriminate the young cashier, and *I didn't want that on my conscience, did I?* She grinned at me, her smug satisfaction reminiscent of the enemy lawyer after he makes what he thinks is a watertight closing statement in *The Defense Rests* (Stark Lucie, 1957). I was pulled by the elbow through the sliding doors (the teenage cashier looked up this time, finally noticing me, no doubt because I'd stopped holding my breath) and into the street. They stood in the doorway, arms crossed, the sliding doors trying to close every few seconds. The detective wore an expression that let me know that his preferred approach would have been less gentle. He looked familiar. Had he been tailing me for a while? Was he waiting for me when I got off the train? Was he following me to make sure I didn't commit some kind of time crime and erase a slice of history while I was travelling back to 1993 from 1994? (And was this what *M. Jainet's Eternal Zigzag* [François Lepin Eziot and Françoise Lepin Eziot, 1941] was actually about?) I tried to memorize his face for future or past reference.

Come on son, the lady said. *You look like you've got somewhere better to be.* She was right, of course, on many fronts. I thanked her for her timely reminder, and walked away, in a straight line towards the inevitable. No fear now, no flanking manoeuvres, no tricks. Like the nun walking into heaven in *What Have I Been Waiting For?* (Nancy Huffman, 2006) I was heading for something that I'd been circling for what felt like forever. *It was always meant to be, I always knew it,* she says, when her epic hike leaves her on the doorstep to St. Peter's Gate, and her paperwork proves to be in order. *Why didn't I come sooner?* To which an admin assistant to St Peter replies, gently and with humour, *you had other things to do first. Your timing was always going to be perfect.*

It was suddenly quite obvious that my timing was always going to be perfect. A calm took over me as I walked through the dark and empty pedestrianised town centre, my breath slowing to match every five steps. Any time anxiety I had was falling away, as if I was walking into the past like the Navajo elders who discover a time machine in *Night Follows Day, Which Is After Night* (Johnson Michael Nighthorse, 2022) and know that they can save their ancestors. I had flashes of the future as I walked, a symptom of going backwards, I suppose. As I walked past Maddy's, the place that underage drinkers could get served, I could see my friends at sixteen and seventeen, drinking without me. But these glimpsed glory years, which might have previously caused me great sadness because I wasn't there and wouldn't be there, now drifted by gently. There were other pictures, bigger ones. I sniffed in the cold, and some knowledge crept up and

in the room, and not letting her eat.[144] This isn't obvious when watching

---

crawled all over me: one day Maddy's would be turned into a series of less and less successful
pub and bar enterprises, before finally dying and becoming flats. Urban zen. One day we'd all
die and become flats. Like all truths this was both startlingly novel and completely obvious, all at
once.

I turned onto the ring road and into a breeze. My stomach started to settle and my
legs were more solid again. The traffic moved clockwise around the town and I walked the other
way, past a shop that I used to go to, but don't look for it it's not there (*Don't Look For It It's Not
There* [Alma Bebey, 1987]), on past the closed library, where a sign in the window said *Librarian
of the Year Ms Josie Werner.* She looked like a Golden Age film star or one of my old teachers.
I breathed again, cold in, warm out, cold in. I was so close. I realised I'd always been heading
towards L's, every day of my life, but never quite getting there, and here I was, finally arriving, finally being born years after my birth. There was the roundabout where the dead centre of England
sign used to be, but now in October 1994 it was covered in flowers, a circular garden that no-one
could visit. But I knew I should cross the road to it, and take a ceremonial knee, acknowledging
the true centre of the country or mourning its diminished status, whichever it was. I'd soak up
some ley line power or I'd offer a prayer to a false god. Either way, I'd rest a few seconds and
slow my heart. I was nearly sober now, I was sure.

When the traffic thinned I ran across the road and onto the green island. I heard a skid,
a car horn, and a shout behind me. I dived into a pile of lavender where I was quickly invisible,
holding my breath in the middle of the roundabout in the middle of, maybe, depending on who
you believe, the dead centre of England, and I just wanted to close my eyes for a second before I
went on to the final climactic scene.

[144] *not letting her eat:* I know what you're thinking: *hasn't Mark seen the Greek tragedy courtroom drama with the Latin name* Mea Culpa *(Max Ophüls, 1955)? In which brilliant prosecutor
Jim French (James Mason) is on the verge of putting away half of a corrupt City Hall when he is
discredited by an indiscretion from his past that has been discovered?* (Key line: *don't you see,
Dolly. Now everyone knows. I'm no better than them.*) *Can't Mark see that he is Jim French, ac-
cusing Andy of bad behaviour with regard to Tanya whilst forgetting his own with L?* I know. *Mea
culpa.* I'm obscuring her even while I talk about her, relegating her to that role with no agency,
the muse. I'm sucking her dry and licking what's left off my fingers. I'm burying her voiceless in

the original film *Andy Warhol Presents: Ryazantsev* (1970). This film is my own story.

But I'm way ahead of you. I'd like to think, and I hope that this document supports it, that our relationship is more like a tentative collaboration, in which both might take a turn at any point as director. It's not anything as tacky as a classic love story, both L and myself are too clever for that. But my interest in L has lasted a little bit longer than Andy's with Tanya Ryazantsev, I think we can agree. Besides, Jim French *was* better than *them*. But I digress from my digression:

I woke up. I was on the roundabout. I don't know how long I'd been there, but it was now completely dark. I got up and ran across the road, through the churchyard, past the old stones and started to sprint when I hit the path. I ran past the large Justice building, and for a moment it seemed to flicker and be a garage again with an empty car park, just like it used to be, but I couldn't think about that now. With no strategy I came straight down her road, and stopped at the front gate. My heart was a few strides ahead of me. When I turned to look at the door it was already open, and legs were coming down the stairs, black trousers, then red shirt, our school uniform, then L's head. She stopped at the bottom of the stairs when she saw me. She looked back down the hallway behind her then came out onto the step holding the door closed behind her back.

What are you doing here, she said.

I don't know, I said.

I can't invite you in, she said.

I know, I said.

I think I-, she said.

-Shh, that's all in the past, I said. I stepped towards her. She took my face in her hands and finally it happened. She kissed me perfectly like van Veen and Ada in *Ada or Ardor* (Peter Weir, 1989) or Eve and her clone in *Eden* (Susan East, 2013). I thought, as William Shakespeare said, or was it Dennis Hopper in *True Romance* (Tony Scott, 1993) *Mmm ... she does taste like peaches,* even though she didn't, not quite. And then quickly it was done and she leaned back and looked at my face, still holding it in her sleeves, she looked into my eyes and said words I'll never forget just like in *Words I'll Never Forget* (Fatima Lahti, 1962): *I never wanted to get you in trouble with the McGintys,* she said.

Except her lips didn't move.

I was dizzy.

Who are the McGinty's?, I wanted to say. Instead I heard my voice saying *don't you*

characteristic of Warhol films of the time in its stark simplicity, with Ry-

worry about those boys they're just hoodlums.

I always wanted you to love me, Jake, she said, and again, her lips didn't move. She began to look confused now.

I always did, my mouth said, against my wishes. Panic began to set into her face, her eyes searched mine, and I must have looked panicked too, because I was starting to realise what was going on, the words coming from our mouths were beginning to make sense to me, because I knew them. She looked through me, frozen still like a paused tape and I knew I was in the middle of a dream sequence, that this wasn't happening, there was no kiss, I was still asleep drunk on the roundabout, waking up and I was trying and trying to hold onto the dream. The scene wasn't real, it was not ours, it was borrowed from *Malignant Ranch* (Tom Bach, 1957). Word for word.

I tried to say something, but nothing came out. So I tried to remember the next line from *Malignant Ranch.*

And that's why I had to go, I heard myself say, just like in that film, and at this L began to move again, as if the tape had been unpaused. She stepped forward to put a hand on my chest just like the script says, and she began to talk with a different tone, a different voice, and now she was using borrowed grown-up language to explain that this wasn't working, that we both needed space, and it wasn't until I said *I don't know what space means* that I became aware that I was now echoing Victor Mature's line in *Humanity Farm* (L.C. Arnold, 1956), when told by a Martian diplomat, in kind calm words, that mankind is so bereft of sense that it should euthanize itself for the good of all mankind. The streetlights seemed to dim a little, as if to mark the end of an act, but I kept talking, trying to prolong the scene, even though an alarm was rising in my head, and had been for some time now (when did I first notice it?), an alarm that grew louder and louder, telling me more and more clearly that I was dreaming. I reached out to touch L's arm but I was too far away. If I could hold the details of the surroundings in, hold her face in, cement our postures, mark our marks, I might have prolonged the moment, this fraudulent dream moment, kept it in my brain, a fake kiss remembered as a real one, but it was sliding away. I tried some dialogue, the best I could remember, Cary Grant at the end of *The Awful Truth* (Leo McCarey, 1937) in the moments before his and his wife's (Irene Dunne) divorce is finalised. He is slowly realising that they could yet get back together, something that she already seems to know: *You're wrong about things being different because they're not the same.* I said, just like Grant. *Things are different except in a different way. You're still the same, only I've been a fool... but I'm not now ...* The scene receded

azantsev captured on Super 8 film posing against a series of backdrops.

almost completely, Technicolor fading to white, and I knew I was waking up, grass in my mouth, I focused on the details of my soliloquy, I *was* Cary Grant: *so long as I'm different don't you think that... well maybe things could be the same again... only a little different, huh?* I said, but I was almost awake now, I could hear the traffic, but to try and linger longer I began to recite names of roads, facts, stats, numbers, if I could list the solid truths of this world then maybe this construct would survive, because numbers are real. *Population 79,641 making this town the largest town in Warwickshire, Ordnance Survey grid reference SP361918, 9 miles north of Cov, 20 miles east of Brum*, these were facts that meant I was here and this was real, what other stats could I remember, but I was waking up now, and if I woke up then I knew I had to go back to my new home which wasn't here, *hold on, stay asleep stay asleep population 79 Ordnance Survey grid reference oh no I'm smelling lavender I'm awake but if I keep my eyes closed I won't be on this roundabout this totem the dead centre of England it won't be five am but the first train is coming soon dead leg dead fingers dead cold bye bullseye see ya L see ya everyone*

  For those not following along, that part was a dream sequence, as Mel Brooks says at one point in *History of the World, Part One* (Mel Brooks, 1981). I don't think that I'm legally bound at this point to state that L and I have never kissed, but I feel duty bound: after falling asleep on the roundabout, I stayed asleep on the roundabout. But, like Sandy Omaha says in *Empty Beaches* (Hal Calistan, 1993), *some things are truthier than truth. And that's the truth.* So I'm including the above detour as a kind of suggestive placeholder. Cut to the roundabout, Mark waking up:

  Now a man was standing over me.

  You ok, son, he said. I sat up slowly. My back was stiff. My head was a brick. My mouth was polystyrene.

  I'm surprised you can sleep with all the traffic, he said. I looked around. Cars circled us clockwise. I sat on flattened daffodils.

  I'm sorry, I said.

  Come on, he said, pulling me to my feet. *Do you live round here?*

  I looked at him.

  Do you hear me, son?

  I blinked.

  Hello. Can you hear me? Do you live round here?

Warhol, the story goes, lost interest in the star long before he'd finished shooting her, passing the film project onto Factory associate Morrissey. He pieced this footage together belatedly in 1970 to show at the Manhattan Film Festival that year. It was billed as *Andy Warhol Presents: Ryazantsev*, with the final film edited by Morrissey, who was given a director credit. Characteristically perhaps, Warhol found the film to be among the finest work that he himself ever produced. Just like many of the silk screens produced by assistants that Warhol never laid a hand on, his essence is often most present in the work of others.

Years later, another Factory regular David Salle made a new version (known as *Andy Warhol's Ryazantsev*) which included shots from a second camera. This footage, in colour, is mostly focused on Warhol as he directs Tanya, and underlines some of her discomfort. Warhol doesn't talk *to* her but *about* her, saying things like *won't somebody do something about her hair*, or *she doesn't know how to pose on camera*. Even so, a narrative emerges of Tanya learning from Andy how to be seen, and by the end they can be seen exchanging jokes.

The original rushes were passed to Ryazantsev by a member of Warhol's inner circle (without Warhol's permission). She made a new edit, which included extended sequences from the original shoot showing Warhol complaining about Ryazantsev's performance, and about food, and money. The effect is unsettling, especially when Warhol

I shook my head.

Lucky lad, he said. *Let's get you on your way, then.*

makes disparaging remarks about Ryazantsev's body. His bitchy misogyny is on full display, notably when Ryazantsev poses with her hands over her eyes and Warhol can be heard saying, from behind the camera *she has hands like an old man. Aren't they ugly?* In response Ryazantsev pokes her tongue out. In the original film, as put together by Morrissey, this sequence has no sound except for a minimal piano played by John Cale. In that version, Ryazantsev's gesture appears flirty and playful, but with the original sound recording included and the dialogue added back in, it seems more like defiance in the face of a bully.

Ryazantsev never complained directly about Warhol. In interviews she talked about him like he was a crotchety old aunt, someone to whom she was loyal despite her annoyances. But she was firm on certain things: *I was not discovered by Warhol*, Ryazantsev said. *He only ever discovered himself.*[145]

---

[145] *discovered himself.* By accident or design (and I often speculate which, because maybe I'm like the lucky general in *By Accident or Design* [Tom Collins, 1956] who inadvertently wins a war because his cowardly attempts to escape the battlefield lead his pursuing enemies to their defeat, washed away in a freak storm) Nuneaton *went dark* to me after my drunken visit.

I was lucky, in a way. My roundabout humiliation was almost entirely without witnesses, so much so that I sometimes wonder if this night ever happened, or whether it is a borrowed embarrassment, like the love android in *All My Dreams Are Second-Hand* (Olga Petrova, 1971) who says *most of our desires are facsimiles of more imaginative creatures, why not our nightmares?* But I knew one thing: like Billy in *Billy Liar* (John Schlesinger, 1963), destiny had been there for the taking, and I had backed down. I decided that L would go her way and I mine.

It's hard sometimes to remember the absoluteness of exile in times before the internet. For about a decade from early 1994 onwards, L was a figment of my imagination. I had no photo updates, no messages, no reports. I examined the paltry evidence I had to hand (a piece of her geography homework that had fallen out of her bag on a walk home once, which included an elaborate doodle that I checked against a book of symbols from the library, with no obvious conclusions) and wondered if she was real. It was hard to imagine what kind of grown-up she might be. Jo kept writing to me for almost a year, but after my secret Nuneaton trip my enthusiasm had waned, and besides, there was little of note in my new life worth reporting. I went from being a bad pen-pal to no pen-pal at all. Eventually Jo moved a few times, and so did I, and that was that. We lost contact, and the Midlands may as well not have been there, like the outlying planets that get cut off from the the intergalactic community in *Distant Suns* (Juan Takeshi, 1966).

A decade after leaving Nuneaton, I left England. I moved to America to work, if somewhat peripherally, in the film industry. Maybe being somewhere new made me think of the old place, like Tandy in *Paradise* (Theo Brandt, 1957) who moves to the home of her dreams and believes she is being haunted by dead relatives who were poor their entire lives. By now it was the 21st century, and there was the internet, and the time/space void between then/there and now/here was bridged. Jo and I found each other online. She sent me her new address, in a flat in Cov, where she lived with an older man she didn't really like. I tentatively asked about some of our mutual friends, but we both avoided talking about you-know-who. Jo wanted to know about America, so I told her, in a series of emails.

America was like the films I'd seen, only weirder and less familiar. I bought Jo a postcard with Travis Bickle on it, emailed her to tell her I'd bought it, but didn't send it. I liked walking around in New York, overwhelmed by the hundreds of tiny ways in which things in America were different to things in England (whereas the longer I have spent here now I live here, the more I notice the ways in which they are the same), and felt on high alert all day.

I fell asleep early and well each night. In a new country, a trip to a shop to buy food is as fantastical as a trip to a museum or gallery. I went to Safeway, a shop with the same name as one in England, but different. The labels on the products were confusing because they evoked products I thought I knew, but didn't. They used words I knew, like *sausage* or *gravy*, but the pictures were not ones that looked like sausage or gravy. These tiny differences were amplified by the bored comfort with which everyone around me was filling their baskets. Here and there were snatches of familiarity: certain crisp packets looked the same. I walked to the back of the store and back to the front again before I began shopping, vaguely reading words as I went. Details began to accumulate like a poem. I saw the name of my old head teacher on the label of some

deliberately large on the poster, as if to draw attention to the artificiality

of the idea of eliciting a *real* Tanya from the compromised work. (*They

are like fingers holding my name in place,* she said at the premiere when

---

tinned tomatoes, the name of my geography teacher on a tin of sardines. An entire aisle filled up with products made by a company with the same name as the one teacher that L and I shared. I walked faster, picking out names everywhere, and they were getting more pertinent, they were arrowing in on a bullseye with L at the centre: chocolate bars made by a company whose name was the same as a kid who lived on her street, then a breakfast cereal that shared the name of L's street. I became convinced that I'd reached the edge of the world's imagination, that I was at a point where any new things could only be made for me by repurposing previous ones, and they would race past me in a blur, like the backgrounds in an old Warner Bros. cartoon (think *Bunny on the Moon* (1949), in which Bugs, running away from the aliens, notices the purple trees he keeps running past are repeating. He turns to face the camera and says *Hey, draw me some more variety, will ya? A bunny gets bored.* A large hand appears, and quickly paints in a beautiful and diverse scene. Bugs stops, says *Wow*, and the aliens catch him and put him in a prison cell with no window.). At the very back of the store there was a row of fridges. A woman next to me hooked her basket into her elbow nook, said *excuse me*, and pulled open the fridge door. As she struggled to get a carton of milk into her basket, I held the door for her. She looked at me. *Thank you,* she said. I smiled and looked into her eyes. They were L's eyes, but older. I thought of Damo Shinmi in *Her Eyes In His Face* (Todd Berryman, 1971) when he tries to kill a stranger who has eyes remarkably like his dead mother. This woman seemed to feel a significance too, as she looked back at me, smiling. We stood there looking at each other. I wanted to speak, but I didn't want to break the moment. I imagined forward: she and I would drop our baskets and go and get a drink, and then another, repeating over and over that we couldn't believe the coincidence that we'd run into each other on the other side of the world, *how long has it been, a year, five years, ten years* she'd say, *fourteen this July,* I'd say, and then finally in a silent moment she'd look at me and—

The woman coughed.

Honey... you should probably close the door. Keep the cold in, she said, and turned away, looking at her list.

I wrote all of this to Jo, except the part about L's eyes. I somehow knew I should leave that out.

asked about the oversized quotation marks, *they have to be big otherwise I might run away*). It was shown only once, at the *Tic Toc* club in New York on Halloween, 1978. Before the show, Ryazantsev gave a speech in which she said that too many actresses were objectified by directors, placed in compromising positions, and forced into uncomfortable nudity. Performers, she went on, must seize opportunities to reclaim their art and their bodies wherever possible. That this new version of the film contained more naked Tanya than the other two surprised many in the audience that night. *It's my nudity in this film, not theirs*, she said. *I'm sharing it. It's not being stolen from me by some creep hiding in the bushes.*

In an interview around the same time, she addressed the fact that she wasn't taken seriously in America:

I'm like Yoko Ono. In the West they laugh at her because she seems like this avant-garde joke. As if she doesn't understand that screaming on stage or being naked might be funny somehow. As if everyone else has a sense of humour except her. No-one realises that she is Andy Kaufman. And I am too.[146]

＊＊＊

Hollywood is filled with foreign actors whose exoticism, rather than their skill, is a perfect fit for American cinema. Ryazantsev seemed

---

[146] *Village Voice*, November 1979.

poised to become one of them, but apparently wasn't that interested. She starred in only a handful of films in America, and even then seemed to choose her projects erratically. She supposedly turned down many heavyweight directors over the years, only to say yes to low-brow efforts like the made-for-TV John Milius flick *Death Or Death*—the kind of work, critics seem to feel, that betrayed her talent, or confirmed her lack of it. In an interview with George Plimpton in 1985 she said:

> *There is still an idea that, despite our better judgement,*
> *we'd all be famous and talented if we could. We'd swap*
> *everything to be able to cry like Meryl Streep or make*
> *a passing shot like Arthur Ashe, and more importantly,*
> *to be famous like them. And even if we don't want to be*
> *President, or on television, we feel sorry for those that*
> *have a piece of fame, and then after a while, don't have it*
> *any more.*[147]

***

Ryazantsev returned to Russia in 1990 to *walk the countryside and breathe the air. That is all.* If her departure from cinema threatens to lend a Garboesque tint to her narrative, a kind of look-at-me-don't-look-at-me glamour, the robust *quietness* of her post-fame life quickly mutes such fancy. Garbo quit the screen because she cared about how she looked, Ryazantsev because she couldn't care less. She gave an inter-

---

[147] *Interview,* March 1985.

view for Russian television in 1991 to explain her exile. She appears in shadow, and with her voice disguised, like a witness being interviewed about a violent crime. This appearance fuelled rumours that Ryazant-sev had aged dramatically, or had changed her appearance with several surgeries. Some speculated that this wasn't her at all, but a double, and that Ryazantsev wasn't in the country or had even died. Few seemed to consider the idea that she just might have thought it was funny.[148] The interviewer asks her why she is retiring from acting. She says:

> Sometimes it feels like we're just stringing things along, waiting for meaning, waiting for happiness, waiting for something. But why wait? Do something else! It's all make believe anyway. These films that people care about so much, it's all pretend. Meaningless. Some idiot wrote it from his own head then boom, millions of dollars and millions more words are written about it. That doesn't mean it is worth any more than some idea you had in your head when you were walking in the woods or shop-ping or sitting on the toilet. A film that costs a million dollars and has Burt Reynolds or Kim Basinger in it is no better than the dream you had last night. Even if you don't remember your dream, or you do, and it was dull. Or maybe especially if you don't remember it, or it was

[148] *When a woman tells a good joke, no-one's first thought is that she wrote it, and is therefore a good writer and a good comedian. Least of all other women. (Interview,* March 1985)

dull.

When the interviewer asks how she will fill her days, she says:

I refer you to my previous comments...gardening is more important than cinema. Cinema is like a boy who was in my class at school whose name I don't remember.

The interviewer is exasperated. He doesn't understand why anyone would walk away from the glamorous life. *Won't you miss it? Being in the middle of everything?*

In the middle of what? Attention is just pretend. There is no middle of everything...maybe there is a middle of something that is an equal shape, like the sphere of an orange, or...look at a map of France maybe or Colorado or Wyoming, they have a middle, they're almost squares... but remember, maps are flat...abstractions...of a globe anyway...if there is a middle of everything I'm more likely to find it digging in my garden than in Hollywood.

***

In the final shot of the film that sealed her fame across Communist Eastern Europe, дневник моего заключительного года (*Diary Of My Final Year*, Lev Mikhailov, 1955) the girlish Ryazantsev conjures a frown so delicately indecisive that the viewer feels tricked; its ambivalence strikes a contrast with the repeated mantra of her inner monologue, *You have to love yourself before you can hate anybody else, you have to love yourself before you can hate anybody else...* which spins ever onwards, until the words collide on the soundtrack, overlapping, and splitting, much like Alvin Lucier's sound piece *I Am Sitting In A Room*. The words become hollow and meaningless in repetition, and the young actress smiles as the words break down into lumpy syllables. *The more I talk, the less I say,* she says. Warhol, you'd guess, might relate.

ANDY WARHOL PRESENTS: *RYAZANTSEV*

Directed by Paul Morrissey. Produced by Andy Warhol. Written by Paul Morrissey. Starring Tanya Ryazantsev, Paul America, Joe Dallesandro, Gerard Malanga. Factory Films Release Date: Oct 1970 (US). 79 mins, Tagline: Don't Stare.

ANDY WARHOL'S *RYAZANTSEV*

Directed by David Salle. Produced by Andy Warhol, David Salle. Written by David Salle, Tanya Ryazantsev. Starring Tanya Ryazantsev, Andy Warhol, Paul America, Joe Dallesandro, Gerard Malanga, Billy Name. Factory Films. 88 mins. Release date: June 1976 (US) Tagline: Yes. No. Maybe Not.[149]

---

[149] *Yes. No. Maybe Not...* was a catchphrase used by Factory regulars to let one another know that their judgement may have been chemically impaired. Someone might ask *have you seen Nico?* Or *Do you like Andy's new work* or *what about Lou's new song?* And the reply would be *Yes. No. Maybe Not.* Meaning: *I have no idea. I'm high.* In 2010 Gunther Patnik used it as the title for a book about inner circle codes among celebrities in the age of social media. In his introduction, he talked about how *now we are all famous, we don't even need to communicate as much as bear witness to one another's performances. Even our deaths become, through social media, an ever-evolving sentimental play.* Patnik also points out that the name *Facebook* is another Warhol reference. At the height of his fame, a certain Manhattan restaurant would only let in patrons who had had posed for a Warhol Polaroid. The Polaroids were kept at the door in an album known as *the Facebook.* It was a place only for the chosen few.

Jo and I continued to write emails to each other, and we also connected on various so-cial media sites and message boards, usually with pseudonyms. She'd argue with a stranger about anything, and then I'd adopt a counter-position, whatever she said. That was our game. Harrison Ford would improve any film. *Oh no he wouldn't.* Cats are geniuses. *Oh no they aren't.* Racism is bad. *You're wrong and here's why.* One or other of us would get suspended or kicked off one place, and we'd go to another, making new virtual friends and enemies as we went, like the play-ful octogenarian grifters causing havoc across Texas in *Eighty To Life* (Paul Mazursky, 1987).

Occasionally we'd bump into an old friend online. As the networks became more popular and codified, we saw even more. Myspace, Frendy, Netwerk, Kreed, Facebook. The fantastical androgynous amorphous pseudonyms fell away, more mundane versions of ourselves stepped forward, and there were many of my old school friends, emerging from the shadows. We quickly collected one another like stickers for an album, exchanged the occasional comment about the old days and what we're doing now, sharing anecdotes about a particular teacher, many of which, I was disappointed to discover, my peers didn't remember properly.

At this point it is easy to forget the feverish early excitement of that particular part of the internet age. We're now embedded in it, we're used to our online lives, and our online deaths. At least four of my school friends on Facebook have passed away. Their profile pictures are frozen tributes to themselves, not as I remember them, but at a point between 2007 (when the site began) and now. Their last status updates serve as epitaphs. A girl in my English class (cancer): *Surprise breakfast in bed from hubby. So lucky.* A boy whose head obscured L from me in science (car accident): *What's with this government?* And David H (unnamed disease): *Saw this video and had to share.* Just a few hours of life undocumented between the choice to share these thoughts and death.

I'd not seen David H for nearly two decades when he died. Our online relationship was perfunctory: I sent him a friend request in 2008. He accepted a few days later, and that was that. I didn't need any more from him, and perhaps he felt the same. Maybe, like a pop culture reference in a contemporary film like *Guardians of the Galaxy* (James Gunn, 2014), the moment of recogni-tion was enough: *Ha. I remember that.* Anyway, David H, that ambassador to the outer reaches of taste whose contraband (and there is a reason that illegal copies of records and films are called *pirated*) blew our young brains apart, had at a certain point, stopped going *there.* He had a list of his favourite films and records on his profile page, but there was nothing newer than, I noted with precision, September 2001. It was as if some catastrophic event had occurred that month (He got a real job? Became a father? Family death?) that took his taste for adventure away, and ever since he'd been coasting on yesterday's refried YouTube clips.

Many other friends may be dead too. Or at least inactive. Surely Facebook now has enough raw footage that nothing new need ever be shown on the vampirically-named feed. Old status updates about traffic, celebrity deaths, sporting occasions, birthdays, family holidays, are numerous enough that they can be cycled in or out when appropriate. Is that photo of your friend's Christmas tree from this year? Or 2009? Or 2020? Is their *I live this weather* update from now, yesterday, or last month? Does it refer to today's bright sun or the wet October just past? Or something else, somewhere else? And is *live* a typo? There is enough hyperbolic language online to be recycled indefinitely, to be posted on our behalf as appropriate commentary on even the most unforeseen cataclysmic event. This, in its way, is comforting, and explains the becalming appeal of this safe online suburb, the fridge that fills itself.

I know, I'm stalling. I know what you're waiting for. But it's coming, here at the end, in an extra sequence enjoyed only by those who stay after the credits and the ushers who clean up the popcorn. Here goes (*Here Goes* [B.F.Kinji, 1961].):

One day L showed up. Not in plain sight. But like the doppelgänger of himself that Jake Gyllenhaal spots as an extra in a film in *Enemy* (Denis Villeneuve, 2013), she appeared in a blink-and-you'll-miss-it-cameo, in a comment on Little Gav's page. He posted a picture of his two daughters. Underneath someone wrote a comment. *So Cute*, and I thought immediately of Fairuza Balk in *So Cute* (Walter Murch, 1990). (In one science class [I could dig out the date, I wrote about it in my journal] I complimented L's choker and said it was like the girl in *So Cute*.) The author of the comment was someone called Bethany Blue, clearly a false name. L's middle name was Bethany. The profile picture, a flag of a European country where there had recently been a terrorist attack, told me little. I immediately sent a friend request. When she hadn't accepted an hour later I sent her a message. *Hey, remember me? Hope you're well, X.* The next day I considered the situation and wrote again. My profile had a false name too, and although my identity was quite clear to anyone who knew me as well as L, she might not investigate too far. (Ah, here it is. April 4th, 1993. That's the day I compared L's choker to Fairuza Balk's in *Valmont* [Milos Forman, 1989].)

I wrote: *Hey L. It's M. I understand that things between us got a bit strange, but I want*

Directed by Tanya Ryazantsev. Produced by John Johnson, Tia Encarta.

Written by Tanya Ryazantsev. Starring Tanya Ryazantsev, Andy Warhol.

Godless Films. 65minsRelease Date: Oct 1978 (US).

Tagline: Please Don't Contact Me Again.[150]

to assure you that my intentions are innocent. I'm just hoping to catch up and see how you are. Regards. Concerned about the legality of my approach (internet search: *do restraining orders expire?*) I considered withdrawing my message, and enjoyed the subsequent delicious heat of realising that it was too late. I didn't hear anything, but played it cool for three days. Then I sent another message, this time asking no questions, just telling her what I'd been up to for so many years. My film work, my writing, the travelling, living in America, and so on. An open-hearted confessional, like the letter from the innocent man in prison in *She Brings The Rain* (Gerd Möller, 1971). That letter ended up falling off a truck and into a ditch. I trusted that my message would fare better. I thought perhaps that this might be too long-winded, a bit much. So I sent another message immediately, telling her that I didn't want to go on about it, but I'd thought of her many times.

[150] *please don't contact me again:* Soon after my second, more direct message, I got a response: *Oh hey. If I wanted to be in touch with you I would rite back. I don't appreciate messages from unknown senders, especially when they turn out to be you. U are criminal and wierd. Please don't contact me again.*

    At first it seemed like a straight-forward message. You might even read it as a simple goodbye. But L knew her audience. She understood that my critical thinking and power of analysis and abstract thought was beyond most of our peers. It always was. (Once in English after I'd read out a lengthy analysis of the opening shot of *2 Up* (Tom Whelton, 1986) I argued, quite persuasively I thought, that the image of a sparrow landing on a branch served as such a thorough metaphor for the film that it was possible to surmise every beat of the subsequent story from this three second shot. Mrs White cut me off about halfway through, before I'd got to some of my most potent points about the colours in the bark and how they foreshadowed the death in the bog, and the physics of the bouncing branch, and how it completely spoils the result of the life-changing decision at the end, if you're paying attention, and most people aren't – *Well, Mark. I'm quite... I'm speechless... I find it staggering that you found 10,000 words from these three seconds of film... thank you... really. Your perspective is always... unique.* She laughed a little. I saw L smiling out of the corner of my eye, the corner that I'd trained so well to see her, and knew she was impressed.) And I knew L better than almost anyone. Our relationship had always been about discretion and subtlety. I read the message again. And again. A plethora of references fell out. In re-reading, the subtlety began to slowly emerge, and like a Shakespeare soliloquy, the hidden depths and rhythms came through. She was providing a clever subtext.

The line *messages from unknown senders* put me in mind of *Letter From An Unknown Woman* (Max Ophüls, 1948), a film which is framed by a letter from Joan Fontaine to the love of her life, Louis Jourdan. He is a brilliant concert pianist, and she the doting fan who adored him as a teen, then had a date with him, spent a night with him, bore his child, and despite several meetings over the years, was ultimately not recognised by him. She was just another of his many women. His heart-breaking question to his servant upon reading the letter, *did you remember her?* (the servant, of course, does) sends chills, and a reading of L's reference here might be that she is implying that I am the doting fan, and she the distant figure who didn't remember me. After all, I wasn't ever foolish enough to think that she liked me as much as I liked her. I didn't need her to.

But there was more. Her choices were deviously clever: the misspelling of write *was* a definite nod to Bruce Rite, star of *Bunny Dee I Miss You* (Su Carpentier, 1993) which, research tells me, came out in UK cinemas on the same Friday in March 1993 that I told the gang at length about the film I'd seen the night before, which happened to be *Letter From An Unknown Woman*. Ha! (That Friday L and Vicki had walked on ahead, and when Jo shouted after them and asked if they wanted to hear about the end of the film I was describing, they ran. *We don't want any spoilers; we want to see it ourselves!*) That L could be so specific in her memory of these moments was striking. I was touched, yet again, that her brilliance was so subtle. I couldn't wait to ask if she'd finally seen the Ophüls film, and in particular the wonderful performance of Joan Fontaine whose love is not noticed by Louis Jourdan.

There's more. The phrase *criminal and weird* is also a quote from *Batten Down The Hatches* (Jude Mills, 1985) a zombie romp in which a despicable scientist, claiming to be trying to find a cure for the undead, invites nubile teenagers to intern with him and *come, let us be criminal and weird, and help me save humanity...* this was an invitation maybe to break the order that had been put in place by her parents, if it hadn't expired at this point. (The misspelling of wierd can itself be read as a nod to *Wierd Waze*, an album by forgotten early-90s shoegaze/dance act Weird Ways, but this might be a stretch, as the band have no significance to either of us that I can place. Further investigation is required. There may be a specific course of action that I need to undertake that I'm not seeing. I have goose bumps at the prospect.)

But it was going back to the first two words that told me the most. *Oh hey* was such an uncharacteristically un-L greeting, I pondered it for days. Then I noticed that she had written that, if she had wanted to write back, then she would have. But she *had* written back. This was it. Then I realised that she was instructing me, cryptic crossword style, to write what she had written back(wards): reversed, *oh hey* spelled *Yeh Ho* (Rubens Gold, 2005). I hadn't seen this film, and managed, after a search, to find it illegally online. It tells the story of a woman who is in love with her childhood sweetheart and can never tell him, because she has been married to another man for years. Well played, L.

Message received. I sent another message that simply said *I'll Wait*. (In *I'll Wait* [Den Sparks, 1991] Ione Skye vows to wait for her boyfriend to return from Vietnam. We know what she doesn't know: he has gone to Canada instead, and asks a buddy to write home from the war imitating him. Ione Skye falls in love with this version of her boyfriend even more than before.) That message came back, with a second one from an administrator saying that I had breached rules. My account was suspended for a week. When I could get back in, I couldn't view L's page completely, meaning I had been blocked. But I could see her profile picture: herself when she was around sixteen years old. Taken just after I'd moved away. A final sign, telling me that our story would continue from where it had been broken off all those years ago? Maybe. I might be finding narratives that aren't there. I know I do that. This book is full of them. But this time, I think I might be onto something.

Either way, I'm paying attention.

Mark Savage is an author and musician from Portsmouth, England. He lives in Portland, Oregon. Contact him at legendarymarkpetersavage@gmail.com.

CPSIA information can be obtained
at www.ICGtesting.com
Printed in the USA
LVHW091615020421
683322LV00010B/452